T0209264

In a future laid waste by environmental catastrophe, one woman in a shielded megacity discovers a secret hidden within—and the nightmare of what lies beyond.

The Skyfire Saga

Her designation is H124—a menial worker in a city safeguarded against the devastating storms of the outer world. In a community where consumerism has dulled the senses, where apathy is the norm and education is a thing of the past, H124 has one job: remove the bodies of citizens when they pass away in their living pods.

Then one night, H124's routine leads her into the underground ruins of an ancient university. Buried within it is a prescient alarm set up generations ago: an extinction-level asteroid is hurtling toward earth.

When her warning is seen as an attempt to topple the government with her knowledge of science, H124 is hunted—and sent fleeing for her life beyond the shield of her walled metropolis. In a weather-ravaged unknown, her only hope lies with the Rovers, the most dangerous faction on Earth. For they have continued to learn. And they have survived to help avert a terrifying threat: the end of the world is near.

Visit us at www.kensingtonbooks.com

Books by Alice Henderson

The Skyfire Saga
Shattered Roads

Published by Kensington Publishing Corporation

Shattered Roads

The Skyfire Saga

Alice Henderson

REBEL BASE BOOKS
Kensington Publishing Corp.
www.kensingtonbooks.com

First Electronic Edition: April 2018
eISBN-13: 978-1-63573-046-3
eISBN-10: 1-63573-046-5

First Print Edition: April 2018
ISBN-13: 978-1-63573-049-4
ISBN-10: 1-63573-049-X

For all the people out there, who, like Jason, are fighting to preserve wildlife and our amazing planet

Chapter 1

Ben had barricaded the door and been as quiet as possible, but now they'd come for him. He could hear them pounding on the door. He scrambled out of his hole beneath the floorboards. He'd found tunnels down there. Rooms. Maybe there was a way out, a tunnel he could escape through. But he wasn't sure, and he could die down there if he got trapped. He just couldn't stake his life on it. He hadn't had enough time to explore.

He knew they wouldn't find the hole. They wouldn't know to look for it and wouldn't waste the time anyway. He spent precious seconds heaving himself up through the hole and then replacing the floorboards. As he threw the rug in place, the strange beeping emanating from those parts below stopped. It had started a few days ago, coming from somewhere under the building, in that dark catacomb of rooms. He'd never found the source. And now the Repurposers were here.

He shouldn't have unplugged from the network. He knew that now. But he had had to unplug because of the chatter. How could he listen to the mysterious beeping over all that chatter? He'd never noticed it before, the constant talking. But suddenly, when he tried to concentrate on that strange alarm coming from below, he realized he couldn't hear anything but the monotonous drone of meaningless voices: *What handbag was the star of High Rise Living carrying in last night's episode?—Win 80,000 creds by playing the beta version of Maximum Shopping!—Get a new look for your avatar!*

They must have immediately noticed his absence from the network and sent the men. He had to get out of there. He ran to the barricaded front door, ready to throw the furniture aside. When he peered through the peephole, he saw men waiting in the hallway. They'd covered this escape route.

There was no other way out of his apartment. No windows that worked. No back doors. Just the front door and the tunnels beneath, which as far as he'd explored had not led out.

A deafening buzz erupted on a wall he shared with his neighbor. They were cutting through. He had to get out of there. He grabbed a chair, ran up next to the wall. As the plaster caved in, he waited until a head appeared. He brought the chair down hard. The man crumpled, but another took his place, and Ben struck him too. He grabbed the second man, pulling him through the hole, then dove through the opening into his neighbor's living pod. He'd never seen the neighbor in person before, though he'd lived next to him his whole life. There he was, sitting on his couch, eyes fixed on his display, hands flying over the virtual keyboard. The man didn't even turn.

Ben ran. He threw open his neighbor's front door and dashed into the hallway, smashing into one of the Repurposers waiting there. Then he bolted in the opposite direction, not knowing where to go. He'd only been out in the hallway once before, when they first installed him in his living pod. He had to make it to the street that he'd seen so many times from his window. Maybe someone could help him. He banged on doors as he ran, shouting for help. No one came out. No one even stuck a head out to look at him. Even though he knew the building was filled to capacity, it felt dead inside.

At the end of the hall he saw a door. He burst through it, and sudden heat struck him in the face. He stared around, not sure which way to go. He bolted left at random. He sucked in the torrid air, happy just to be outside. He'd only been outside once before, the day he came here all those years ago. Back then it had been freezing.

The streets lay empty. No one walked around. He could hear noises from the living pod buildings all around him, huge structures that reached into the amber sky. Light and sound emanated through the windows, coming from thousands of displays and entertainment channels. He shouted again for help, then thought better of it. No one was even coming to the windows to look, and shouting only gave away his location. For someone to help, they'd have to detach from the network. That's what he had done, and now they would make him pay for it.

He spotted a shadowed place next to a building and ran to it. Pressed into the dark, he heard the whirring of some kind of machinery coming from inside. The wall felt hot, hotter than the sticky air. He caught his breath, then dared a look around for the men who followed him.

As his eyes adjusted to the shadows, he saw an old metal door in the wall. He ran to it and yanked on the handle. An even hotter blast of air hit him, along with a dazzling light. Squinting, he stepped inside, closing the door behind him. Raising his hand, he shielded his eyes against the glare of overhead lights. He stood on a steel platform with stairs leading down. Below him stretched a hive of activity. White steam billowed in the air, and the whirr and groan of machinery almost deafened him. Dozens of people milled around long tables, some folding laundry, some preparing food cubes. One man sat at a bench repairing a food delivery drone. The people weren't using displays. They didn't have keyboards. They weren't plugged in.

He glanced this way and that. No sign of the men who'd come after him. He ran down the stairs toward the man fixing the drone. The man looked up as Ben reached him.

"Can you help me?" Ben asked, trying to catch his breath again.

"What's wrong?" The man put down his tools.

"Men are after me!"

"*After* you?" The man's brow furrowed. "What do you mean?"

"They mean to repurpose me."

The repairman stared at him, noticing the network jack in the side of his head. "You're from the living pods?" he asked, looking amazed.

"Yes."

"And you aren't plugged in?"

Ben glanced at the others. They took no notice, just continued their work.

"I thought you couldn't live without being plugged in."

"What do you mean?"

"That's when the corpse cleaners come. When someone has unplugged from the network."

Ben shook his head. His mouth had gone dry.

"You die without it."

He backed away. "I don't think it works like that." He'd been unplugged for days now, and he was fine.

"The men will come and plug you back in," the repairman assured him.

Ben turned. He had to get out of there.

He ran back toward the stairs, but just then the door banged open. The three men from his living pod stood on the platform, pinpointing him on the busy warehouse floor. He pivoted and ran the other way, but not before two more men entered through a different door.

Closing in from all sides, they homed in on him. Panic swelled up inside him. He made a dash toward all the people folding laundry and making food. He sped through them, his pursuers close behind. Then one of the Repurposers tackled him, sending him sprawling across the floor. In an instant the rest fell on him, grabbing Ben's hands, wrists, and legs. He thrashed, crying out for help. The workers stared down at him, and one advanced, but the Repurposer waved her off.

"No need," he told her. "He unplugged from the network and is going a little crazy. We need to take him back to his pod and reconnect him."

She nodded and went back to folding laundry.

"No!" Ben shouted. He kicked his legs, but still they carried him toward the metal door. They lifted him up the stairs and dragged him outside. As he thrashed in horror they retraced his footsteps, hauling him back to his building, down the hallway toward his living pod, in through his neighbor's place, and through the hole.

"It's not killing me to be disconnected! You've got it wrong!" he screamed.

The men remained stoic. They pulled him into his bathroom. He thrashed, knocking over his supply cabinet, spilling towels into the shower. A vase fell off the sink and shattered. Still they held him tightly. None of them made eye contact. He wasn't a person. Just a thing.

"Hold him down," one said. They flipped him onto his stomach, and one knelt on his back.

He felt the man's gloved hand on his head, pressing down, parting his hair over the network jack in his skull. The man brought out a gleaming metal instrument with a circular saw on one end.

Ben kicked out on the cold tile, but the others held down his arms and legs.

The man brought the tool up to his head jack, and Ben felt a blistering pain in his head. Everything went gray, then black-and-white. All their voices became muffled.

"The jack is corrupted," he heard the man say. "I don't think we'll be able to repurpose him. There's dust in here, some weird debris. What has this guy been up to?" He felt the men readjust their weight on him. "I'll give it a try."

He brought the tool in again, and a searing flash of heat erupted inside Ben's head. He flailed, fought against them, but all he could smell was burning flesh. Suddenly a white-hot eruption filled his eyes, and his brain felt too big for his skull. He screamed as it swelled, his teeth cracking against the tile. He squeezed his eyes shut. An agonizing pain racked his body. His legs skittered on the floor. His fingers opened and closed. His eyes fluttered, and he couldn't breathe. Blood leaked out of his eyes, drowning out his vision. Then the black came, seeping over him, filling up all the cracks in his view. His body went slack. "We're losing him," one of the men commented.

"Looks that way," said the one with the tool.

Air rushed out of Ben's lungs as the black took over his mind.

Chapter 2

H124 waited outside the door, closing her eyes and concentrating on the theta wave receiver by the door lock. She mentally sent the message "unlock," and the door hissed open. Quietly she stepped inside with her gear, then stopped as she heard noise coming from the main room. Someone still lived in this pod. Her employers had told her that the only way to access the corpse was through the neighboring pod. Weird, but she didn't ask questions. Maybe the deceased's lock was broken. Still, she'd never been inside someone's place while they still occupied it, and she felt uncomfortable, a stranger in someone's home.

She crept into the main room. Her instructions told her they'd created a hole in the wall there. A light flickered on the wall as she moved forward. Not wanting to disturb the occupant, she stepped lightly in her work boots. She knew she'd get in trouble if she interrupted him. She stepped around the corner and saw him, seated before his display, his button pad shimmering in midair just below his hands. The light from his display hovered in the air before him.

She knew about these display setups and button pads that most people were equipped with. But she'd only been in these living pods to clean out the previous tenants after they'd passed on, so she'd never seen the equipment turned on before.

Just ahead, she could see the ragged, dark hole in the wall, but her eyes returned to the floating display.

She'd never seen anything so beautiful. She knew she wasn't supposed to, but she stopped before stepping through the hole. Unable to help herself, she stared at the display. Six windows filled the screen, and the man's eyes darted from one to the other. Both hands fluttered over the button pad, fingers pressing down in such a rapid sequence, she didn't know how he could possibly make sense of what he was doing. In one window he controlled an image of a little man who moved through different rooms of a building, pulling levers and pressing buttons on walls. In another flashed a sequence of unintelligible numbers. Another window held an animated avatar of someone else, a woman, with text flying across the screen just beneath her face. Every few seconds, his hands would stream over the buttons and more text would fly by. A group of people talked in yet another window, sitting around a table chattering about someone named Phil, and how they couldn't believe that he had opted for the small swimming pool when he could have had the bigger one. Along the bottom of the screen scrolled more text: *THIS YEAR'S MOST IMPORTANT DECISION! Pick the right candidate! Vote wisely! Watch the candidates' videos! Yes! Vote for your favorite reality TV star in this all-important election to determine which show will be renewed!*

In yet another window a little graph fluctuated up and down, beeping out sounds every now and then. Whenever it beeped, the man entered text in the window, pressing some more buttons until it stopped beeping. His eyes never left the display, and his fingers never stopped working at the keypad.

It fascinated her that he could attend to so many things at once. What was he even doing in each of the windows? She had no idea.

He stood up suddenly, and she leaped back into the shadows. He walked to his wall slot as a delivery drone clattered in the vent and came through. The display followed in front of the man, while his fingers kept typing away. The drone hovered briefly, laid down the man's new food tray with the food cubes, then took away his empty tray from earlier that day. It buzzed and vanished back into the vents. Rapidly the man reached out, grabbed the squares, and shoved them into his mouth. Then he returned to his seat, his attention on the display not once faltering.

Her face burning, H124 realized she'd been standing there far too long. If her employers found out, she'd be ticketed. Or worse. They could assign her even more extra duties. She was lucky the man hadn't noticed her. She stepped forward quietly and reached the hole in the wall. Without a sound, she stepped through it into the dead man's apartment.

She could smell the corpse before she saw it. She wondered why they'd waited so long to call her onsite. She followed the sickly sweet smell down a dark corridor to the bathroom. He lay sprawled on the bathroom floor, legs twisted at an odd angle. His bloody head lay in a pool of crusted red on the white tile. She crept closer, staring down at him. She'd never seen a death like this before. She'd seen heart attacks, disease, a broken neck once. But this was different. Violent. She didn't see how he could have done this to himself, even if he'd slipped and fallen on the tile, cracking his head open. She bent closer, looking at his skull. It wasn't a fracture he'd bled from. It was an evenly cut hole in his skull.

She'd heard that if jacked-in citizens unplugged from the network, they risked death. Is this what happened? Had the man's cranial implant malfunctioned?

She slung her tool bag off her shoulder, placing it on the floor. The coppery scent of blood hung strongly in the bathroom, lingering above the fetid smell of decay. She tried to breathe through her mouth and pulled out a thick plastic body bag from her supplies. Kneeling over the body, she rolled him onto his back. She tugged on his shirt, and his face came free from the dried pool of blood. He was heavy, tall and flabby, probably around thirty-five or so. She unzipped the bag and moved it along the floor until it lay flush to him. She sat back on her heels, preparing to roll him into it.

Grabbing his arm, she stopped. A sound echoed up from beneath her. A beeping sound. She paused, listening. It was muffled, like it wasn't coming from this unit. Cautiously, she stood up and walked back into the hall. Craning her neck, she tried to pinpoint the sound. She moved back toward the hole in the wall, thinking it might be coming from the next living pod, but it wasn't. She walked back toward the bathroom. The beeping grew louder. She walked past the bathroom toward the man's bedroom. She stopped at the end of the hallway, just before its doorway. The sound was loudest here, an incessant, unfamiliar beeping. She knelt down, and it stopped.

She waited, but after minutes of silence, she stood up and returned to the bathroom. Stooping down, she rolled the body into the bag. She began zipping it up and looked back at the man's head. The wound was circular and clean, right where his implant should have been. Curious, she leaned closer, staring at the hole. The man's implant hadn't malfunctioned; it was completely gone, and something had seared his brain tissue. She stared down at the blackened flesh, wrinkling her nose at the acrid smell that wafted up.

She looked around the bathroom, seeing a shattered vase, a group of towels spilling out of the hutch above the toilet. Her gut roiled around inside her. Something wasn't right. This wasn't a natural death or an accident.

His brain had been destroyed, *violently*. He had struggled, fought against someone.

Who had removed his implant? And where was it now? Who would have had access to his pod? Only her employers or a worker like herself.

Maybe someone had tried to save him when his implant shorted out. She didn't like it, and she grew nervous, wanting to finish the job.

She finished zipping him up inside the thick plastic, then tugged him out into the hallway. Straightening up, she looked back into the bathroom. Blood had pooled under him, crusted and dried. She pulled out the bleach and scrub brush and went to work. When a new person was installed in this living pod, it had to look spotless.

She scrubbed and wiped until the white tile floor gleamed. Then she went through the whole pod, righting an upended lamp in the hallway. Housekeeping would take care of the rest, resupplying the bathroom with new linens and other necessities.

She returned to the body bag. He was heavy. She'd have to drag him out with the harness. She pulled it out of her bag and stepped into it. Tightening it around her chest, she was glad he lived near the corner of the building. Even so, it would take a lot of effort to get him down the exterior hallway to the incinerator.

She pulled out tow ropes and attached them to the body bag with carabiners. She was about to attach him to her harness when the beeping started again. She stood silently in the darkened hallway, listening. She waited for it to stop, but it didn't this time. Dropping the ropes, she walked to the end of the hallway where it was loudest. A red-and-black carpet covered the floor there. The sound was coming from *underneath*. She was sure of it. She knew the utility tunnels well, having been navigating them since she was four. They didn't run under this part of the building. It should be just dirt under there.

She peeled the carpet back and stared at the floorboards. Faint scratches marred their plastic edges. While all the planks still lay flush together, she noticed their nails had been removed. As she bent lower, she found a broken fingernail. She leaned back on her heels. Stood up. On a thought, she returned to the body bag and unzipped it. Pulling out the man's cold arm, she found all of his fingernails bloody and torn. He'd been scratching at the floor.

The beeping continued, insistent, demanding. *What was it?*

Then, just as suddenly as it started, it came to an end. She waited, but it didn't resume.

Taking a knee, she traced her fingers along one of the boards. At the end she tugged upward, and it came free, revealing a support beam beneath. Under it lay darkness. She lifted up a few more boards, laying them quietly to one side. Glancing back toward the hole in the wall, she made out the faint glow from the man's display in the next pod. He had taken no notice of her. She felt exposed, crouching there, exploring, not doing her job. Her heart hammered, and her mouth went dry at the thought of him peeking through the hole, or, worse, her employers showing up for an inspection. But no one came through the ragged hole in the wall.

She grabbed her headlamp and her tool bag and returned to the opening in the floor. Donning the light, she switched it on and pointed it down into the darkness. The beam traveled over rubble from an ancient ceiling, more support beams, and strange shapes clustered in shadow. It was a whole other room, she realized, a room beneath this one. Her nose wrinkled as a moldy odor stirred upward.

She swung her legs over into the darkness. Sitting on the edge, she hovered between two worlds. What lay beneath this living pod? She always thought it had been built on the ground floor.

Before she even knew she'd made the decision, she gripped the edge of the floor with her hands and lowered her legs down into the unknown.

Chapter 3

H124's feet thrashed inside the hole until they found a stable spot on the rubble. Slowly she lowered her full weight onto it. With only her head above the floor of the deceased man's living pod, she glanced one more time toward the hole at the end of the hallway. Nothing had changed.

She turned away, aiming her light down into the black. The rubble angled downward, so she slid and stumbled her way to the base of the pile, reaching a sloping floor. Dust motes hung in the air, and a thick blanket of gray covered strange rectangular shapes around the room. Stopping to listen for any sounds above, she stared up through the hole. Then she turned, playing her light over the shapes. A large desk stood against one wall with a chair in front of it. Two items sat on top of the desk. She brushed the thick layer of dust off them. The larger one was a plastic box with black glass on one side. In front of it lay a flat plastic rectangle with buttons. Each button had a letter on it, along with some other symbols she didn't recognize. As she moved around the room, her light dancing over more strange shapes, the headlamp's beam fell on a door. Another room? She rushed to the door. It had no theta wave receiver. She pushed against it, and it swung open, revealing another room beyond. This one held a number of large tables, each with its own sink. Posters hung on the walls. She studied each one, but she couldn't make sense of them. One showed a series of color-coded squares with letters and numbers in them: *Ag 47. He 2. C 6.* Most of the poster was ripped, decaying, pieces of it lying on the floor. Another showed a diagram of a circular object with smaller circles surrounding it.

She couldn't believe it when her light fell on yet another door. The hole in the floor hadn't simply led to another room. This was vast. She was sure she was under one of the adjoining pods. The whole living unit building had been built on the ruins of some other structure. The place was ancient. Of that much she was sure. It smelled old, musty. She walked up to one of the large tables and wiped away dust. Glancing back at the mysterious posters, she walked across the room. A glass case on the far wall held small silver rocks. They weren't like the landscaping rocks outside of the living pod units. These were shiny, metallic-looking. She reached inside and picked one up, finding it unusually heavy. Uneasy, she slipped it inside her pocket.

Even stranger shapes lay enshrouded in dust on a table along another wall. She brushed them off, finding equipment of some kind, but she had no idea what it was. She'd never seen anything like it, bizarre tubes of glass and metal with knobs and dials. She wondered if they powered on, so she sent theta wave signals to them. They didn't respond. She touched the pieces, finding them clunky.

She passed into the next room. Shivering in the damp, she noticed signs and drawings covering the walls. Another desk sat against the far wall with the same ancient equipment sitting under a layer of dust, a tall black rectangle standing on its end, and a bigger rectangle on a stand of some sort. Shelves stood on either side of the old desk, filled with peculiar objects. She walked to one of the walls, her feet kicking up dust. She coughed. The signs on the wall were very thin, tacked there with rusted metal pins. She recognized letters on the page, but didn't understand most of the words. One sign focused on an image of a huge rock pocked with holes. She walked along the wall, taking in the images when she couldn't make out the words. The next showed a destroyed building with a massive pit next to it. An inset image showed another giant rock with a burned crust. The next few signs held images of fires consuming city blocks. She tried to read the writing beneath the images, but other than *building, fire,* and *fell,* she didn't understand them. She'd never seen so many different words in her life. Some of them were so long, an archaic form of English. Her written instructions always came to her in abbreviated format, like today: *Crps clnp bldg A pod 25*. These words were long, clustered together in dense sections.

Suddenly the beeping noise returned, louder than ever. She was in the room with it. She snapped her head toward the ancient desk. A tiny red light glowed. Quickly she moved to it, afraid someone above would hear her. The beeping came from one of two little boxes next to the bigger rectangles. She sent it a theta wave command to lower its volume, but nothing happened. Then she sent an off signal, to no avail. Finally she sought out the red light, finding a dial on one of the little boxes, which she tried to push, but ultimately twisted. The beeping grew much quieter, then with a click, it went away entirely. She turned it back on, leaving the volume very low. She felt along the bigger rectangle with the glass, finding a small button. She pushed it, and it began to glow beneath the dust. Wiping it off with her sleeve, she found a blank blue square staring back at her. It was a screen, she realized—an ancient one. It didn't hover in the air, but glowed outward from the sheet of glass, held within a plastic casing.

She moved her hands over the upright rectangle next to it, feeling for another button. She found one and pushed it. Something hummed, then the sound of a small fan filled the silence. In a few moments, the screen showed symbols, *circles.*

She couldn't believe the equipment could still be turned on. But she knew the whole building had been nuclear powered for a long time. She didn't know for how long, only that the maintenance crew for the power plant had tales going back generations. This thing must still be plugged into that power source.

The words *Sentry System* appeared at the top of the screen. Below them was a bright yellow circle. The third dot read *Earth.* She'd heard an old man in the laundry facility once talk about how there were more planets than theirs, perhaps as many as nine. But this diagram showed smaller objects among the planets. Three of them were flashing red and black, two small dots followed by a very big one. As she stared at the moving diagram, the flashing triad moved ever closer to Earth, crossing into its orbit. The three smaller dots collided with Earth. A series of numbers flashed across the screen: *Fragment 1: 3.7 km. 0.00002 lunar distance. COLLISION CERTAIN. Torino Scale 9. Regional Damage. Fragment 2: 3.2 km. 0.00031 lunar distance. COLLISION CERTAIN. Torino Scale 8. Regional Damage. Fragment 3: 942 m. 0.00014 lunar distance. COLLISION CERTAIN. Torino Scale 8. Regional Damage.*

The animation continued. The big dot missed the earth and continued its loop around the sun. It wheeled around, repeating its orbit. Once again it entered Earth's trajectory, but this time they collided. A series of numbers read: *Main asteroid: 9.2 km. 0.00011 lunar distance. COLLISION CERTAIN. Torino Scale 10. Global Climatic Catastrophe.*

The diagram changed now, zooming in to the little dot that was Earth. As the detail increased, drawn outlines appeared on the earth, forming different shapes. She thought they might be the profiles of the lands. Then the animation showed exactly where the first two fragments would hit. A large portion of one of the landmasses bloomed red. Then she saw where the main object would strike on its next swing around the earth.

As it struck the planet, a red circle bloomed out from the area of impact. It swept outward, covering the entire earth.

She looked at the dates on the collisions. The first fragment was due to hit in two months, the main asteroid the next time it swung around the sun. She brushed off a lump in the dust, finding a plastic oval with two buttons. A wire ran out from it, plugging into the upright metal box. She clicked on one of the buttons, and the diagram with the circles vanished. The beeping stopped at once. She stared at a black screen with a blue icon that read *Previous Impact.* When she moved the oval, an arrow moved on the screen. She clicked on the icon, and several small images appeared. She hovered over one of them, then clicked the button again. Something new filled the screen: a movie. It was just like the videos she could create on her personal recording device, but instead of emanating on a floating display as it did on her PRD, it appeared on the glass screen itself.

A woman was standing before a burning building, smoke billowing upward, the sky filled with black ash. The woman's voice came from the beeping device: "Since the catastrophic disaster on the mining asteroid *Free Enterprise* was first reported, we have been dreading this day. As underfunded government space agencies raced unsuccessfully to prevent the impacts, this nightmare has become a reality. Several fragments of the asteroid have landed here in Chicago, destroying a huge part of the downtown area. Residents have evacuated as more debris is expected to fall. Critics blame the current administration for not granting NASA enough funding to track near-Earth objects."

H124 could hear strange wailing noises in the background, mechanical and haunting. Flashing lights reflected off the building, and she could hear people screaming.

"More fragments fell north of this location, causing a factory to catch fire and burn down several city blocks."

The movie finished.

She clicked the little button on the hand device, and the video played again. Now she clicked on a different image on the screen. Another movie opened. A man stood in front of more burning wreckage, the blackened shell of a building behind him. She heard his voice coming through and adjusted the small dial so it would be quieter. "The fourth of the huge fragments has devastated downtown Chicago," he said. "These are just small parts of the asteroid that have broken off after the catastrophic disaster on *Free Enterprise*. Scientists at NASA are now saying that the asteroid and its remaining fragments, far larger than the ones that have crashed here, have been knocked into an unknown orbit. NASA and the

Jet Propulsion Lab will have to calculate their new trajectory before we know if these disastrous pieces of space rock will endanger our planet in the future. Though from what we've been told by our Washington, D.C. affiliate, while this has certainly been a devastating day for the city of Chicago, scientists have at least eighty years—possibly as long as two hundred and thirty-two—before the main asteroid and its larger fragments pass this close again."

The movie stopped, and she watched it again. She didn't understand a lot of the words the man and the woman had said. *Chicago? Asteroid? NASA? Washington?*

She clicked on the other image, and the animation opened again, showing the orbits of the planets and the flashing dots. She now knew what she was looking at. Those eighty years—or two hundred and thirty-two—had elapsed, and these things were coming fast.

She whipped out her personal recording device. The room's technology was so old that she couldn't find a way to pair her PRD with the screen itself, so she had to settle for just using her camera. She filmed the animation, then the two movies.

Plugged into the upright machine was a small metal-and-plastic device. It glowed along one side. She found several more in one of the drawers. On one end of each device was a shiny metal plug. She grabbed all of them and pulled the other one out of the machine. Something beeped when she did. In the drawers beneath the little devices was a small binder full of gleaming discs. She put that in her bag as well.

She was just figuring out how to detach the machine itself when she heard shuffling on the floor above. She froze. She guessed that someone was coming down the hallway that led to the dead man's living pod. Only two people would use that hallway: another cleaner or one of her employers. Maybe they were checking up on her progress. If they found her down here . . . She shuddered. She slung her bag over her shoulder and raced through the doorways back the way she'd come.

Chapter 4

When H124 reached the rubble at the bottom of the hole, she stood, listening. All she could hear were the building's ventilation humming and the distant sounds from the neighbor's display. She climbed the pile of old rubble and peeked out into the man's living pod. She tensed, listening. Nothing unusual met her ears. The body still lay in the middle of the hallway, sealed inside the body bag. The smell of bleach hung heavily in the air. She didn't catch the sound of any more footsteps. Maybe they'd gone past this place, heading for a different living pod.

She pulled herself out and quickly replaced the floorboards, slinging the carpet back in place. The foreign devices weighed heavily in her bag, even though she knew they were only a couple of ounces. She had to get out of there fast.

She strapped the body bag to her harness and began dragging the man down the hall. She peered out through the hole in the wall. The neighbor still sat on his couch, display gleaming in front of him. He entered text in one small window while watching a show about two girls shopping in a megamall.

He didn't turn as she hefted the body through the hole and hurried toward his front door. She started to close her eyes to use the theta wave receiver to open the door, but instead leaned forward, staring through the peephole. The hallway was clear. She sent the message to the TWR to unlock the door, and it hissed open. Glancing up and down the empty hall, she lugged the body out, dragging it along the floor. The incinerator stood at the end. She bent with the effort, clenching her teeth. Her mind sped along, wondering what to do. Her body was on autopilot, dragging the corpse toward the incinerator the way she had countless times before in other living pods. The corridor lighting flickered overhead. If she told her employers about the asteroid, they'd know that she had been exploring, not just doing her job. She'd heard about other people who got distracted from their day-to-day tasks. Some were repurposed, moved into other, more menial positions. Others simply vanished. She knew she couldn't tell them. Even if they listened, could she trust them to go to Public Programming Control so they could broadcast the information? Her best bet was to go straight to the PPC herself. After she incinerated the body, she'd head to the media building, and her employers would be none the wiser.

At the end of the hall, she stopped in front of the incinerator's TWR. She sent the thought for it to open, and a gleaming metal door slid open on the burner. An incinerator stood on every other floor of each residential building. It was easier that way. She unclipped the harness and stepped out of it. Unzipping the bag, she took one last look at the man and his head wound. Then she rolled him into the furnace and commanded the door to slide back, closing him inside. She sent the mental command to burn. She packed up the body bag, straps, and harness, returning them to her tool bag.

At the exit door, she used the TWR to open it, and a gust of hot air swept over her from the outside.

She didn't see the men until the outside door hissed closed behind her. Then she saw them, one at the end of the street, the other only a dozen feet away, staring at her. The closer one pulled out a gleaming metal tool and advanced. She recognized the black uniform, the armbands with the red insignia, the wide-brimmed hats worn low over their eyes. They were Repurposers, and they'd come for her.

Chapter 5

For a terrifying moment H124 froze. The man with the gleaming tool met her eyes. His face was unnaturally pale, dark eyes glistening beneath a crop of short black hair. His black suit blended in with the shadows, and his face seemed to glow. The other Repurposer moved behind him, two more joining them from the shadows. She stood at the top of the cement stairs, a metal railing at her back.

The men advanced, and she forced her feet to move. Turning, she vaulted over the railing and landed hard on the asphalt beneath. She cracked her knee, but got to her feet quickly, taking off. Her tool bag slammed against her side. It was too heavy. She thought of ditching it, but she couldn't lose what she'd found.

Ahead of her towered the other residential buildings of New Atlantic. Her ability to use the TWRs would get her into any of them, but she knew that the Repurposers used them, too. They'd be able to see that someone had passed through the door recently, and could use it to track her. She wondered if they were tracking her even now through her PRD. She pulled it out of her pocket and switched it off.

She had to think of something, maybe find a door that didn't require a TWR to open. She knew that would be more likely in the older part of town, so she raced east. The city's floating light orbs provided scant illumination above her, casting everything in a sickly orange glow.

Her boots pounded on the pavement, the noise alarmingly loud to her. They'd hear her. She chanced a look behind and saw the three running in the shadows, closing in. She darted down an alley between two of the residential skyscrapers, the stench of uncompacted trash assailing her senses.

Normally the trash dispensers came through and destroyed the garbage nightly, but they must not have come through yet. She leaped over the waste, smelling offal and excrement and blood. The end of the alley branched off into three separate passages. She shot left, trying to keep buildings between her and her pursuers.

The bag slammed against her back as she ran. She wasn't going to make it if she didn't ditch it. She rounded a corner, then another, heading deep into the labyrinth of residential complexes. She turned every chance she got so she wouldn't be in the men's direct line of sight.

Her lungs gulped for air. Why did they want her? What had she done wrong? Did they know she'd taken a break from her work and explored under the man's living pod?

Her foot skidded on something slimy in the trash heaps, and she went down hard on her back. The bag swung to the side, the strap twisting on her neck. Up ahead she saw an alcove in the wall, an old battered metal door without an electronic lock. She scrabbled to her feet and ran for it. She pushed its battered handbar, but it was locked. She ran ahead, pressed against the wall behind a mound of trash, and listened. The footsteps were close, but she'd gained ground on her pursuers. They must have taken a few wrong turns. She kept running, turning left and right so many times, she knew she'd have to use her PRD if she ever wanted to navigate back to her quarters.

Then it hit her.

She could never go back to her quarters.

Her life as she'd known it was over.

If these men caught her, she would never be the same again. She'd be one of those wiped automatons she'd seen in the underbelly of the warehouse she lived in. Button pushers. Vacant stares. Complacent. Unaware.

Panic bloomed in her chest, and suddenly she didn't know where to go. She'd had nightmares like this before, running and running from some terrible evil, never able to gain enough ground. Never able to get away. She could hear the men's footfalls, closer now, and she turned down another alley. At the end, an old metal door stood open a crack. She raced to it, finding it rusted and loose on its hinges. She didn't know what lay beyond. But she had to stop, had to catch her breath and figure out where to go. She stepped into the shadows and quietly swung the door closed behind her. Her grasping hands found a deadbolt on the inside of the door, and she engaged it.

As blackness took over her world, she ran her hands along rough brick. She had her headlamp, but she didn't dare switch it on. She didn't want the men to see the light under the door. Her groping hands found another door, but it was locked. She heard the men run by. They didn't try the door. Her chest heaved, her breath coming in ragged gasps. Her side burned with the effort of running. She slid her tool bag off her shoulder and felt around the contents. She tossed out as much as she could—her cleaning supplies went first, followed by the body bag. She kept the rope, the harness, her headlamp, her multitool. She could feel the cold, round discs she'd found, along with the small plastic and metal devices. She zipped them up safely in an inner pocket. Now her bag weighed much less, so she slung it over her head, then tightened the strap securely against her.

She listened, waiting for the men to come by again, terrified to hear the rattling of the doorknob as they tried it. But it didn't come.

Her own body finally quieted, and her breathing eased. Her heart slowed. Then she heard something else. Someone was breathing, only feet away.

She grabbed her headlamp and flicked it on. Crouching against the same wall she leaned against was a male about her age. But she'd never seen anyone like him. He met her gaze, his blue eyes bright and sharp beneath a crop of short, spiky blond hair. He hadn't shaved in a few days, as evidenced by the golden whiskers on his jawline. Colorful tattoos covered his tanned arms. She'd seen tattoos before, but they were always utilitarian, like marking the location of someone's living pod. But these were elaborate, decorative . . . *beautiful.* His clothes were ragged and artistic, sewn together from different pieces of cloth. He wore knee-high black boots over a ripped pair of red pants, and a black tank top that clung to his muscular frame.

She stared, not saying a word.

He smiled.

She heard distant footsteps, and he brought one finger to his lips in the universal symbol for *quiet.* He reached out and touched the lamp she was holding. She switched it off. She could feel his warm fingers touching hers. The men ran by. This time they did try the door, rattling the doorknob. But the deadbolt held, and they moved on. She heard one shout, "Split up!" and the footsteps faded away, heading off in different directions. When they were gone, she switched the light back on. He removed his hand, stood up, and slung a tattered gray canvas backpack over one shoulder. Cautiously he went to the door. He opened it, glanced both ways, then turned to her.

She stared at him there in the doorway. His tanned face was not the lax, apathetic face of a citizen, and he had no head jack. He grinned at her once more and entered the alley, closing the door behind him.

She was too scared to move. She switched off her light and huddled in the darkness. Before long she realized he wasn't coming back. She switched the deadbolt back to its locked position and waited.

Minutes dragged by. When a half hour had passed, she knew she'd eluded the men, at least for now.

But she couldn't go home.

She had no idea where to go.

Where had that guy gone? What was he doing, hiding here?

She thought of the discs in her bag, of what she'd learned in that forgotten building. She had to warn someone.

When what felt like an hour had passed, she stood up, her legs aching from sitting tensely for so long. She unlatched the deadbolt and peered out.

Beyond lay the city, and gleaming in the distance rose the Tower, the spire that housed media operations. It was far. She didn't know exactly how far, but miles for certain. But if she could make it there, maybe someone would listen. They could call off the Repurposers when they heard what she had to say. Surely this was more important than her taking a break from her duties. This was something that would change the face of the earth forever.

Peering down the alley both ways, H124 emerged from her hiding place. She let the door close behind her, and ran for the Tower.

Chapter 6

She darted down the alley, listening at each corner for sounds of the Repurposers. It seemed she'd lost them—for now, at least. She ran on, knowing it would take at least an hour to make it to the Tower.

The residential complexes stretched on and on. She'd never known there were so many. This was the longest she'd ever been outside, the farthest she'd ever traveled. She knew she was at least two miles away from her living quarters.

The air hung like a wet weight, so heavy she sweated from every pore. Her shirt clung to her, and her feet swam in her work boots. Above the skyshield, the gray clouds of the night sky hung low, their undersides lighted by the orange wash of the city lights. The streets lay empty. She wasn't surprised. At this hour, only a corpse cleaner like herself would be out. The laundry, food, cleaning crews, all would have finished by now. An electric buzz hung in the air, filling the silence.

As she ran past the residential skyscrapers, she tried to count how many people must live in each, then how many buildings stretched to the horizon. Would anyone notice her? Help her? Every few blocks, she passed industrial complexes like the one she lived in, massive warehouses that contained the laundry, food-making, and baby facilities, as well as the living quarters of other workers. The dull throb of machinery thudded outward from these buildings, the ever-present deafening cacophony of laboring equipment, hidden away from the residential buildings, all that menial labor out of sight of the residents.

She sped on, navigating by the landmark of the Tower. She passed another industrial building. Light poured out from an open door, and she felt the blast of heat from clothes dryers working overtime just inside the entrance. Her body ached for a drink of water, but she forced herself onward.

As she passed the mouth of an alley, she heard something move behind her. She staggered forward as someone struck her in the back of the head. Blistering pain erupted inside her skull, and she went down hard on one knee, collapsing on the hot asphalt. Hands grabbed her arms and pulled her down the alley. More hands grabbed her legs, and she felt herself propelled forward, into the dark shadows of the stinking, trash-filled back street. Her head throbbed in pain as she fought a grogginess that stole over her body. Her limbs felt like great manacles held them, and though she tried to thrash, her dull headache slowed her reflexes.

"Place her down here!" one of her captors said. She turned her head to see the same dark-haired Repurposer she'd seen before. Sweat streamed down his face from under the brim of his hat, and his dark eyes glistened eagerly. He pulled out the gleaming tool, switching it on. The anticipation in his eyes chilled her. This was not just a job to him. He enjoyed this.

"Should we blast her first?" another asked, reaching for his energy discharge weapon.

"Then she wouldn't be awake," the dark-haired one said simply. He had the air of their commander. "Hold her down!"

Her head started to clear. She craned her neck around as they pinned her down on her stomach. Four men gathered around her, all dressed in the dark uniform of the Repurposers: the efficient, tight-fitting suits, the shiny shoes . . . She kicked the one holding her legs square in the face. His nose erupted in a crimson spray, and he fell backward.

"What the hell are you doing?" their commander barked to him. "Get up!"

He struggled to grab her legs again as she tried to wrench free from the men holding her arms. Panic seized her as she felt the man grab her feet again.

"Sit on her!" the commander shouted. She felt a crushing weight as the man pinning her left arm sat down on her rib cage, forcing all the air out of her lungs.

Now the leader came forward with the tool. He revved its tiny motor, and she heard the whir of the bone saw inside it. He was going to cut right through her skull. She thrashed her arms, flailed her legs, bucked her hips, and tossed her head around. As her head connected with the leader's hand, he almost lost hold of the tool. Cursing, he grabbed the back of her neck, forcing her face down hard against the asphalt. She fought with everything in her, hands thrashing against the pavement until they bled.

She felt the cold metal of the tool connect with her scalp. A searing pain cut through her skin.

Then a swift boot appeared, and the tool went flying. She heard a grunt. The leader flew backward, slamming against a brick wall. The weight off her back vanished, and she lifted her head as the Repurposer slammed back against the wall. The man holding her legs cried out, and suddenly she was free.

She punched the last man holding her right arm, sending him crashing onto his back. She was up, braced to fight.

Standing in front of her, holding one of the men in a head lock, was the tattooed stranger. As the Repurposer struggled in his grip, another came toward him. The stranger wrenched his elbow upward, cinching tighter around the man's neck. She heard the snap of bone, and the man slumped lifeless at the stranger's feet.

Against the far wall, the leader leaped up. She faced him, expecting his men to jump her all at once. But the man on the opposite wall ran for the end of the alley, vaulting over a fence there. Another followed. The leader watched them go, eyes enraged, then turned to her.

He brushed off his jacket and calmly bent down, picking up the shiny metal tool. "I might have to do more than Repurpose you," he said, walking toward her. "I might have to accidentally botch the operation."

Fear shot through her like an electric jolt. Her mouth went dry, her limbs heavy as cement bags. He didn't even acknowledge the outsider. The tattooed stranger stepped over the fallen Repurposer and stood next to her. She could smell him when a gust of hot wind hit them, a curious mix of unidentifiable spices, sweat, and an earthy scent. The leader took in his fallen worker, then gazed slowly up at the blond-haired stranger.

"I have no interest in you, wastrel. Go back to whatever sewer you crawled out of."

He advanced on H124, but she fought the urge to bolt, knowing he'd only catch up to her again, bringing more reinforcements. But she'd never fought in her life before tonight. He came forward, and she stepped back, keeping a safe distance while she figured out what to do. The tattooed stranger did the same. Then hands grabbed her from behind. The two men had circled, not run away. The leader sneered. One of the men grabbed the stranger, but he bucked him off, whirling around and kicking him in the face. H124 kicked out as the leader approached, landing a solid boot right to his knee. He went down hard, cursing. She thrashed, trying to throw off the man who held her arms. His fingers dug into her flesh as he held onto her relentlessly. The stranger's attacker had recovered, holding on to his ruined nose. Blood streamed through his fingers. The outsider charged, sending the bleeding man sprawling into a fetid pile of garbage.

As the leader advanced, bringing up the tool, while the other man held her head still, H124 saw a blur of motion. The stranger leaped up onto the leader's back, twisting his body around. She saw genuine shock seep over the commander's face as he fell back, arms flailing. The stranger grabbed the gleaming tool and pressed the trigger all the way. The machine whirred to life, flashing light from one end. The stranger brought it to the leader's chest. H124 watched in horror as the bone saw cut through the man's clothes and rib cage, and hit his heart with a violent crimson spray. The leader fell limp.

The stranger stood up, tool in hand. Releasing her from his grip, the man who was holding her turned and ran down the alley. The other one picked himself up from the garbage, nose seeping blood, and limped after his partner.

"The commander's dead!" one shouted into his PRD as he retreated.

"We need backup," yelled the other. "Now!"

H124 stood in the alley, alone with the stranger. He tucked the Repurposing tool into his satchel and glanced around at the carnage.

He then rummaged through the clothing of the two bodies, removing their PRDs. He looked up, meeting her eyes. A pleasant thrum buzzed through her, his gaze a visceral force.

"You have to get out of here," he said. "Stay in the shadows. Leave the city. It's not safe for you now. You've been marked."

"Who are you?" she asked, finding her voice.

"Rowan. And you?"

"Um . . . I don't have a name. My worker designation is H124."

"Nice to meet you, H." He smiled again, then turned and sprinted down the alley, vaulting over the fence at the end.

Now she was truly alone, her attacker's blood pooling at her feet.

Heeding Rowan's advice, she followed suit, taking the same course as he had. She would take these side alleys as far as she could toward the Tower.

Chapter 7

When she got within a block of the Public Programming Control Tower, H124 stopped to catch her breath. Leaning against a brick wall in the shadows, she stared up at the immense building. City lights reflected on the underbelly of the clouds above the shield, making the night sky a luminescent orange. Bright lights flashed along the Tower's height. The building was massive, easily ten times the height of the surrounding buildings.

Now that she was here, she didn't know how to proceed. She'd never been this far away from her station. Through the glass of the lobby entrance, she spotted a guard at a long desk. A bank of floating displays gleamed above his head. She checked the street for Repurposers but didn't see anyone. Her scalp stung where the Repurposing tool had cut into it, but at least the bleeding had stopped.

She hurried toward the front door. It didn't open, so she knocked on the glass. The guard peered out, then minimized one of his floating displays to get a better look at her. He stood up, brow furrowed, and came around the side of his desk.

She knew that the media officials all lived in this building. She wondered how many people actually came and went through the entrance. Most probably worked and went to sleep with nothing more than a floor separating their work and living spaces.

The guard stopped in front of the glass door, staring out at her. Finally he moved to the TWR on his side of the glass. The door slid open.

H124 entered, her legs aching.

"Where did you come from?" the guard asked.

She decided to skip all that. "I need to see someone in charge."

He leaned from side to side on his stocky legs to examine her head. "You don't have a head jack." Deep concern wrinkled his face. "What are you doing out there? Where is your office?" He took her arm and gestured her all the way inside. The door slid shut.

"I have important news," she said, "and I need to talk to someone in charge."

He moved back to the large desk and called up one of the displays. "Not many people up at this hour."

"Anyone will do. I have information that needs to be passed on."

He scrolled through a directory, his moving eyes causing the names to cruise by. At last he stopped at a name glowing in red.

"James Willoughby is still in his office. I could call him."

"Yes, please," she said. She had no idea who that was. As a worker, she lacked a head jack and had no way to watch the media broadcasts. But meeting with anyone was preferable to standing out in the open like this.

She waited nervously while he activated the comm link. "Mr. Willoughby, someone is here to see you. She says she has important information." He waited. "I don't know. She just walked in. I don't know why she didn't use the comm link." He frowned in confusion, then turned to her. "We'll need to know your name for the log before we send you up," the guard said.

She stared around at the lobby. Already the black behind the glass doors felt oppressive. If the Repurposers came this far to find her, she was an easy target right now in this overly lit room. "H124."

The guard stood up abruptly. "What? You're a worker?"

"Corpse cleanup."

He spoke into the comm link. "I'm calling security, sir. Don't come down."

He pressed a button on the floating keyboard. An alarm erupted in the lobby.

"Just stay there," he commanded her, coming back around the desk. He pulled a weapon off his belt, a thin black cylinder with two metal prongs. An arc of blue electricity sprang from one prong to the next.

A flurry of footsteps echoed from a corridor at the end of the hall. There a metal door burst open, and a dozen armed men in black uniforms stormed through. The guard pointed at her, and H124 ran. She raced to the front lobby doors, but they'd locked again. She faced the TWR, but when she commanded it to open, it didn't. She knew how to do workarounds with locks, but there was no way she had the time right then.

The security team poured into the room, all pointing weapons at her, long-snouted things with currents buzzing at their ends. She saw another door, one behind the guard's desk, and ran for it. The guard tried to grab her, but she slammed an elbow into his face, and he reeled back.

She heard a strange *ding,* and a voice that yelled, "Wait, wait, wait!"

H124 tried the door behind the desk. It was also locked. The security team closed in, forming a tight semicircle around her.

"Wait!" sounded the voice. From the security corridor came a man dressed in an elegant suit. His black hair was perfectly styled, and kind blue eyes twinkled in a pale face with chiseled features. "I want to talk to her. There's no need for all of this. Timmons!" he barked.

The guard, grabbing his bloody nose, stood up. "Yes, sir?"

"You should have cleared this kind of action with me before you did this. There's no need for this show of force."

The man stepped closer as the armed men lowered their weapons.

"Miss?" he said to her, gesturing for her to come forward. "I'm very interested in hearing the information you brought." He flashed an angry glare at the guard. "Timmons, you don't want the higher-ups to find out you escorted a perfectly good story to the brig without even finding out what it was, do you?"

The guard shook his head. "No, sir."

"Well, then." He turned back to her. "Miss? If you'd kindly come to my office."

H124 took him in. Something about him made her trust him. He was good. Her gut could feel that. She came toward him, letting him usher her past the guards to the bank of elevators. They stepped inside.

"Short ride," he said, smiling. "Only a few floors to my office."

When the doors slid shut and the elevator began to rise, H124 let out a huge breath.

He studied her. "I'm fascinated. How did you get here?"

"I've got some very important information."

"That I gather. But how the hell did you make it all the way here?"

"It wasn't easy." She furrowed her brow. "But I needed to."

"Fascinating," he said again and turned to watch the numbers growing higher as the elevator climbed.

They got off on the fifteenth floor and walked down a short corridor. He used the biometric scanner on a door, and it hissed open. "My office," he said, waving her in.

She entered, gazing around at the immense space. It was easily twenty times bigger than her living quarters. "This whole place is yours?"

He smiled. "Yep. Took a long time to get it. Had to produce a lot of hit shows."

She tried to guess his age, wondering how long he'd been working toward this. He looked to be at least twice as old as she was.

He took her in, looking at her head. "Of course, you've never seen any of my shows."

"No, not really, not up close."

"That's good," he mumbled. He waved her over to a chair as he sat down behind his desk. "So what is this pressing news?"

She hesitated, then pulled out her PRD. She really didn't want to turn it back on, but she knew that he'd have to see the animation and movies. She studied him, still deciding if she could really trust him. He wasn't checked out like the residents she'd seen over the years. She glanced at the side of his head and saw that he didn't have a head jack either. Before now, she thought only workers like her didn't have them.

She glanced over her shoulder, half expecting his door to slide open and the Repurposers to charge in. She met his gaze. "I don't have much time. I'm being chased." She held up her PRD. "As soon as I turn this on, they're going to know where I am."

"Who?"

"The Repurposers."

He stared at her, a hint of fear stealing over his face.

Then, steeling herself, she switched it on. Scrolling through the contents, she pulled up the movie she'd made of the animation, showing the collision course of the asteroid.

She handed it to him, and he watched the animation as it floated in the air above the device. When it finished, he squinted up at her. "What is this?"

"I didn't know at first either." She pulled up the rest of the files, the ones she'd recorded of the destruction.

He watched them in silence. "I don't understand what this is."

"I found something. The ruins of an old building under one of the residence structures. There's technology down there, old tech. And a warning system."

"Warning of what?"

"Earth's destruction."

He took a deep breath and ran his fingers through his hair.

She leaned forward, triggering the animation to play again. "See . . . this shows the path of three objects that are going to collide with the earth." The display showed red across the globe. "The fourth one is the biggest threat. It's going to destroy everything."

Willoughby blinked, looking down at the PRD. He was frozen. Silent. His relaxed demeanor vanished.

"We have to warn people," she urged him. "We have to stop it."

He looked up again, incredulous. "Stop it?"

"Yes."

"How?" He watched the animation and gestured at it. "We don't have the ability to stop something like this."

"What do you mean?"

He threw up a hand. "That knowledge is gone. Wiped out. So long ago it's almost legend . . ."

"I don't understand."

"No one would know how to stop something like this now. This kind of scientific knowledge vanished so long ago that there's simply nothing left of it."

Her heart hammered. "I thought . . . I thought the PPC knew everything."

He gave a disheartened laugh. "Hardly. We don't know anything. Nothing useful, anyway. Just how to keep people tuned in. How to gain more power." He gestured at the animation. "Are you sure this is right?" He frowned. "Maybe the calculations are wrong. Maybe this is old information. Maybe the person who gathered it was a crackpot."

"That could all be true, I guess. But you should have seen the photographs of the destruction this thing caused before. They were plastered all over the walls. That was real."

He ran his hand over his chin. He watched the movie again, studying the havoc it had wreaked. "They say on here we had eighty to two hundred years for us to figure out how to deflect the asteroid and its fragments. But there was one thing these reporters didn't count on."

She raised her eyebrows.

"That we wouldn't continue to learn," he went on.

She felt sick.

"What about these ruins you found?" he asked.

"They're under Residence Building A-12."

"There might be more information there. Something we could use."

"There could be. But they didn't know how to stop this thing either. Just a few fragments destroyed an entire city. It says these three fragments are much bigger." She looked down at her PRD. "This time the destruction is going to be a lot bigger than parts of a single city. And that's not even the main one that's going to hit later."

He fished around in a drawer. Pulling out another PRD, he quickly copied the contents of hers onto it, then handed the new one to her and powered down her old one. "Use this. They can't track it. I need some time to think." He hid her PRD in the same drawer and slid it shut.

Suddenly the door behind her slid open. Framed in the opening stood two Repurposers with building security. "We have orders for this one," one of the Repurposers told Willoughby.

He stood up, hurrying around the side of his desk. "We were just discussing something very important." He stood in front of her, blocking their way to her. "I told the guard that security wasn't required. She has news."

"That isn't relevant." The Repurposer moved forward, followed by the members of the security team.

H124's mouth went dry. She backed up, looking for another exit. A second door stood behind Willoughby's desk, and she ran for it. The men crashed through the furniture behind her, shouting to each other. She got to the door and wrenched it open. It was a fire door of some kind, opening to a gray utilitarian hallway. She dashed through, her boots sliding on the smooth tile floor.

"Don't let her leave this building!" a Repurposer shouted.

Not knowing where the corridor led, she ran on, the men close behind.

Chapter 8

She raced down the hall, hurrying to the end of the next corridor. She careened around that corner before the Repurposers saw her. A steel door at the end of the hall opened to a staircase. She slipped inside, taking the stairs two at a time, heading down to the next floor. She was sure they'd cover the exits to the building. She had to think of something else.

She went down three floors, then opened the stairwell door and stepped into a quiet corridor. Maybe they'd expect her to rush toward the exit on the ground floor.

Emerging quietly into the new hallway, she glanced in both directions. It was empty. She knew they had to have an incinerator on one of the nearby floors. Most residential buildings had one on every other floor, and she had to hope this building was no different. She chose to run to the left, but a few feet down the corridor, she saw that it ended at another stairwell.

She bolted in the opposite direction, tearing past the stairwell door she'd come from. No incinerator in that direction either. She doubled back, slipping through the door and descending to the next floor.

Cautiously, she opened that door and stepped into another quiet hallway. A line of residential doors greeted her in both directions. She chose to run to the right. She was relieved to see an incinerator door at the end.

She raced toward it, hoping she could crawl inside the shaft, climb down to the incinerator room, and get out through some basement egress. Most basements had ancient, forgotten openings. She'd used them plenty of times in buildings when different theta wave receivers had been on the fritz, which had happened more times than she could count.

When she got to the incinerator, she slid to a halt in front of the TWR. She closed her eyes, concentrating, sending the thought for the incinerator to open. It didn't. She heard it whirring and clicking on, listening to her, but it wouldn't obey her commands. She tried again, with no result. She opened her eyes, muttering a curse. Of course she didn't have access here in the PPC tower. They probably had a select few workers who could move around the building. The usual commands were not going to work.

She had to try a work-around. Glancing back down the hallway, she found it empty. She closed her eyes again, sending the incinerator a conflicting message. She told it to open and close at the same time, to begin and end incineration simultaneously. It whirred and clicked, and she smelled an electrical fire.

Reaching into her bag, she pulled out her multitool and flicked open a blade. She pried off the plate covering the TWR. Flames smoldered inside, so she blew them out. The incinerator door lock disengaged. Then she replaced the cover, making it look just the way it had before she'd hacked it.

She slid inside the incinerator, pulling the door shut just as she heard the stairwell door bang open around the corner. She froze, barely breathing inside the tight confines. With the TWR fried, she hoped it wouldn't malfunction and switch on suddenly. Outside, footsteps ran in the opposite direction. She used the time to switch on her headlamp. The shaft led straight down to the ash collection area in the basement. She shinnied along the warm metal, past the body disposal area and into the narrow shaft that the ashes blew through.

She stopped when she heard the footsteps double back and head nearer. She switched off her light, holding her breath in the dark. The shaft was unbearably hot. Beads of sweat ran down her back.

"Anything?" a voice yelled.

"Negative, sir," said a man so close to the incinerator door that she opened her eyes wide in the dark and hoped with everything in her that he would move away. "This hallway is clear!"

The footsteps ran back. She heard the stairwell door *thunk* open, then swing closed again with a clank.

She switched her light back on, chasing away the darkness. She shinnied to the edge of the shaft, peering down into the abyss. Her headlamp couldn't penetrate it.

Carefully she swung her legs over the edge, then lowered herself into the vertical shaft. She braced her back against one wall, her feet on the opposite, and began crawling down.

Steadily she worked her way to one floor, then another. She was down five floors when she heard an incinerator door open somewhere above her. Light flashed inside the shaft.

"She must have gotten into one of these," a voice barked. "Send a man up and a man down."

She froze. She was trapped. In the shaft above her she saw a headlamp flashing, and the metallic thudding of someone crawling in after her. She rushed down to the next floor and climbed into its corpse deposit area. Switching off her light, she lay on her stomach in front of the door and quietly lifted it up, grateful for the fail-safe built into the incinerators that allowed them to be opened manually from the inside in case someone got trapped. This floor was dim and quiet, another residential floor.

She slid out, shutting the door behind her and gazing around in horror. Where could she go now?

Suddenly the PRD the producer had given her vibrated in her pocket.

She jerked it out, bringing up the floating display. His face hovered above the device. "I'm unlocking a door for you," he whispered, his face close to the camera. "I can see where you are through my PRD."

The door to her right clicked, and its biometric scanner glowed green. She heard footsteps, and the stairwell door on her floor banged open. She had one second to decide.

She glanced back at the incinerator door, then turned and fled through the unlocked unit. The door whooshed shut behind her, locking just as the men turned down the hallway and ran to the incinerator door.

"Climb inside! She's not down to the basement yet, so she's got to be between these floors."

She peered through the view porthole, seeing two men lift open the incinerator door and crawl inside. As they slipped out of sight, she turned slowly. The living pod was dark. She saw no glow from a visual display, heard no hint of movement from an occupant.

Willoughby flashed back on the display. "Most people are sleeping right now. Try to be as quiet as possible. I'm going to get you out of this building."

"Why are you helping me?" she whispered.

"I believe your story. We've got to get the word out somehow, and that doesn't involve your brain getting . . ."

"My brain getting . . . ?"

He didn't answer her. After a moment of silence, he said, "Listen. We won't know how to stop that asteroid here. But there are others who might."

"What others?"

"We call them the Rovers. I've heard stories that they continued to learn, that their knowledge of science hasn't dwindled."

"Where are they?"

He frowned. "That's the challenge. No one knows. Though I might be able to find a lead. But . . ."

"What?" she whispered.

"They're not inside the city."

She gaped. How could anyone not be inside the city?

"I'll explain more later. When you get out of the city, just head west. Far west."

She shook her head. "When I get *out* of the city?" She didn't know it was possible to leave New Atlantic and live. She'd never known anyone who had, only rumors of people dying as soon as they left.

"For now, we have to get you out of the building." On the floating display, he looked around his office, peering nervously toward the door. He turned back to look at her. "Okay. There's an airshaft that goes from the computer server room straight out to the exterior of the building. I think that's your best bet."

"Where is the computer server room?" she whispered.

"It's on the third floor. I can unlock the door for you when you get there. It's got a high encryption on it, and they won't assume you have the time to crack it. Hopefully they won't look there until after you're long gone and they've checked everywhere else."

A map flashed up on her display, with an arrow pointing down the hall toward the stairs.

"But you're going to have to navigate the stairs on your own. I can't help you there."

H124 took a deep breath. Her hand shook as she held the PRD. She was on the fifth floor. Two floors down felt as far away as another world. And security was crawling all over the hallways.

Everything in her rebelled against the thought of going back out there. She wanted to stay here in the darkness. To run out there felt like running into a fire.

"I might be able to buy you a little time," he said. "Draw them away."

She gripped her PRD. "Please."

It was a simple word, and one she'd never had the occasion to use before.

"Okay. Get ready to run," he told her. Then she heard his voice over the PRD. "Quick! Security! She's come back to my office! Hurry!"

H124 opened the living pod door and peered out. The hallway was clear. She could hear shouts through his PRD as the security team returned to his office. She could also hear them clambering in the incinerator vents.

She muted her PRD and ran, pausing at the door leading to the stairwell. She heard men running up the stairs. "Get up to the fifteenth floor!" one of the men shouted. They passed her floor and kept going.

She slipped inside the stairwell, then leaned over the railing and listened. She could hear the men above her, but no one below. She took the chance and raced down the stairs, leaning heavily on the railing so she could jump down several stairs at once. She reached the landing of the fourth floor, then stopped to peer over the railing again. Above her, security teams shouted and ran, but below her it was still quiet.

At the door to the third floor, she stopped, pressing an ear to the metal. The hallway beyond sounded quiet. She opened the door and slid inside. The arrow floating above her PRD pointed left. She followed it, arriving at a nondescript steel door with a biometric scanner glowing red. When it turned green she slipped inside. The dimly lit room was so cold that her breath frosted in the air. A large air-conditioning unit labored along one wall. Huge servers covered the floor of the colossal room. She followed the vents for the air conditioner along the ceiling until she saw an open access hatch.

And then her heart sank. It was too high up on the wall. She couldn't reach it. She hurried around the room, looking for anything she could drag over to the access door to stand on.

She was eyeing a large metal bin over in one corner when she heard movement outside the door. She pressed against one wall, out of sight. The door slid open, and someone entered. She slid along the shadows to a nearby bank of servers and hid between two rows of blinking machines. The door hissed shut, and moments later she heard more footsteps rushing past. They didn't stop at the server room.

The person moved into the center of the room. She froze, not even daring to breathe. His shadow fell across the floor, moving along the bank of servers on the opposite side of where she hid. When he passed by a rack that separated them, she caught a familiar scent of exotic spices. She looked again at the shadow. It had spiky hair.

He rounded the corner, and she moved quietly to the next row. She caught the briefest glimpse of him between two server banks. It was Rowan.

She stepped out of the shadows, feeling her whole body shaking with adrenaline. "Rowan?"

He spun around, eyes fixed on her. Disbelief swept over his face. "What are you doing here?"

"Trying to get out," she told him.

He looked grim. "Me too. It's not going very well." He patted the satchel slung over one shoulder. "But I have what I came for."

"You risked your life to steal something?"

"It's a game changer, believe me."

An alarm suddenly erupted in the room, a deafening, high-pitched klaxon. A red flashing light swept through the shadows.

"I think they know we're here." He turned to her with the hint of a smile. "You know, if I'd known we were going to infiltrate the same building, I'd have suggested we team up."

The footsteps in the corridor returned. They were running out of time.

"We need to get out of here!" she whispered. "This way!" Together they hurried back to the vent opening. "It's too high," she said. "We need something to stand on."

"Give me a boost," he told her, "and I'll pull you up."

She bent her knee. He placed one sprightly boot on her thigh, jumped up to the opening, and hung there for an instant. Then he pulled himself up and out of sight.

She waited for a tense moment as she heard movement in the vent. Was he leaving her?

Then his head popped out above her. He lowered his arms. "Okay! Grab on!"

She reached up, closing her hands around his wrists. He lifted her up almost effortlessly, backing up inside the vent until her belly lay on the cold metal.

Now he pivoted again in the confines of the shaft and started crawling out. She checked her PRD to make sure they were headed in the right direction. They came to several T's in the ductwork, and always Rowan chose the same one Willoughby had indicated. She got the distinct feeling he'd broken in here before.

They took a few more turns in the tunnels, crawling on their elbows and knees. Only one more and they'd be out.

When they turned the last corner, she could see the orange glow of the night sky through holes in a vent cover. Rowan reached it and pounded on it with his fist, sending it flying outward. "Almost home free," he said.

She heard something hiss through the air. A plastic net flew into the opening of the vent and gripped Rowan, cinching tightly around his torso. He thrashed as it suctioned to the shape of his body. Arms pinned, he bucked around, smashing the sides of the vent.

Then something started pulling him out into the street. She grabbed his legs, planting her weight on him. But the pull was too strong. "Hold on!" she told him, but a second later his feet slipped through her fingers, and he flew from the vent. She heard him hit something twice. All went quiet.

She shinnied to the edge of the vent, careful to stay out of sight. Below she saw him lying in an alley among heaps of trash. The white fibrous net covered him from head to waist, attached to a cable. Two Repurposers held the other end, hurrying to where Rowan lay prone. They'd been three floors up.

She saw now what he'd hit first. A ledge protruded from a second-story window; his body had crashed through it. Broken masonry lay scattered about the alley. She peered through the hole he'd made on his way down. Though he might have broken bones, the ledge had probably slowed his fall and saved his life.

As they approached him, they didn't notice her. Maybe he'd used this escape route before, and they had been waiting for him.

The shorter one bent over his body.

The other Repurposer stood, pale and gaunt. She recognized him as the one Rowan had kicked in the nose earlier that night. Crusted blood covered his upper lip and mouth. "Does he have anything on him?" Broken Nose asked his colleague.

The short one patted Rowan down. Rowan wasn't moving. She saw wet crimson pooling beneath his head. "We'll have to cut the net. It's too tight."

Broken Nose pressed a button on his utility belt. The net retracted back into a tiny holster on his hip.

Still Rowan didn't move.

They started patting him down again, searching his pockets. His satchel still hung around his torso. Whatever he'd stolen, it must be important, and it was in that bag. She had to do something. She had no doubt that once they'd taken everything off him, they'd kill him. Or worse.

Rowan groaned, rolling over on his side. He pushed their hands away weakly.

"He doesn't have a head jack."

"Then you know what to do," Broken Nose answered. "He can't be allowed to enter the city again."

While they bent over him, searching through his clothes, H124 quietly pivoted inside the narrow confines of the vent. She swung her legs over the edge, out into the open air. Her body flooded with adrenaline. Right now she was vulnerable, her legs swinging down into open space. If they happened to look up, they'd see her.

Lowering herself to hang from her fingertips, she gazed down to the ledge below. She aimed her feet for the unbroken section, then let go.

With a thud she landed squarely on the ledge, out of sight.

"What was that?" she heard the short one ask.

"There's someone up there."

"Get your gun."

The window next to the ledge was bricked up, a long time ago from the look of it. Her only way out was down. She knew the Repurposers stood right beneath her. Bracing herself, she leaped down through the hole to the alley below.

Chapter 9

H124 came down with a crash, her feet hitting the shorter Repurposer squarely in the head. She knocked him over, then sprawled into the alley. Broken Nose reached for his energy discharger. She flung herself on the shorter one's body, her quick hands closing around the weapon on his belt. She brought it up, firing at Broken Nose before he unholstered his weapon. Bright tendrils of electricity lit up the alley, burning her retinas.

She rolled off the other one and fired again. Light enveloped him, flashing again in the darkness. Struggling to her feet, she moved to Rowan. "Can you get up?"

She could see all the blood now, too much of it. "How badly are you hurt?"

He brought a hand to his head, and it came away crimson. "Feel sick to my stomach," he slurred.

"We have to get you out of here."

The short Repurposer groaned, holding his head and trying to stand up. She hurried back to Broken Nose and grabbed his weapon. But when she tried to shoot them, it wouldn't work.

"It's fried," Rowan said behind her. "A flash burster's one weakness is being hit by another one."

She took the one good weapon she still had and shot both of them again. Their bodies jittered on the black asphalt and then lay still. She returned to Rowan. Handing the weapon to him, she hooked one arm around his waist and draped his arm around her shoulder. He gripped the gun. She half dragged him out of the alley with a hammering heart. They had to get out of there.

Struggling under the Rowan's weight, H124 dragged him through darkened alleyways.

He drifted in and out of consciousness. Sometimes he was dead weight, and other times he managed to stumble. They couldn't keep this up for long.

"What about your place?" she asked when he came out of a stint of unconsciousness. "Could we hide there?"

He looked at her groggily. "My place?"

"Yes, how far is it?"

"I don't live in the city."

"What? I don't understand."

He met her eyes. "I come from outside the city."

"Outside the city?" She raised her eyebrows.

He managed a smile. *"Outside the city."*

"But . . . I've heard that you can't survive out there."

"That's not far from the truth. It's a nightmare."

"How long have you lived out there?"

"My whole life. I was born there. And that's where we have to go."

Her mouth fell open. "I can't . . ."

"No choice. You've been marked. I have to get this to my people." He placed his hand on the satchel where he'd hidden his stolen prize.

"How far is it to the edge of the city?"

"A couple miles or so."

"Which way?" she whispered.

He pointed vaguely west, so she dragged him in that direction. She looked at him as they walked, too afraid to stop. A deep gash along his temple was already turning purple and red. Blood streamed down his neck, soaking his sleeve and the back of his shirt.

"Can't seem to focus," he mumbled.

She ripped off a sleeve from her shirt and pressed it against the wound. "Can you hold that there?"

He tried to focus on her, though his eyes wandered. "I'll try."

She readjusted his arm over her shoulder as she continued to hurry down the dark alleys. A few times they had to cross over the main streets, the orange lights gleaming down on them. She felt exposed and terrified, hastening to escape into the shadows.

She lugged him on for what felt like an hour, Rowan half awake and stumbling. "My head . . ." Progress was agonizingly slow.

He almost fell, but she caught him. "You're going to have to dump me," he slurred.

"No."

"Those Repurposers won't be out long."

"No way."

Then they heard footsteps behind them. They'd caught up, closing in fast. A blinding light flashed down the alley. Rowan shoved her away with unexpected force. She stumbled in the dark, crashing to her knees.

The weapon fired again, and she saw Rowan light up, the snaking current enveloping his body. He gritted his teeth and went down, sprawling onto the asphalt.

She started toward him, but he waved her away. The Repurposers raced forward, now only feet away, but they hadn't seen her. She crawled back as they hit Rowan with another burst of energy.

Staying low, she crept to a nearby corner and crouched in the darkness. *Damn it,* she thought. He had the gun. It was probably fried. The two Repurposers had replaced their weapons before resuming their pursuit.

"Hit him again," Broken Nose said. "I've had it with this guy. He's dead." In the sickly pale glow of the orange light, she could just make out Broken Nose's pale face slick with sweat.

They stood over Rowan's prone body. The short one glanced around. "Any sign of her?"

Broken Nose peered into the darkness. "We'll find her. Let's deal with him first. Got to get him to lie still." From inside his long jacket, he pulled out the same gleaming tool they'd used on her. As the short man held down Rowan's shoulders, a flicker of sick pleasure turned up the corners of the Repurposers' mouths.

Broken Nose leaned over Rowan, starting up the blades on the gleaming tool. As the man lowered it to Rowan's head, H124 looked around for anything she could use. Some fifty feet away in the gloom lay a pile of rusted rebar and an ancient sawhorse.

She knew she couldn't reach them in time. The tool would have bitten through his skull by then. Instead she began to run back toward the rebar, shouting, "Hey!"

The two Repurposers looked up. As her hand closed around the heftiest piece of rusted metal she could find, she whirled around.

The two men had left Rowan, chasing her instead.

"That's her!" cried Broken Nose.

"We can deliver them both!" the other said eagerly.

She ran down a side alley, doubling back on them. Once out of sight, she ran back for Rowan at a crouch. Just as she was almost on him, Broken Nose cut her off. "Going somewhere?"

She gripped the rebar tightly. He reached for his weapon, leering down at her. She steeled herself, then swung with everything in her. The metal connected with the side of his temple with a sickening crunch. He crumpled to the ground, a heap of loose bones. She pivoted, facing the second Repurposer. He looked down at his fallen comrade. "What have you done?" he shouted, eyebrows knitted together

She wanted to reach for Broken Nose's weapon, but she knew the other would fire before she had the chance.

She started back as he circled her, sizing her up. As he took aim, she dove to the ground and rolled, cracking him in the knee with the rebar.

He screamed in agony, toppling to the ground. He rocked back and forth, grabbing his knee, eyes squeezed shut. She raced forward, grabbing the gun off Broken Nose. She shot them both and snatched up the gleaming tool.

Rowan stirred with a groan.

She kneeled over him, finding him barely conscious. She grabbed his arm. "We have to get out of here!"

Over her shoulder, one of the men stirred, but he didn't get up. "C'mon!" She hefted Rowan's arm around her shoulders and twined her other one around his waist. Heaving him to his feet, she supported his full weight. He moaned, bringing a hand to his head.

"What the hell . . . ?"

Behind her the short man moved, fingers grasping the pavement.

Rowan came around a little more, taking some of his weight off her. She spun him around, weapon at the ready. She hit both their assailants again. They skittered on the pavement.

Why wasn't the weapon knocking them out? She looked at it to see if it had some kind of intensity setting, but couldn't find anything. It fizzled, the acrid stench of burning circuits billowing up. It was fried. She tucked it into her bag in case it could be repaired later.

She found her bloody sleeve lying on the ground and gave it back to Rowan. "Keep pressing this on your wound." She wheeled him around and made for the end of the alley. "Are you sure this is the fastest way out of the city?" she asked.

He lifted a weak arm, pointing farther west. She closed her hand around his where it rested on her shoulder, lugging him along. She took every corner she could, still trying to keep out of the men's sight.

"Did they find us again by chance, or do you have something on you they can track?"

He shook his head. "Nothing to track."

She thought of the PRD in her pocket, praying that the producer hadn't double-crossed her. She switched it off just in case.

"How far is it to the city's borders?"

"A mile or so," he gasped. They hurried, his feet dragging a little. He tripped a few times. "Think I'm feeling better," he said after some time, taking some weight off her. They picked up their pace. His head had stopped bleeding.

She glanced back, thinking of how Rowan had killed the Repurposers who had come for her. Should she have done the same back there? She'd never hurt anyone before tonight. The guard's bloody nose in the PPC Tower had been the first time she'd made someone bleed. She couldn't just kill two prone men, could she?

She snuck a glance at Rowan, whose head was sagging. What was his life like, and what was it like out there?

She gazed up at the city's atmospheric shield. "How do we exit?"

"Exiting's no problem. There are huge carbon dioxide vents at the city's perimeter. They pump all the CO_2 out of the city. We can get out through there. It's getting *in* that's the hard part."

"How did you get in?"

"I know someone on the inside. He opened doors for me. But I didn't have much time. It's got to be a quick in and out or they start to notice the open doors." He hooked his thumb back the direction they'd come. "Let's hope those guys stay down."

As they hurried onward, H124 started to feel sick to her stomach. Was she really leaving the city? This place was the only home she'd ever known, such as it was. It may not be a good life, but it was familiar. As far back as she could remember she'd lived in her tiny pod, going from cleaning vacated living pods to cleaning corpses six years ago, when she turned twelve.

How could she leave? Where would she go? She knew nothing about the world outside. She barely knew the city. Maybe she could stay. Maybe she could explain to her employers about the asteroid. Maybe they'd understand and let her stay as she was. Maybe Willoughby could explain to them that she knew something important, that she hadn't been shirking her responsibilities, but discovering something vastly more important. Maybe she could go back to her little bed, her tiny, comfortable room, the bland but easily acquired food cubes.

She started to slow down. She thought of the PRD in her pocket. Maybe she could call Willoughby and see what he thought.

"What's wrong?" Rowan asked. "Why are you slowing down?"

She looked up at him. "I—"

He gazed back at her, lifting his eyebrows.

"I don't think I can do this," she admitted.

"What?"

"Maybe I could explain to my employers . . ."

He gently took hold of her elbow. "Look, I don't know why those Repurposers are after you. I don't live in your world, but I do know a lot about it. You're a worker. A cog. You don't even have a name. Whatever you've done, they won't listen to you. They won't spare you. You're a machine to them. A machine made of meat. You go back there, and those Repurposers will wipe your mind. It's not worth their time to listen to you." He stared at her with compassionate eyes. "If you go back there, you're signing your own death warrant."

She thought of Willoughby urging her to leave the city. If he had enough sway to keep them from harming her, wouldn't he have mentioned that? They hadn't listened to him in the Tower, at least not for long.

She looked up, thinking of the asteroid out there in the darkness of space, on its way to Earth. Would her employers really do something to stop that? Willoughby said no one even knew how to stop it, except maybe these Rovers. Even if she talked to her employers, and they let her back without wiping her, that wouldn't change the fact that soon the earth was going to experience the biggest destructive force it had ever known. She could sit in her comfortable little room, clean up more corpses, and then one day fire would fill the sky, and she'd be obliterated along with everyone else.

She looked back at Rowan. His eyes met hers. They gleamed with an intensity she'd never seen in another person. Hope filled them. She had to take this chance. Had to leave the city. She would never forgive herself if she went back now. And besides, if she went back and they wiped her, she wouldn't even remember about the asteroid. Nothing would save them. All would be lost.

She adjusted the strap on her tool bag. "Okay. Let's go."

He nodded, then squeezed her shoulder. She felt a pleasant zing of electricity at his touch. They hurried onward.

Above the atmospheric shield the gray clouds roiled. Lightning flashed. She'd never been outside of the shield. She didn't know anyone who had. Until now.

"What's it like out there?" she asked.

"Rough. Be ready."

They walked on, staying to the shadows, listening to every sound behind them. Relief flooded through H124 when they reached the edge of the atmospheric shield. It was the first time she'd been this close to it. She could hear it buzzing all around her.

"Where are the vents?"

Rowan pointed toward a series of large holes in the concrete base. The concrete swept around them, a one-hundred-foot wall encircling the entire city. On top of it, force field generators jutted into the sky. She smelled the crisp scent of crackling electromagnetic energy. It tickled the inside of her nose, and she fought off a sneeze.

Rowan pointed to one of the vents. "You can go out, but you can't come back in. It's a way of pumping out the bad air, and not letting more bad back in."

She frowned, staring at the large dark mouth of the tunnels. "Is it really so bad out there?"

He put a hand on her shoulder. "I won't lie to you. It's like nothing you'll have experienced here in the city." He left his hand there, and she felt that sensation in his touch once more, a warmth she hadn't known before. When he took his hand away, she felt strangely disappointed.

"So what now?" she asked.

"We go through the tunnels. My inside contact hasn't checked in with me, so we need to find a different way out. You can operate TWRs right?" He pronounced it like *"twirs."*

She nodded.

"Okay, then." He went first, choosing a particular tunnel. When they reached the entrance, she saw that it extended much farther than she'd thought. The concrete wall must have been at least a thousand feet thick. The tunnel stretched on into inky blackness. She took out her headlamp and switched it on. It didn't even begin to penetrate the gloom.

Rowan looked at her. "Ready?"

She frowned. "This is the only place I've ever known . . ."

He nodded.

She bit her lip. "Let's go."

"There's a barrier here at the entrance," he said in a hushed tone. "It's a semi-permeable membrane. But a shield protects it. You'll have to take down the shield first."

On the wall next to the entrance, she saw a theta wave receiver. Concentrating, she sent a message to the membrane shield to disengage. When she felt it turn off in her mind, she said, "Okay. It's down."

He went in front, entering the tunnel and moving quickly through the darkness. She turned as they passed through the shield controls and turned it back on. Then she caught up with Rowan, keeping close, her headlamp's beam bouncing off the curved walls. The cement beneath glistened with damp, and about hundred feet in the air grew chilly.

She walked behind him, watching his back, the satchel moving against his side. His muscular frame moved with a kind of grace. Now a mildewy smell filled her nostrils, and she fought off another sneeze. When she felt like they'd walked a mile in the darkness, Rowan slowed in front of her.

"What is it?" she asked.

"There's another barrier here in the middle, another shielded membrane." He stopped to face her. Her beam shone on his handsome face, set jaw, and powerful blue eyes. "Something worse than death awaits you if you stay in the city, but I want you to be certain. Are you sure you want to leave?"

She gave him a quiet stare.

"I, for one, think you should. But it's got to be *your* choice."

And some choice it was. If she stayed, the Repurposers would wipe her mind, and the asteroid would wipe out more than that. But out there, she'd be vulnerable to a world of dangers she'd never even dreamed about.

She studied Rowan's face in the shadows, then gave a resounding, "I'm ready." They moved forward through the stifling air. "I feel light-headed," she told him.

"It's all the CO_2. It's really concentrated down here."

As they moved deeper into the tunnel, she felt her lungs gasping for a decent breath.

"We're almost there," he reassured her. "The air will be better on the other side."

Her vision began to tunnel, and the air grew even more dank and foul. Her side started to burn, as if she'd been running. She saw the TWR for the second membrane and sent a signal for its shield to come down.

"It's down," she confirmed.

They walked to the other side. Her ears popped as cooler air filled her waiting lungs. She ordered the membrane to activate again.

They walked a few more feet. "There's additional security here," Rowan told her. "A field beyond the membrane incinerates anything that moves through. Watch." He removed a food cube wrapper from his satchel and threw it back the way they'd come. She saw it freeze midair, with blue volts swarming over it. Then it was gone, leaving nothing but a tiny puff of smoke. "Same thing with organic material, so don't go back that way."

He started moving again, and she followed him. "Where did you get in?"

He glanced at her over his shoulder. "My inside man opened a spot along the perimeter. But it'll be closed by now. He can't risk keeping it open for long."

An entirely new scent reached her. "What's that?"

"What?"

"That smell."

He grinned back at her, that contagious smile that made her stomach light. "Rain."

She raised her brow. "Rain?" She knew the city collected its rainwater in huge tanks outside the atmospheric shield. She also knew they maintained large desalinization tanks that pulled water from the nearby ocean. Not that she'd ever seen the ocean, no matter how near it was. And rain? She'd always been fascinated, wondered what it would be like to be outside, where water fell freely from the sky.

"I've never been in the rain." She felt herself smile. The gesture felt strange, strained, something she'd only done a couple times in her life. It was a small smile, short of showing her teeth, but she felt the corners of her mouth turn up. It almost hurt.

"Hey, keep that attitude! A lot of people can't stand the rain. It gets to them." He regarded her with kind eyes. "You know, you're pretty refreshing. Unlike anyone I've ever met. I think you're going to make it out here."

He started moving again, navigating the tunnel as if he'd been in it countless times.

"Just how many times have you broken into the city?" she asked.

His laugh was a rueful sound. "Too many to count. Been coming here since I was a kid."

The smell of fresh air grew stronger, so they hurried on. Soon her headlamp picked out the edge of the concrete tunnel. Beyond was the most pitch-black landscape she'd ever seen. At least while inside the tunnel, her headlamp had reflected off its close walls. But out there, the space was immense. Her headlamp reached out into that abyss and simply ended.

She stopped. "What's out there?"

He turned. "Everything."

"I'm . . ."

"Afraid?"

She nodded.

"I don't blame you. This is huge. But you can make it." He held out his hand, and she took it. His skin felt rough and warm as his strong fingers closed around hers.

As they reached the mouth of the tunnel, the stale air gave way to a fresh gust. She heard a roar, like the drone of distant machinery locked away in some residential building. "What's that sound?"

He stuck his head out of the entrance. "A storm."

She'd never been in a storm. Weather in the city was always the same. The same temperature. The same humidity. The air out here felt cold and windy, like nothing she'd experienced inside the city.

Then she heard something crack in the sky, a deafening cacophony of sound. It cracked again, and this time she felt the vibration in her breastbone. She backed into the tunnel, her hand withdrawing from his. "What was that?"

He walked back to her. "Just thunder."

"And the drone?"

He smiled. "That's the rain." He took her arm gently. "C'mon."

She let him lead her out through the opening. Rain poured from the sky, instantly soaking her hair and shirt. The wind picked up, so loud it roared. Rowan said something to her, but the wind carried it away. He leaned closer. "Let's find some shelter!" he yelled, running out into the storm.

She followed, finding herself on a ruined street amid giant crumbling buildings that leaned on each other. Old bricks and stonework littered the decaying road. Pieces of shattered glass crunched under her feet.

Rowan ran for a recessed doorway in one of the buildings. He dashed inside and turned to wait for her, but she was mesmerized. She couldn't help but stop and look up. Now she saw the clouds roiling above, illumed by the orange lights from the city. Behind them the huge cement barricade swept away on both sides. Inside the atmospheric shield loomed the tremendous buildings of the city.

Then it hit her. She couldn't go back. She was on the outside now. She felt strange, floating, her anchor gone. How was she going to survive? She felt the pang of homelessness, her roots ripped away beneath her. Tearing herself from the sight of the city, she reached the recessed doorway and ran inside, joining Rowan.

"You okay?" he asked.

She peered out at the storm. "I've never seen anything like this." Lightning flashed in the clouds, making the surrounding terrain go from night to day and back again. Rain gusted by in a level sheet. "I had no idea storms were so intense!" Wind whipped inside the doorway, so powerful it pushed her backward.

He gave a mirthless laugh. "I hate to tell you, but this is a break in the storm." She faced him.

"It's going to get a lot worse." He took the satchel off his shoulder and placed it on the ground, crouching down beside it. "Listen. I have to leave. But you're going to be okay." He started pulling things out of his satchel and stacking them on the floor.

She stared at him. "What?" Panic filled her. He was her lifeline, the only way she'd been able to get out of the city.

"Where I'm going . . . it's dangerous. You can't come."

"More dangerous than what we just went through?"

He lowered his head, then looked up at her with regretful eyes. "Yes. I'm afraid it is. I can't bring you with me." He took her hand again. "You can do this. You can survive." He dug through his bag. "Look, I've got some food here, and a bottle of water and a filter to collect more." He reached into his pack and pulled out an aluminum bottle and a little filter and hose. He handed them to her. "And here are some MREs."

"MREs?" she asked.

"Meals Ready to Eat," he explained. "They taste pretty bad, I won't lie. But they get the job done." He handed her all the rations he had.

"You've got to keep some for yourself!" she insisted, handing them back.

He pushed her hand away gently. "I can get more. And so can you. Do you have a PRD?"

"I do. I was told it couldn't be traced."

She pulled it out, and Rowan took it, flipping it over and removing the back. He whipped out a small tool and removed the circuitry board. "Damn. You're not kidding. Never seen one like this. It doesn't even have a slot for a tracking chip." He put it back together and turned it on. Pulling up the map function, he waved his hand through the floating display, scrolling to an area about thirty-six miles away. "Go here. It's an old weather shelter, built a long time ago when the megastorms first hit. You'll find a place to sleep, a water purification system, and lots of MREs to replenish your supply." He typed in something else. "Put in this code when you get there."

She watched him enter it, feeling hopeless and lost, then dug around in her tool bag and pulled out the fried flash burster. "Any chance this will work again?"

He took it from her and turned it over, then used his tool to open the casing. The circuitry and electricity generator were fused as one. "Sorry. This thing is done for."

She decided to take a chance. "Have you heard of the Rovers?"

He snapped his gaze up to her. "Not since I was a kid. They were the ones who allegedly built the network of weather shelters, but I don't think they're around anymore. No one has seen them, anyway. We've all wondered, though. I grew up, moving from shelter to shelter, thinking about the people who built them. But all we have are stories, all made up, I think." He looked back at her. "Why do you ask?"

"I need to find them." She told him about the asteroid and its fragments, and how Willoughby had told her that they might know how to stop it.

Rowan parted his lips as he listened. "How much time do we have?"

She bit her lip. "Two months before the first fragment hits, followed by two more. A year before the main one collides."

His eyes widened. "Small window."

"I know." She stared out at the rain, thinking of the devastation heading their way.

"Maybe a long time ago we could have stopped it. But now?" He stared out into the storm. "We're all just rats hiding in a hole. Your friend is right. If anyone would know what to do, it's the Rovers. They held onto things. Onto *knowledge*. You'll get a sense of them when you get to the weather shelter. They left books."

The word was new. "Books?"

"They're old and strange, but cool. Printed on weird stuff. And they're full of information. Some people take them from one shelter and leave them in the next. So the inventory changes."

"What kind of information?"

"Old stuff. Like what the world was like back in the day. Strange animals. Maps of places that have been gone a long time. You wouldn't believe the things that used to be out there." He stared out at the driving rain, the wind blowing it sideways down the street. "It's all gone now."

She followed his gaze, shivering in her wet shirt. "What's out there now?"

He met her eyes in the growing dark. "Heat. Death. Storms." He pulled a jacket out of his satchel and handed it to her. "You'll need this. It's waterproof."

She accepted it reluctantly. "Won't you need it?"

"I'll be fine." He rummaged through his satchel and pulled out a clear pouch. "This'll keep the rain out of your PRD." He handed it to her.

"Where are you going?" Fear gripped her stomach. Was she just supposed to walk to this place alone, with no idea how to survive out here?

"I have to go north, to my people."

She felt awkward. "And I really can't come?"

He met her eyes. "They're, uh . . . not very nice. You don't want to meet them. And whatever you do, if you meet anyone out there in the wastelands, don't tell them that you were a worker in the city. Don't let them know you can access TWRs, or that you can do work-arounds to open locks. Don't ever reveal that information."

She tilted her head. "Why?"

"Because people will kidnap you for that information. That, and your ability. And if you don't cooperate, torture's the least of your problems."

A new wave of fear stole over her, the most sickening feeling she'd had yet. "I don't think I can do this."

He closed his hands around hers. "You can. I've seen you in action, remember?" He nodded toward the city. "It's a hell of a lot more dangerous for you in there than out here. Now there's more distance between you and the bad guys."

"That doesn't make me feel better."

"Don't worry. You probably won't run into anyone." He looked out at the wind-tossed rain. "It's the weather that's the killer."

He lifted his satchel and swung it back over his head. "Good luck, H." He walked to the edge of the recessed doorway. Then he turned back. "You should think of a name for yourself. Your current designation will be a dead giveaway."

She met his eyes. "Is this the last time we'll see each other?" She barely knew him, but the thought was a painful knot twisting inside her.

He took her hand again, something hanging heavily in the air between them. She wanted to move closer, to bask in his scent one more time.

"My people have a way to communicate," he told her. "Devised over years of trial and error. Like Morse code."

"Morse code?" She'd never heard of it.

"Ancient way of sending messages by tapping out a rhythm of long and short tones." He pulled out his PRD and brought up a hovering screen. "We had to alter it from the original, in case our enemies still knew about it. The idea's the same, but the letters are different, and we've added some other elements to make messages harder to crack."

He held up his PRD. The floating display showed a communication window with a button for a short tone, and one for a long tone. A section of the screen showed each letter of the alphabet followed by its equivalent of short and long tones. *A* was a short tone followed by two long tones. Numbers one through ten also had codes.

"You type in who you want to send the message to, then enter the code for each letter as it appears on the screen. The codes change multiple times a day, but the program saves the date and time you sent the message, so you can always decipher it if you knew what the code was at any given time." He gazed at her. His eyes were so intense, she fought the urge to look away. "If you need me," he told her, "contact me this way."

She pulled out her PRD. They touched devices, and the program automatically uploaded to hers. When she double-checked it was there, she lowered her device, looking back at him. She'd never felt so drawn to someone, but she didn't know what to do. He'd led a completely different kind of life—free, adventurous, full of risk. She'd only known that which she'd been born into: raised in the machine of the city, fulfilling her duties.

She hadn't known anything else was possible. She'd always felt unsettled and alone, like she was missing something. And now, despite the fact that she had no home to go to, and was soon to be left alone in this chaotic wilderness, something felt like it was falling into place. She felt connected to Rowan, a feeling she'd never had with another human.

He gripped her hand one more time and forced a smile. But there was a deep sadness in his eyes. He let go, moved back, and stepped out into the storm. She watched him walk down the street. He stopped at a corner and turned back to look at her. Something stirred within her, a strange kind of longing. She wanted to run to him. He stood there for a long moment, gazing back as if memorizing her features. Then he raised a hand and gave a sad wave. She did the same. She watched as he reached the end of the street, gave her one last glance, and rounded the corner of a building.

And then he was gone.

She stood alone, shivering in the doorway, the howling wind cutting through her clothes. She'd never been so cold before. The city was always too hot, too humid. She watched the rain pelt the cracked pavement. She pulled on the jacket Rowan had given her, huddling in its dry warmth.

As she stared out at the gray, she noticed something green poking up between the cracks of the crumbling black road. She pulled the jacket tightly around her and crept outside. She reached out, touching the wet, green strands. They were flexible. It was a plant, she realized, not the flat-leafed ones she'd watched the food workers grind up into food cubes. This was something different. She looked down the stretch of the road, seeing more tufts breaking through the asphalt.

The loneliness sank in. The ancient road stretched into the abyss, the crumbling buildings immense and empty, their brick guts spilling from their decaying bodies. She shivered in her jacket. Hurrying back to the doorway, she checked her PRD. Noting the direction of the weather shelter, she turned off the device, tucking it into the weatherproof pouch he'd given her. Then she walked out into the storm, not knowing what lay ahead, or if she'd even live to see the next day.

Chapter 10

She walked alone, listening to the howling wind and the rain lashing at the shattered windows around her. She thought back to that feeling of sitting in the tiny room where she'd first encountered Rowan. When he'd left, disappearing into the night, she hadn't realized the full gravity of her situation. Now she did. She was alone in the middle of a torrential storm, with only a spot on a map to guide her.

She rechecked the PRD. The arrow still blinked in the direction she needed to go. She'd walked a few miles now, her surroundings never changing. The ruins of crumbling buildings loomed in the distant glow from the city dome. Strange sounds hung in the air, the drumming of the rain, the whistling of the wind through empty windows. Nothing sounded or looked familiar. She'd always been acquainted with her own company and a vague sense of loneliness that plagued her some nights when she lay in her narrow bed. But this was true solitude.

Somewhere out there, above those swirling clouds, doom sped toward Earth.

She took another look at the blinking arrow, then powered down the PRD and replaced it in the weatherproof bag. She estimated another five hours of darkness. The lights from the city reached this far, but as she stared into the distance, she saw only an endless black cluster. At least she had her headlamp. She could recharge it in five hours with UV. Her PRD too.

She didn't think the Repurposers would come out this far to get her, but she felt exposed this close to the city, so she didn't use the headlamp just yet. She wanted to get out of this creepy, desolate area, these decomposing ruins of a people who had come before.

She walked where the arrow pointed her, winding down streets between immense skyscrapers.

She stared up in awe of them. Most had only one or two standing walls. Crumbled brick lay in piles at their bases. Some, comprised of steel and glass, stood like skeletal monuments to a long dead people. Crunching under her feet, dirty, shattered pieces of glass littered the ground. She saw more tufts of the green plant in cracks along the road. She passed a teetering steel structure reaching up into the sky. Wind shrilled around its exposed girders.

Wild gusts shoved at her back, while the rain soaked her legs beneath her coat. Her chest stayed warm and dry, though. She was grateful to Rowan for the jacket. She nestled into it more, bringing the hood closer around her face while the rain drummed on it. She caught a hint of his scent in that hood, the same spicy smell she'd caught back in the city.

A sudden draft hit her so hard she flew forward, knees landing on the run-down pavement. She struggled to her feet again, hurrying down the road. Rounding a corner, she escaped the brunt of the wind. She waited for a few minutes for the squall to abate. Rowan had said this was a break in the storm. When the loud whooshing died down a little, she continued on. Monstrous metal poles lined the roads. Many had toppled, but some still stood, with shattered glass at their crowns.

She kept checking behind her, half expecting to see the Repurposers, half hoping she'd see Rowan coming to take her safely to his people.

But there were only shadows.

She kept moving, walking until her feet dragged. She opened her water bottle and let the rain fill it. She sealed it and drank through the filter. It tasted cleaner than the water in the city. Purer, somehow, without a chemical tang. She saved the food, not wanting to eat until she felt too weak to go on. She didn't know how long it would take to reach the weather shelter, and she didn't want to waste her rations.

Thinking she couldn't take another step without falling asleep on her feet, she slowed to a stop.

The pavement ended beneath her, and a dark expanse stretched out ahead. The tiny green plant she'd seen rising out of the cracks was everywhere before her. She'd never seen anything like it. No more cement, but a verdant carpet, stretching as far as the eye could see. The glow from the city was now very faint. Soon she'd have to switch on her light or start tripping and running into everything.

But for now the dim orange glow illuminated the wet, spiky strands of the plant. She bent down, running her fingers through its softness.

As she crouched there, her eyes grew more accustomed to the dark. She made out something huge standing fifty feet away. She stifled a cry, thinking it was a man. She froze, and simply stared at it. More details came steadily into focus. It stood tall, with massive limbs stretching in all directions. Its top billowed out. The wind tossed it violently, its limbs quavering as little objects flew off it. It wasn't moving, not the bottom part anyway. She stood up and crept closer. At last she pulled out her headlamp and switched it on, looking up. Green filled her field of view. She'd never seen such a vivid color. The billowy top was actually thousands of flat leaves. Its base was hard and thick. She reached out, touching its rough skin. It creaked, and the wind sighed in its leaves. She'd seen leaves before in the food processing plants of New Atlantic, but never knew where they came from. This whole thing was a plant, she realized, only colossal. Beneath it, the rain couldn't reach her. The plant sheltered her, and she didn't feel the pang of the cold as much. Her eyes burned from want of sleep.

She breathed in the great stalk, welcoming its fragrant scent into her lungs. She pressed her face against its cool exterior and closed her eyes.

She'd come miles from the city. She could spare her lids a few moments' rest.

She let her body sag to the ground, sitting on the wet, spongy plant cover. Switching off her headlamp, she turned her back, leaning against the shelter of the magnificent giant. She huddled more snugly in the jacket. She would let her eyes stay closed for a minute. Just a minute.

* * * *

H124 jerked awake to the sound of a cry. She leaped to her feet, looking in all directions. She'd fallen asleep for too long. Light streamed through the thick layer of clouds. The rain fell less violently, and the wind had died down. She shivered, her clothes positively soaked.

The cry came again. She pressed against the giant plant and scanned all around. It sounded strange. Not human.

A flicker of movement in the tree above her caught her attention. There was something there. H124 took off, racing across the expanse of vegetation. She glanced back over her shoulder, spotting a black form moving among the limbs. She ran harder, leaving the plant far behind. She sprinted up a small hill and found herself before a bigger group of gigantic plants. Their leaves shaded her from the bright clouds and the rain. She slowed, listening. She couldn't hear the cry now. Little paths wound between the giants, with strange, rusted barrels toppled over on their sides. Some still stood next to decaying benches. A short distance away, the gathering of giant plants ended, and more decrepit buildings blocked her view of anything beyond.

She turned. From the top of the little knoll, she could see all around her, far into the distance. A drizzle fell, blanketing everything. And for the first time in her life, she saw the sea. She'd heard it was near the city, heard tales of a colossal body of water that had no end. And there it was, its blue-gray stretching to the horizon.

Winds tore across it, forming great white waves. She stood, awestruck. She spotted things poking out of its surface. Way out, she saw a huge green arm holding a cup of fire. Closer in, buildings rose up from the waves, some blocky and square, others with spires. One in particular flashed in the light. Ornate arches decorated its sides, one stacked on top of the other, tapering to a point. She'd never seen such an elaborate structure. All the buildings in New Atlantic were stark, utilitarian. Even the PPC Tower, the tallest and best lit structure, was all straight lines and functionality. No adornment. But this building was something else.

The sea met the shore some distance closer, and even nearer stood New Atlantic, its atmospheric shield gleaming. From her vantage point the city looked a ghastly deformity against the backdrop of that wind-tossed sea.

A violent crack brought her eyes up. The clouds roiled, a swirling mass of gray and black. Lightning flashed, illuminating the underbelly of clouds in brilliant streaks, but this time she couldn't see the actual bolts. The rain grew heavier, drumming down on her hood. Reluctantly, she turned her eyes away from the ocean and the submerged buildings. A strange, ancient world now drowned and dead.

She walked on, watching the rain drip off the edge of her hood. Beneath the jacket, her skin felt clammy and cold, and she wondered if she'd ever be warm again. She thought of her tiny room back in the city, of sweltering nights in her narrow bed, where it was often too hot to breathe. Workers didn't have the luxury of air-conditioning like the plugged-in citizens did. She always welcomed the cool, dry air of their pods.

But out here, her nails turned blue, and she started to shiver. The rainfall grew louder and sharper, and began to hurt. Something heavy bounced off her hand, and she peered out into a world of white.

Hard pellets clinked on the ground, bouncing off the pavement and old rusted machines that lay along the sides of the streets. The ice amassed, building up a thin layer of white. Then the pellets became small balls. One hit her arm, and she ran for cover, not sure where to go. She scanned the street for a recessed doorway, but didn't see any. This street was different.

None of the tall brick buildings she'd first encountered. Here they ended in pointed roofs. Some had overhangs in front of their doors, but they'd long since become rotten. These buildings looked more unsafe than the balls of ice. She spotted one of the machines that stood along the road. It was more intact than the others, and the space beneath it was tall enough for her to slide under if she lay on her back.

As the ice slammed down on her shoulders, she covered her head and ran for it. Jagged rusted metal made up most of the machine. She dove down and slid under it, tucking in her legs just as the sky let loose another crack of thunder. Suddenly spheres of ice rained down, bouncing all around her, splashing in growing puddles and *thunk*ing on the roof of the machine.

Icy rainwater swept past, flooding the pavement, sweeping in torrents around her chilled body. Her teeth chattered, but she couldn't even hear them above the din of the storm. Now she saw what Rowan had meant about it being a break in the storm. She peered out, past the rusted wheels into the gray world beyond.

Her eyes burned with exhaustion, and her shoulders and legs ached. As the cacophonous roar of the storm filled the air, she shivered, wrapping her arms around herself. The ice continued to fall. She tried to roll into a tight ball, crossing her arms over her chest. She felt so heavy. She let her stinging eyes close.

A second later she jolted herself awake, banging her head on the underside of the machine. She was amazed she'd fallen asleep. Cold water had seeped in through her sleeves. The ice-choked water had risen, reaching her ears as she lay flat on her back. She cursed as the water swirled around her. It was rising past her ears, and started to cover her face. She would drown if she stayed there. Wiping the water from her eyes, she looked out into the streets. The ice balls had quadrupled in size. If one of them hit her on the head, she could fall prone into the water and drown. She could hear them striking the metal above her, the entire machine now rocking under the weight of the impacts. The ice churned in the rising water from the earlier rain, creating a frigid soup that carried trash and debris down the street.

The cold water streamed in the gutter. She craned her neck, seeing a choked drain hole about twenty feet away. So much debris clogged it that she doubted it had drained any water for decades. Trash protruded from the opening, mostly shards of metal and plastic.

Water seeped into her boots and down the neck of her jacket. Now it was up past her shoulders, so she lifted her head above it, pressing her face against the cold underbelly of the machine.

The ice continued to hammer down.

She waited, hoping it would abate, but the water level was still rising. She had only inches of air left beneath her shelter.

She had to get to higher ground or find better cover. She thought of the empty buildings around her. They weren't like the living pods in the city and looked uninhabited. All she had to do was break into one of the dwellings with an intact roof.

Thrashing in the water to get a better look, she twisted around. About five feet away lay a rusted piece of rounded metal. If she could just grab it . . .

Taking a deep breath, she submerged herself and wriggled out from under the machine. She leaped up, running for the piece of metal, arms flung over her head for protection. She reached it and lifted it up, finding it surprisingly light. She whipped it over her head just as one of the tremendous chunks of ice slammed into her hand. Her fingers went numb, and she nearly dropped the metal disc. But she didn't.

She ran.

As ice pummeled her back and the ground around her, H124 ran for the nearest building. A flight of six stairs led up to the door. She raced up them, hand throbbing where the ice had struck it. She reached the door and pressed against it. A tiny overhang provided a little cover.

The door was a complete puzzler. No TWR. No biometric scanner. Just a strange round metal knob. She grabbed it and pulled. Then she pushed. It gave a little, turning to the right, so she twisted it. The door came open in a rush, and suddenly she was inside.

Thin light streamed down from a scatter of holes in the ceiling. She shut the door and looked around, lowering her metal shield. Now that she had a moment to look at it, she saw that it had a handle in the center, and was rusted through in several places. It looked like a lid. She placed it on the ground and moved into the room.

All the while, ice pummeled the roof, but it didn't reach her.

She caught her breath, wringing the water out of her hair. She glanced around, realizing she might even get dry in here.

She walked into the building, taking in the ruined space, wondering what the place must have been, what *all* these places along the street must have been. She walked down a narrow hallway, from which several rooms branched off. The first one she came to, with a missing wall and a portion of collapsed ceiling in the far corner, held strange, rusted appliances. One looked like a refrigeration unit, but it was big, taller than she was. A granite counter stood in the center of the room. Corroded utensils lay scattered upon it, while above hung pots and pans dripping with rust-tinged rainwater. She left the room and entered the next one.

The remains of a couch sat against the far wall. Different objects stood against another wall, including a huge rectangle like the one she'd found under pod A25. But while this box held a similar glass screen, it was much bigger. Several other plastic boxes sat on dilapidated shelves under the large screen. A thick layer of dust covered them, and she wiped away the front of one, but had no idea what it was. The letters *PS* were still barely legible.

Another cabinet stood against the far wall. She walked to it, finding several ancient glass items, tiny sculptures in abstract shapes. The objects originally held in plastic frames, with shattered glass at their bases, had long since rotted away. She scanned these frames, finding one pushed to the far back of the shelf that still had its glass intact. Inside was an image of a man, woman, and child, all smiling, the sun streaming down on them. In the background was an ocean of sapphire. The occupants of the image beamed like the sun, looking happier than she'd ever seen anyone.

She picked it up, staring at their faces. She'd never seen a photo of someone so obviously from outside the city. The fact that they were with a child was even stranger. The only people who had contact with children in her city, New Atlantic, were the caregivers, and they didn't single out any one child like this. They were efficient, trained, able to raise a physically healthy child. But this was very strange. She set the photograph back on the shelf.

Leaving the room, she resumed her walk down the corridor. A set of stairs climbed up. She passed them and entered the last room on the left. She walked inside, finding a huge bed, bigger than any she'd ever seen. But it was mildewed and ruined, the covers black with mold and the mattress decayed, springs emerging through tears in the fabric.

The ceiling had held up well in this room. Cabinets lined one wall, and she opened them one by one. Most were empty, water-stained, and reeking of mold. But in one she found a strange device with a decaying hose attached to it. On the bottom of the device was a bristly brush mounted on a roller. A snaking black cord was wrapped up on its back. She had no idea what it was for.

She spotted a metal box high up on a shelf and pulled it down. Placing it gently on the floor, she lifted the two silver latches that held it closed. She gasped as she opened it. Inside lay more images like she'd seen in the other room, again reproduced on physical sheets. But these were still pristine. She flipped through them. The man, woman, and child from the photo in the other room were in most of them.

In some they were running and laughing outside, and in others, it was a posed image where they sat perfectly still, smiling out at the camera.

Other images baffled her. In one, the child sat behind a round, white object aflame with colorful sticks. He was grinning and wearing a cone-shaped hat. She didn't know what to make of it.

In another photograph, the woman sat at a huge contraption with black-and-white hand levers and metal foot pedals. Perhaps it was some kind of primitive locomotion device? Again, she had no idea.

But one thing became clearer the more she looked at the photos: These three people had lived together in this place. The child had grown up here. From image to image he got older, bigger. They hugged and smiled. She wondered if they'd somehow kept their own child.

No one lived together where she came from. People were assigned a pod when they grew old enough to take care of themselves. If you were a citizen, you were given a head jack and set up in the kind of pod she cleaned out: luxurious, equipped with a network connection, no need to ever leave your living quarters. If you were a worker, they denied you a head jack. You got a tiny living space in the subbasement of a building. Who would be a worker or citizen was decided when people were infants. She didn't know how they determined which one you ended up as, but there were far more citizens. People like her were rare.

Even rarer were the Menials, who had head jacks but weren't connected to the network. There was something wrong with them. They shambled about their jobs, which usually involved pressing a button every few minutes or throwing a lever. They stared and never talked. Some had seizures, writhing on the floor, and were removed after that to some unknown place. They made her sad when she saw them, like a part of them was gone, and they could never get it back.

She looked back at the photo, at the happy adults embracing the child. It was alien to her.

If you were a citizen in New Atlantic, you could conceive one child. To do so, you trolled through profiles of other citizens online. If you found a person you liked, you sent a message. If the other person liked you back, the Automaton Controller came into your pod and got the necessary ingredients from both of you. Babies were raised in a central child-rearing area by workers called caregivers, then children were installed in their own pods when they reached a self-sufficient age. If you were their mother or father, you could watch your child age and progress via its online profile. She herself had never been online, though, so her parents, whoever they were, definitely hadn't watched her grow up. When she was six, she was assigned her worker duties and installed in a cramped living pod.

She looked back at the photos. It *did* look like this kid had actually grown up with the same two people, who could well have been his parents. She tried to imagine what that would have been like. To know your own parents? To live and grow with them?

She didn't know why, but her eyes started stinging, and a painful lump grew in her throat. She put the photos back in the case and latched it shut.

She found a relatively dry corner and curled up against the wall, pulling her knees under her chin. She shivered in the damp, listening to the incessant beating of the rain outside, the wind howling through the jagged walls and empty spaces.

* * * *

She awoke to light filtering in through the missing walls. The sun was up, but once again, thick clouds filled the sky. She shivered on the floor. Sitting up, she stretched. The scalp wound from the Repurposer's tool still hurt, but it was starting to heal. While she used her tooth cleaner, she laid out her headlamp and PRD beneath a hole in the ceiling, letting the UV recharge them. When her tooth cleaner beeped, her PRD and headlamp also emitted a tone, letting her know that they were fully charged. She scooped them up, placed them in the bag, then studied the map on the PRD. She had to head west and a little south. Reluctantly, she left her shelter.

Throughout the day, she walked along countless streets, from town to ruined town. A few times she walked on crumbled roads that stretched between ancient cities. Huge signs, long since bereft of their messages, rose on both sides. Above her the sky churned gray, and a steady drizzle rained down on her.

The sun faded into the west, and she pulled out her headlamp and switched it on. The wind intensified, the cold rain falling in bigger drops, slashing across her face as she tried to see into the dark. She had to find shelter and rest.

She came to a huge building that still had three of its walls. Many windows lined its sides, but all had lost their glass long ago. Rusted rebar stuck out of old brick. It looked industrial and roomy. She hurried to it, finding a corroded dock door that was partially up. Squatting down, she ducked under it. She moved farther inside, crouching under debris that had collapsed from the walls and roof. Huge steel girders, tarnished and smelling strongly of iron, sprawled across the floor. Pink, fibrous insulation, soaked from the rain, lay tufted beneath piles of moldy plaster and ancient wiring. The far corner of the building still had a partial roof over it, and she headed for it in the darkness.

With the cloud cover so thick, she could barely pick her way through the shadows, and more than once she tripped on strange shapes that gave off metallic clangs. Thick mud from years of accumulation covered the ground. Finally she reached the corner. She dragged a rusted metal box over and propped it up to sit on.

The rain beat on the roof. An ear-splitting peal cracked throughout the sky until it rumbled away in the distance. Again the wind moaned through the missing walls, and out in the street she could hear the water gurgling down the antique gutters choked with debris.

She rubbed a shoulder pensively, then pulled out an MRE and chewed half of it, not bothering to switch on her headlamp. In her pod back in the city, she never knew darkness. Outside lights burned twenty-four hours a day. Even in the pod where she slept, her walls glowed with dozens of switches for lights, fan, food and laundry delivery, and, of course, the corpse cleanup light that accompanied the message beeping on her PRD when a job came in.

She'd never known darkness like this, and it enveloped her completely. She found it oddly comforting, so quiet, so little stimulus getting in. Just the rain and the wind and the dark.

She finished her half of the MRE and wrapped up the rest, saving it for tomorrow.

Leaning her head against the wall, she let her lids fall shut. If she could just get out of this flooded area, she could cover more ground. Would it be raining like this every day? Would the wind always howl like this?

She had just dozed off when she jerked awake. She'd heard something. Something was moving out there in the dark.

Chapter 11

She listened, trying to separate distinct sounds from the pouring of rain and lashing of the wind. Had she dreamed it? What had awoken her? Every muscle tensed, some primal part of her flowing with fear. Minutes passed, and still she heard nothing out of the ordinary.

She closed her eyes again, figuring it must have been a dream.

Then she heard it again: a kind of hissing sound, coming from outside. It sounded like a long exhale. Something slid debris aside at the other end of the building, where she'd entered. She heard that long sigh again, then more debris overturned and clanged.

She strained her eyes in the dark. She couldn't see anything and didn't dare switch on her headlamp. The sigh was almost human, but something about it was distorted, as if it came from a misshapen mouth. Another piece of metal screeched. She could barely make out the shape of something dark pressing through the broken field of rusted clutter.

The primal fear washed up her back, sending the hairs on her scalp pricking. Pressing her back against the wall, she regretted having cornered herself. But she hadn't seen another living thing since Rowan had left, and hadn't expected to.

Clang. Screeeech. It was moving closer, that exhale through the ruined mouth. Peering into the gloom, she tried to figure out how far along the wall she'd have to move before she reached another ragged hole that led outside.

As the screeching and lifting of debris grew closer, she left her perch on the metal box and moved to her right at a crawl. Shadows clustered so thickly on this part of the floor that she winced with each step, constantly banging her shin or stepping down wrong on shards of trash.

Then a higher, more plaintive breathing met her ears. This second thing was much closer; it must have entered the building through some other hole. She stopped, staring toward the noise. Something shifted in the darkness there, blotting out the tiny portion of the night sky she could see through one ruined wall.

Though she couldn't make out what it was, she had the distinct impression that it could see her perfectly.

Panic welled up inside her. The shadow grew taller, leaning over a boxy shape on the floor. She started moving again, hurrying toward a dim hole she could see in the wall.

The thing on the far end of the building started shoving debris aside more carelessly, making its way toward her. She still couldn't make out if the shapes were human or not. But she could definitely feel eyes on her. She ran.

Leaping over debris, bag clutched tightly to her chest, she raced toward the hole, and the shapes bounded after her. She came to the opening, smelling the fresh air rushing in from the outside. A large grate of some kind stood leaning precariously against the wall beside the opening. She got down on all fours and crawled through the aperture, then reached back through the hole and grabbed the grate. Pulling with all her strength, she slid it over the opening just before her pursuers reached it.

She stood up and ran.

The rain soaked her hair. Her frantic eyes searched the shadowed streets for cover. A short distance away, she saw a series of brown stone buildings, all with staircases leading up to their doors. She raced toward them, picking the closest one whose entryway and walls were intact.

She raced up the stairs, found the knob, and shoved open the door, slamming the thick wood behind her. Her groping hands found an old lock. She engaged it. Then she slumped down, pressing her back against the door, catching her breath. Hopefully, the things hadn't seen where she went. There was a chance they hadn't. Unless they could move the grate, they'd have to backtrack and leave the warehouse through some other hole.

She sat, waiting, listening. She didn't dare move or even sling her bag off her shoulder. She clutched it, ears perked for any hint of noise outside. She didn't hear anything except the rain pounding on the roof. Miraculously, her spot on the floor was dry. Part of one of the upper walls was missing, but the ceiling was largely preserved.

For hours she sat burning with fatigue, tensely clutching her bag.

She fought the desire to sleep, but suddenly found herself jerking awake. She checked her PRD. Four hours had passed. Relief flooded through her. They hadn't found her.

She rummaged through her bag and took a long drink from the rainwater she'd filtered earlier that day. It was still dark out, and she didn't want to leave this place at least until light, when she'd be able to see if those things were still out there.

Reaching up, she double-checked the lock on the door. It was still engaged. Then she slumped against the wood and closed her eyes.

* * * *

She woke to warmth on her face. An unbearably bright light shone down on her. Heat spread over her entire body. Through the empty place in the upper wall the sun gleamed. It was the first time she'd seen it in weeks. She got to her feet, finding her clothes dried. The floor around her steamed as the sun hit it. Normally she preferred stormy days, when the gray clouds bubbled above New Atlantic's shield. But she was very grateful to see the sun. She laid out her PRD and headlamp to recharge in a pool of light. In a few minutes they beeped, and she put them back in her bag. Willoughby still hadn't sent her a message with a lead on the Rovers.

She stepped outside, bombarded by a wave of humidity. After checking up and down the ruined street, she didn't see any sign of movement. She staggered outside, struggling to breathe the heavy air. Yesterday it had been chilly, but today was twice the temperature. She checked the direction of the weather shelter on her PRD and headed that way. She took off her jacket, folded it up, and placed it inside the bag. The sun burned her scalp as she walked. She didn't have a hat, and she didn't want to put the parka back on in this miserable heat.

She walked in the shadow of crumbled buildings whenever she got the chance, trudging along the cracked sidewalk as the pavement shimmered. Tar ran in little rivulets down the asphalt, sticking to her boots. Having to squint made her head ache. As the day wore on, the oppressive air began to smell. It reeked of death and decay, of rotten things decomposing in the sewers below. She gagged. Stopping in the shade of an old stone building, she took a long drink out of her water bottle. She was going through it too fast today. If it didn't rain again soon, she'd have to find another source of water, but she hadn't seen so much as a water storage facility since she left. She realized that she had no idea what an antique water storage facility would even look like. She could have walked past dozens and not known it.

She trudged on, feet swelling and burning in her boots. Her shirt clung to her as rivers of sweat trickled down her back.

As the afternoon wore on, the inevitable happened: She ran out of water.

She stopped, sitting down under the protection of another stone façade. This had the letters B-A-N-K carved in stone above the door. She could feel the building's warmth radiating upward.

In the west, more clouds accumulated. One swelled higher than the others, a puffy white tower. The wind met her, carrying with it now familiar scent of rain.

She picked herself up and continued toward the shelter, keeping an eye on the weather.

As she walked, more clouds clustered on the horizon, forming dark gray layers that crept toward her. Flashes of lightning arced beneath the clouds. The bloated column grew into a massive black wedge. The wind picked up, hitting her hard. Still the sun hammered down overhead. The storm hadn't reached her yet. All the same, the weather shelter lay in its dominion.

She kept walking, the gales shifting her back and forth. Dirt and sand kept hitting her in the face. She bent forward, trying to protect her eyes. Then she heard a creak, and the grinding of stone. She turned to see a nearby building lose a section of bricks, which came crashing down. The next gust knocked her right into the rubble pile. She looked up. Another round of bricks leaned and creaked, ready to plunge down on top of her. She leaped up and bolted toward safety.

She had to find shelter. The clouds moved in, rolling above her in a swirling mass, blotting out the sun. A bolt of lightning jagged out from their gray underbelly. She glanced around for a place where she could ride out the storm.

She ran down the street, stopping occasionally to make sure she was headed in the right direction. Then the rain let loose in another roar. Gargantuan drops pelted down, coalescing in streams along the street. The wind tore at her clothes, buffeting her back and sides. It threw her off balance, and she went down hard onto the rain-soaked asphalt. She staggered to her feet and looked down to see that her pants were soaked.

Nearby she saw a sewer opening that wasn't clogged with debris. She reached it just as ice started careening down from the sky. The opening wasn't wide, but she could fit. Sliding her feet in first, she squirmed through the hole, then dropped down a few feet, splashing into a shallow pool. She regained her balance, then pulled out her headlamp and switched it on. The beam played off a long, curved tunnel.

Ankle-deep water gushed by her in torrents as a noxious, rotting smell filled the air. She pulled her collar over her face to mask the stench, but it did little. Breathing through her mouth, she cast the headlamp's beam up and down the tunnel, wondering if she should try to move underground or wait out the ice chunks.

She'd seen a few buildings a couple blocks down that looked more intact than the others near her, and decided she'd move toward them underground. Already the water in the tunnel had risen to her knees. She didn't want to be trapped down here if the tunnel filled.

She sloshed toward the buildings, stepping over rusted pieces of metal and clumps of thick, gray slime whose origins she didn't even want to ponder. About twenty feet in, she heard something splashing behind her. She spun, aiming her beam down the tunnel. She thought it might be ice coming in through the opening, so she stared hard in that direction. Then she saw a black shape, like the ones from last night. It drew in a sharp, hungry breath and loped toward her.

She ran.

Chapter12

H124 leaped through the water, banging her shin on a piece of submerged concrete. Behind her the splashing grew more insistent, and she knew she didn't have much time. She had to reach the next opening. She tore on, now hearing more than one thing in pursuit. Daylight streamed in through another opening up ahead. She ran clumsily, vaulting over obstacles as they came, but so much debris choked the tunnel that she eventually tripped and pitched forward. Her hands caught the rough concrete walls of the tunnel, and she righted herself. She could hear the things hissing behind her, exhaling, now joined by a kind of ragged sigh. Ten more feet to the light. She plunged forward. She could see the opening, a circle in the tunnel's ceiling, waiting for her atop a short steel ladder.

She grabbed the rungs and swung herself up.

The things hissed behind her.

As her head and shoulders burst upward, a chunk of ice collided with her arm. She let out a cry. She climbed all the way out of the dark hole and raced for the buildings. Another ice ball screamed down beside her, shattering on the asphalt. A second connected with her shoulder, and she cried out. She glanced back, spotting something dark sticking above the sewer opening. She continued to race onward, but when she looked back, whatever it was had retreated back into the tunnel.

She reached one of the more undamaged buildings, noticing that it didn't have a door. She ran on to the next one, relieved to see it still had one. She wrenched it open, slammed it shut behind her, and drove a rusted bolt home. She could hear the ice pummeling the ceiling. She slumped down against the wall, wanting to laugh out loud. She caught her breath, wiping the rain out of her eyes. She pulled out her PRD, seeing how much ground she'd covered. She had to cover more distance today. If the Rovers had built the weather shelter system, maybe she could find some clue to their whereabouts when she reached it. Her body ached, but she had to keep going, at least until night, when those things might be out again. During the day it seemed like they kept to the dark. She hadn't seen any topside while she'd been walking.

She stared down at the gray, featureless map of the PRD. Other than the blinking arrow, Willoughby's PRD had no base map outside the city. Hers hadn't had that either, and she wasn't surprised. People had no reason to leave the city. More than a few times when she was younger, she'd pulled out her PRD and scrolled her city's map beyond the edge of the atmospheric shield. Hers simply stopped and snapped back when she reached the perimeter.

Willoughby's allowed her to scroll beyond New Atlantic, but the map showed no roads, no buildings, no markings at all.

She waited, listening to the ice pound on the roof. When it stopped, she unlocked the door and peered out. Nothing stirred in the opening to the tunnels. Light filtered down from the cloudy sky, and she set out again.

The humidity had lessened after the storm, so she walked on, feeling a little more comfortable. In the distance, something gleamed in the light, a long ribbon cutting through the terrain.

At last she reached it and found a massive body of water coursing by. Kneeling at the bank, she refilled her bottle and took a long drink of the filtered water. Then she topped off her bottle again. Standing up, she gazed across to the other side. She had no idea how to get across.

Then she spotted a bridge, mostly submerged, with just a few ornate towers visible above the muddy banks of the flooded river. She could cross it, but it was going to be tough. Along the swollen banks, the tops of houses peeked out, their roofs covered in slime, algae, and muddy branches twisted in leaves. She wondered how long they'd been like this. On the other side of the river, a road ran through the town, cracked and broken.

Cinching her bag tight around her torso, she waded out into the cold water. Her boots found the surface of the bridge, waist deep underwater. The surface was slippery, and she almost fell back into the raging current.

Windmilling her arms, she managed to stay upright. Inching out, she kept her body low and slid her feet along the slimy bridge. She made it to the first tower and grabbed hold of it. She steadied herself, looking back the way she'd come. So far, so good. She then moved past the tower, trying to hold on to the submerged side rail of the bridge. But it was too slick with algae. She soldiered on, the current more powerful toward the center of the river. As water rushed over her boots, she knew she wouldn't be able to stay afoot at its midpoint.

She crept along a few inches at a time, sliding one boot ahead, then shifting her weight and sliding the other. She reached the next tower, grabbing it eagerly. She shifted to the middle section of the bridge. Here the water gushed in a swirling mass. She didn't think she could remain standing. But she had to try. She pushed onward, concentrating. She hadn't gone more than a few feet when a rush of water hit her, sweeping her feet out. She came crashing down into the waves, arms flailing until they found the railing.

Her fingers gripped the slimy surface, and she laced her arms around the metal. Water shot up under her chin, flooding her nose and mouth. She spat it out, gasping frantically. The faster she crossed, the better. Arm over arm, she shinnied herself along the bridge, the cold water sucking the life right out of her muscles. Finally she reached the next tower and pulled herself out of the water, trying to catch her breath. She coughed up mud.

She then moved past the tower, starting out on her feet once again. The current was less powerful here, so she padded along. Her teeth chattered, and her legs trembled. She soon reached the last tower and took hold. She clung to it, wondering if she'd ever be warm again. Coughing, she left the tower and made her way to the muddy bank on the opposite side. When her feet hit dry ground, she turned around, surveying the length of her feat. A sense of pride welled up. *She'd made it.*

She turned around, staring out at the cracked and sun-bleached road. Glad for the waterproof bag, she pulled out her PRD and checked the compass reading. The weather shelter wasn't far now. She couldn't believe it. Only five miles away, and the land looked relatively flat. She'd be there in no time.

She imagined dry clothes and a solid roof over her head. Though she'd only been gone from her pod for a short time, the memory of its warm, dry confines already felt distant, as if they belonged to another life.

She realized they did.

As she stepped onto the road, the rain returned, pounding on the hood of her parka. It had been raining so constantly that the thrumming of droplets on her head was starting to get to her. The drumming sounded from inside her skull, with every fiber of her being rattling to each drop. Water soaked everything she had, except her shirt under the warm jacket and her meager belongings in the protective bag.

She double-checked the direction and headed off, feeling more robust now that the end was in sight.

She stepped over broken chunks of asphalt, trotted past rows of abandoned, decrepit houses, and threaded her way through derelict vehicles that littered the road like rusted carcasses of a bygone age.

She passed through endless streets of collapsed buildings as thunder boomed overhead. From the time she'd left the city, the edifices stretched on and on. She could see why they'd been abandoned; no way could someone build an atmospheric dome this big. And the weather was out of control. It destroyed everything. Wind shattered windows and swayed buildings; water eroded foundations. Heat cracked and heaved the street.

All of a sudden, in a nondescript spot on the boundless cement, her PRD started beeping. She stood before a monstrous building of white stone with pillars on either side of the door. She knew she was close.

The arrow pulsed softly. This was the place. Like every other building she'd come across, this one stood in ruins. An entire wall had fallen to rubble, and all the windows had shattered long ago. Some letters chiseled into the stone above the gaping door read *Municipal Library*. She recognized the letters, but not the words. She mounted the stone steps, staring upward. She noticed smaller letters had been notched above the big ones. The entire sign read, *The Mall at the Municipal Library*. She walked through the main entrance, assaulted by the reek of mildew. Something else hung in the air too, the sickly sweet, cloying smell of death, an all too familiar scent.

Rain pattered on the floor through a dozen holes in the place's roof. She didn't see how this could be a weather shelter.

Dozens of doorways lined the main corridor. Strange rusted metal racks lay on their sides, scattered in and out of the doorways, lying in puddles of rainwater. Glass glittered all over the floor. In some places, the ceiling had caved in, and a huge chunk of a southern-facing wall opened to a view of the ruined city beyond.

She walked cautiously down the hallway, peering into the doorways. Some glass still hung in walls framed by rusted metal. She realized these walls had once been all glass. As she moved forward, she jumped. Lying on the floor in the next room was a human on his back, one hand reaching toward the ceiling.

She crept closer. Rowan had said she probably wouldn't run into another person. But if weather shelters were as valuable as he'd made out, then people probably came from all over to find one, just as she had done.

She pressed close to one of the few sections of solid wall that was still standing and peered around the corner. The man wasn't moving. It was so dark in the room that she saw only his silhouette.

He was the first person she'd seen since Rowan, and she had no idea when she'd see someone again. Her fight-or-flight urge crept through every limb. She stepped closer, now almost in the same room as the man. Still he didn't move. She allowed her eyes to grow accustomed to the dark. She eased herself closer, ready to bolt, but the man did not move. Finally she switched on her headlamp.

Shadows skittered up the walls. The beam fell on the man. He was fake, she realized. He was completely white, wearing the tattered remnants of some kind of cloth. Shining the beam around the rest of the room, she saw similar shapes, men and women, scattered on the floor.

What was this place? Why all these life-size models?

She left the dark, sodden room and returned to the hallway. Aiming her light above the doors, she read different signs. She recognized the letters as before, but didn't know what many of the words meant.

Mark Twain's Tweens, read one. She scanned down the hallway and read: *Dumas Electronics, Victor Hugo's Fashion Revolution, Sherlock's Better Holmes and Gardens,* and *Oliver Pretzel Twists.*

Then her beam fell on a different kind of sign, a blue one at the end of the hall. It revealed a strange funnel next to the image of a running man. An arrow pointed to the right. She followed it, her boots splashing in the standing puddles in the corridor. At the end of the hallway, some stairs led down, and another sign with the same design pointed down the stairs. She rounded the landing, continued down another set of stairs, and came to a thick steel door. A keypad stood to the right of it. The technology was somewhat recent and looked out of place in this strange, ancient place.

She entered the code Rowan had given her, and the door slid open, issuing forth fresh, sweet air. Inside, shelves upon shelves of MREs, jars, cans, and other objects lined the walls.

She stuck her head in, wondering if she was the only person there. Her ears caught the sound of dripping water on the floor above. But no movement came from inside the shelter. She stepped inside, and the door slid shut behind her. Lights flickered on overhead. She turned, seeing an identical keypad on the inside of the door. To be sure she wasn't trapped, she entered the code, and it opened again. Then she turned toward the shelves, hearing the door whoosh shut behind her.

On the back of the door, a sign described how to reboot something called *the solar relay* if no power was feeding to the shelter. But she had power, and she was relieved.

She eased forward, taking in the space. More shelves lined the walls, and an open doorway stood at the opposite end. She moved through it, finding another room beyond, once more full of shelves. Unfamiliar rectangles lined them. She wondered if these were the *books* Rowan had described to her.

She pulled one off the shelf. A mildewy smell blossomed up, and it fell open. It wasn't a box like she'd pictured, but was comprised of a number of thin, flat pieces, each filled edge to edge with words. She scanned over them, recognizing a few here and there. Again the words used every letter, fully spelled out like in the descriptions she'd found regarding the asteroid. She put the book back and pulled a different one off the shelf. When she opened it, the colors surprised her. Images filled this one, depicting a variety of structures and scenes. She didn't know what to make of some of the pictures. The buildings were stone like the ones she'd been holing up in at night, but they weren't wrecked. Some were quite elaborate, with intricate designs and beautiful stonework. Other images showed vast green landscapes dotted with color; others relayed scenes covered with the same huge plant she had seen on her first day outside the city. One showed a woman standing next to a single colossal plant that dwarfed her completely. The description below read: *The Roosevelt Tree, King's Canyon National Park.* She didn't recognize any of the words, but the object was definitely similar to the giant plants she'd seen.

Forgetting how wet she was, she flipped through page after page, wondering if someone had created these images for a purpose.

Finally she replaced the book. She'd been standing there a long time.

Then she spotted a dented metal box on the bottom shelf. She pulled it out. When she flipped up its small latch, she found a PRD, at least ten years old from the look of it. She tried to turn it on, but the battery was dead. She stood up, placing it on the table.

She turned, spotting a large hanging map with a list of coordinates written on a poster below it. The poster read *Weather Shelter Network*, and listed other shelter locations. Red dots on the map above marked where they were situated across a vast geographical area. She took out her PRD and imaged the coordinates, then the map.

Another open doorway was set in the opposite wall, and she passed through to the last room. Four cots took up half the room, with folded, warm-looking blankets at the foot of each. A small sink, toilet, and a strange space with a protruding nozzle stood on the other side. Nearby were a small table, a few chairs, and some dishes and utensils.

She sat down on one of the chairs, an old green one. She took her bag off her shoulder, then removed her soaked coat. A chill set in at once, so she glanced around for a heat source. Against one wall was a small box with a lever. She walked toward it. The bottom of it sported numbers: 50,

60, 70, 80. The lever moved a red needle up and down across them. It was an ancient kind of thermostat, she realized, controlled by an old analog lever. She set it to seventy, then sat back down, draping her wet coat over another chair. It felt good to sit, to have the weight of her bag off her. She dug through her belongings and pulled out her PRD, checking for messages. Willoughby hadn't contacted her about the Rovers. She would have to wait here. Glancing around the shelter, she wondered if she could find a clue on her own.

Returning to the initial room, she took a cursory inventory of all the MREs. So much food filled the shelves that her stomach starting rumbling just looking at it all. She chose a dinner that was said to simulate something spelled *fettuccine alfredo*, and returned to the little kitchen. Inside one of the drawers, she found a wicked-looking knife. It wasn't a simple food knife, but had the kind of handle that looked like it would be good in a fight. The blade gleamed, and the edge felt sharp. She decided to stash it in her tool bag.

She returned to the table and began to eat, staring at the shelf of books. She realized they held information, like an ancient form of a PRD. If she still hadn't heard from Willoughby by tomorrow, she'd start going through them.

After finishing her dinner, she rose from the little table and made her way to one of the beds, taking the old, depleted PRD with her. She found a portable UV charging station on a small bedside table and laid the PRD on top of it. Then she spread out the blankets and placed two pillows at the head of a bed. Stretching out, she wrapped herself up in the warm blanket. She sent a theta wave message to the lights to turn them off, but they remained on. Then she said, "Lights," hearing her own voice for the first time in days. Nothing happened. A small lamp burned on the bedside table, which she examined for an analog switch. Near the base, she found a button and pressed it. Darkness flooded in. She lay back on the bed and fell into a deep sleep.

Chapter 13

She awoke with a start, sitting upright in bed. Her eyes stared in the darkness, her heart suddenly skittering. She didn't know what woke her up, but she felt that something was in the weather shelter with her.

Her hands fumbled for the small lamp by the bed and switched it on. Welcome light flooded the room, and H124 cast off the blanket, jumping to her feet. Her heart pounded so fast that all she could hear was blood rushing through her ears.

What was that she heard? Her body shook. Had the Repurposers found her? Or was it the nightly hunters?

She listened. A faint noise came, a kind of scratching, some distance away. She tiptoed toward the sound. It grew louder in the kitchen, and more so in the first room, where the MREs were stashed.

She strained her ears. More scratching, like someone trying to get into the shelter. She pressed her ear against the door. The sound wasn't coming from there. She moved along the wall, realizing that something was inside it. She heard more scratching, then desperate scrambling, followed by a crash. She leaped back, hand flying to her chest.

Something *was* in there.

After a moment of silence, she put her ear against the door again. On the other side, rain muffled all other sounds.

The scratching was higher and closer. Snapping her head up, she saw an air vent above the door. Something moved inside.

She recoiled.

A flash of gray fur pressed against the grating, then vanished. The scratching receded. The hole above the door held only a deep blackness. She stared, backing up against the shelves full of food.

Then the scrambling got louder, and she saw the flash of fur again. A thick, viscous red dripped down the outside of the vent. She bent over it. Blood.

A tiny sniffling came from the ductwork, a sad, lost sound. The fur turned, and suddenly she saw a little face staring out at her. Intense black eyes met her own, as a tiny pink nose sniffed at the grate.

It was clearly an animal, but she didn't know what the hell it was. She merely stood there, blinking at the creature. It gave another long, pitiful sniff. Then it vanished, its little feet pattering away. A low wheeze sounded, and the creature returned.

It was trapped in the vent.

H124 stood still, not sure what to do. She'd seen things other than humans before. But those were tiny: maggots on corpses, flies buzzing about the air over decomposed bodies. Roaches in the subbasements where the workers lived. But this thing was huge. She watched it pace, its lonely sounds piercing her heart. It didn't seem hostile.

Making up her mind, she moved to the kitchen and grabbed one of the chairs. She dug through her tool bag and pulled out her screwdriver.

She stood up on the chair and went to work loosening the bolts on the vent. The creature backed away. Once the last screw was off, she pulled off the grating.

The little creature hunkered about twenty feet away, at a turn in the ductwork. The vent was too dark for H124 to make out any details. She felt thrilled and scared and awestruck. This thing was alive, but completely alien to her.

She backed off, wondering if it might come back to the edge. Thinking better of it, she opened up one of the MREs, something called *soy-based meatloaf,* and broke off a chunk. Gently she placed it at the mouth of the vent.

She lowered herself out of sight and returned to the kitchen.

She heard the animal move toward the front of the vent, and then a soft chewing. Quietly she peered around the corner and saw the white face framed in the vent. Its eyes shot toward her at once, two black spheres set in a face of snowy fur. It had gray, rounded ears and a pink nose. She drew closer. She could see blood soaking the fur on its shoulder. As she moved near, it fell over on its side, tongue sticking out.

She stood up on the chair to get a closer look. It was more than a foot long, not including its thick, naked tail. Its little feet were strange things. It had fingers like her, but they were situated oddly. And though it was breathing, it continued to lie there, tongue out.

She reached up, touching the fur very softly. The thing didn't move. Gingerly, she scooped the creature up in her hands and lifted it out of the vent. It lay immobile. She got it over to the table and laid it down. Now she could see a bad wound in its shoulder, a jagged cut. She'd sewn herself up plenty of times, because workers couldn't use the biomed chambers unless they had a mortal injury.

She dug around in her tool bag and pulled out her first aid kit. She looked back at the creature, now standing and staring at her. As soon as she moved toward it, it flopped over on its side again, tongue out.

It lay still as she cleaned the wound. Then she got out her surgical needle and thread. She sterilized the needle with her pocket pyro and carefully sewed the gash shut. Still the creature didn't move. She wondered if it was unconscious.

When she got up to wash her hands, she heard a scuffle on the table. The creature had leaped down from the chair to the floor, its black eyes penetrating her. She leaned closer, and once more it fell onto its side.

She realized it was playing dead, though she didn't know why. She fought back an urge to laugh, which caught her off guard. She'd hardly ever laughed.

Returning to the kitchen, she picked out two small bowls and filled one with water, the other with the rest of the MRE she'd opened. She watched in utter fascination as the creature, largely prone all this time, now opened its eyes. It stood up and began tottering around the room.

H124 remained as still as she could. It wasn't anything like the maggots and roaches she'd seen. It was soft and furry and warm. She smiled, delighted to see it explore the room, sniffing at everything. Finally it found the bowl of water and lapped up a few drops. Then it began eating the MRE.

She thought back to the books with their pictures, and she quietly moved to the bookshelf. She saw one called *The Magnificent World of Animals*, recognizing the last word. She pulled it down and began flipping through it

It showed hundreds—no—*thousands* of images of exotic animals, with maps showing where they were found, and numbers describing their sizes. She stopped, jaw agape. Was this book saying that all these creatures existed? Some had feathers, which she'd only seen on clothing. She hadn't known that those came from living creatures. There appeared to be scores of animals with feathers of every color. She got to a section regarding furred animals and started turning the pages more slowly. A grin cut across her face. There it was, the gray-and-white creature sitting not a foot away. She read the name: *opossum*. She could read only a few of the words in its description, but the image showed one of its kin carrying three babies on its back.

It ate things called *snails, berries, and leaf litter,* among other things. Tomorrow she'd go rummaging for food and let it stay here with her while it healed. She placed the book down.

Exhausted, she returned to bed. The old PRD she'd found glowed softly on the charging station. She checked its battery level. Forty-six percent full. She brought up its hovering display. It was even older than she'd guessed, probably twenty years or more.

The screen resolved to show a series of video files. She waved past them, finding a locator map like the one that came on all PRDs, but these were the only things installed on it. It was completely stripped down. She waved back to the video page. The files progressed by date, so she picked the earliest one, dated a little more than ten years prior.

It loaded slowly, and for a minute she thought it wouldn't load up at all. It might have been too old.

Then the file played.

A young man, probably a little younger than she was, stared into the camera. His black hair hung past his shoulders, framing a handsome russet face. He smiled awkwardly. "Hi, there," he said, his voice deep and soothing. "Thought I'd put my mom's old PRD to some good use." He looked behind him, where a stormy sky brewed. His chestnut eyes stared into the camera. "My name is Raven. I'm out here with my parents while they restock the weather shelters. Someone's got to do it every few years, and now it's my family's turn." She couldn't believe it. He was part of the group who stocked the shelters? Was he a Rover?

"My parents are making me record these entries and place copies in every shelter. We know there are a lot of people out there who don't know what happened, or how we came to live like this. They don't know what happened to the animals who used to share the planet with us. So here I am. A Rover kid. Sharing history. I'll try not to be too boring." His brown eyes twinkled as he tucked his jet strands behind his ear. A shadow passed over him, and he looked up at someone off-camera and smiled. When the person left, he leaned close to the camera and said, "My mom. Checking up. I'm supposed to have recorded five of these things by now, but this is only my first. Don't tell her." He put a finger to his lips and winked.

"Now where to begin?" He donned a more somber look. "The beginning, I suppose. See, a long time ago, libraries started closing down because no one was using them, and universities shut down their math and science programs for the same reason, so a few people decided to come together to preserve whatever knowledge they could. This was the beginning of the Rovers. We came from all regions of the globe, of every ethnicity and age. My parents and I are Diné. That's Navajo." He grinned. "So enough about us. On with the bigger picture." He shifted to get more comfortable. "Okay. Lesson one." He lifted his palms up. "What's up with the weather?"

He sat back, cross-legged. "It started to go bad a long time ago, after the Industrial Revolution. Too much carbon dioxide was ejected into the atmosphere, and everything heated up too quickly. You see, the oceans are a vital part of creating local weather. Even if you're way inland, the ocean still affects you. The majority of heat from the sun is absorbed by it. Since so much greenhouse gas had been pumped into the sky by human activity, even more heat was soaked up by the seas. This heat then circulated the globe via ocean currents, which again drive weather patterns. With all that added heat, weather systems became erratic. Drought and megastorms became common.

"They say that some people wanted to prevent it from getting worse, but they were far outnumbered by those who didn't think it was a problem. So they kept going on as they did.

"It may sound crazy now, but back then people didn't want to do anything about all this. They didn't believe it was real. My mom says humanity is resourceful when it comes to a crisis, but they're not very good at preventing one *before* it happens, especially if it will cost them money." He gave a mirthless smile. "Money. That's what it was all about. But in the end, the damage cost them more than that. Droughts. Floods. Fires. Storms. Preventative measures would've been cheaper." He crossed his arms over his knees, which he tucked under his chin. The wind lifted his hair. "Resourceful when it comes to a crisis," he repeated.

He snorted. "Well, they thought they were being resourceful, anyway. They thought they could fix the climate by messing with it some more. Someone had the idea of cooling down the earth by ejecting material into the upper atmosphere, which would reflect sunlight back into space instead of letting it reach Earth's surface. They got the idea from volcanoes. When one erupts, ash gets trapped in the sky, and the global temperature has the potential to decrease for a few years before the particles settle from the atmosphere. So they had the idea to engineer sulfate particles that would stay up there for decades. It was called the Apollo Project, and it was designed to block out the sun's radiation. No one is sure which country launched the particles. They called it *geoengineering*. There were no laws restricting who could do it, be it countries or individuals. No one knows who was the first, either. We just know Earth was never the same. There was a miscalculation, and the particles stayed up there for too long. Any funds that could have been channeled to fixing the problem were spent on war and surveilling the human population. Then the heat trapped in the upper atmosphere came crashing down, causing disasters worldwide. The crazy thing is that someone tried it again. They engineered a different kind of particle to stay suspended, and come down slowly over time. Only they messed up the design again, and these pieces never came down. They're still up there, messing with the sun's radiation and trapping heat down here."

He looked at the rubble behind him. "The irony. The road to hell is . . ." He shook his head.

He pulled out a newer PRD. "Check this out." He tapped out a command, then rotated the PRD's floating display so it faced the camera. "This is the same spot, if you can believe it. Right here, where all this concrete is now." He held the PRD closer, and she could see a throng of trees like the one she'd seen that first day out, but instead of five or six, so many she couldn't count. Sunlight streamed through their branches. Huge green plants grew on fallen logs. An elegant, long-legged creature with a brown coat sniffed the plants. He lowered the PRD. "That was right here." He stood up, gesturing behind him.

All she saw there now were old roads, crumbling buildings, and fallen signs.

"We have plans to plant these forests again. Since trees breathe carbon dioxide, they would soak some of it up from the atmosphere. My parents planted a plot when they were kids, so we're going back there to check on them soon. I've never seen live trees, so I'm pretty excited."

Thunder rumbled above him, and he looked up at the clouds with darkened eyes. "Looks like I should get inside." His gaze met the camera again. "That wasn't a half bad entry, I hope." He managed a smile. "Stay tuned for more. Others will include: *More Disaster; Wolverines; How to Do a Cartwheel; Really Bad Historical Decisions; What Were Ornithopters?;* and *A Brief History of the Organisms That Roamed Earth before Humanity Evolved and Subsequently Killed Everything.*" He reached up and switched off the recorder.

H124 stared at the dark screen, thinking about what she'd seen. Had things really been so different? She turned off the PRD and placed it on the bedside table. Her eyes were heavy. She closed them, imagining a world of green, a world of life, a world of possibility. . .

She spent the next few days sleeping, eating once or twice a day, and reading. She was starting to pick out more and more words, able to figure out what they meant in the long way of spelling them.

Bldg became *building. Bthrm* was *bathroom.* She read through a series of books called *field guides.* The tree she'd seen that first day once had thousands of varieties and grew in things called forests. The one she'd seen was a sweet gum, she thought, from what she could remember of it. The images in the book showed whole hillsides full of them. She'd only seen a handful when she was outside. Everything else was a wasteland of cement and abandoned buildings like the one she now hid under.

The little spiky plant that had blanketed the ground was called grass, and it too had many variations. In some place called the Great Plains, it had covered vast landscapes.

She read about weather, learning that the ice storm she'd encountered was called hail, and that storms could manifest via tornadoes and hurricanes.

The opossum puttered around the weather shelter, having taken to sleeping under one of the cots during the day. At night it roamed through the small space, eating, drinking, exploring. She changed the dressing on its wound a couple times, and as before, it played dead. But the third time she did it, it just sat there and let her touch it. It sniffed her arm, curious. She felt a shared camaraderie, two lone survivors who could very well be the only living things for miles.

Above them she could hear the rain pelting the outside of the building. Wind roared through the hollow halls. She checked her PRD a few times every day, hoping to hear from Willoughby.

On the third day, she sat down at the table, chewing thoughtfully on an MRE, and decided to watch another video on the old PRD she'd found.

She clicked on an entry, watching as Raven's face appeared. He stood in a forest, but the trees were black and leafless, stark against a searing blue sky. He adjusted the camera, turning it away from himself to expose the view. Blackened trees stretched all the way to the horizon.

Then he turned the camera back on himself. "This was once a vast pine forest, a living place full of animals and plants, like ferns and berry bushes. Woodlands like these stretched all across the western half of the continent.

"But as the earth warmed up too rapidly, the forests died. There were these beetles that laid eggs under pine bark, and their larvae would feed inside the tree. Cold winter temperatures usually kept the population of these beetles in check. But as the earth got hotter, cold winters became rarer, and the beetle population exploded. Drought made trees even more susceptible to beetle attack. Beetles devoured whole forests. The dead trees were more prone to fires, and with all the crazy storms that erupted as global warming increased, lightning strikes constantly set everything aflame. Entire regions burned. Eventually, all that was left were these scarred remains of habitats that were once teeming with wildlife."

He showed the camera around again, and she saw all the burned trunks, the fallen charred logs, the desolation of the barren landscape.

"I've seen images in books and videos of what they used to look like. One really stayed with me. I recorded it." He pulled out his own PRD. Bringing up an image, he held it in front of the camera.

She saw a verdant forest whose enormous plants were clustered in the shade, its wildflowers winding about the tall grasses. In the distance, a massive mammal with sharp claws tore apart a fallen log.

He pointed to the animal. "That's a bear. They'd pull apart logs looking for grubs and bugs to eat. Three species of them used to roam all over the continent, one even living way north where vast sea ice used to form, but now they're just legend." He looked thoughtfully at the bear. "I would have loved to see one."

H124 set down the PRD, feeling a sinking in her gut, and moved to the bookshelf. She wanted to see more photos of these extinct animals. She opened a book on birds only to find it hollowed out in the middle. Hidden inside was a small piece of flat metal, wide on one end, slender and grooved with serrated teeth on the other. A piece of paper folded beneath it showed a hand-drawn map of the street above, with a red X on a street a few blocks away. The words *Allow five hours' charging time* were scrawled underneath the map. She lifted the metal, bewildered. Then she took it along with the map and slid them inside her tool bag. Maybe it was time for a little exploring.

She waited until the thundering of rain became a dull roar, and donned her jacket. Seeing the opossum sleeping soundly under one of the cots, she slung her bag over her shoulder. She exited the weather shelter, sliding the door shut behind her.

Rain cascaded down the stairs as she walked up the slick steps. Its scent greeted her, a smell she was becoming both familiar with and fond of. As lightning flashed, she waited for its boom to follow. It shook the walls of the building. She hoped it wouldn't hail again. Upstairs, she avoided places where the ceiling leaked and stayed to the drier parts. She pulled out the map, studied it once more, then tucked it back inside her bag.

At the doorway to the building, she stared out over the monochromatic landscape. Water flooded the gray streets, gushing down the gutters, carrying trash and jagged pieces of glass and metal.

She jogged out of the building, making sure she was alone. She turned right at the corner, sprinted down two blocks, and headed left. The X lay just a couple blocks up. She closed the distance, then double-checked the map, trying to shield it under her hood. She counted the number of intersections. The map showed the right number of buildings for the corner with the X, though in the drawing they were still standing. Now they lay in ruins around her, but at least the foundations were the same. This was it.

But she couldn't figure out what the X represented. She looked back at the map, and saw that it was just off to the left of the building in front of her.

As the rain pattered down on her hood, she sprinted to the spot. The ground squished under her boots. She mucked around in the dirt, then tripped on a piece of metal sticking up from the sludge.

She knelt down, finding a handle in the dirt. She grabbed it and pulled, but it wouldn't budge. She came around the other side, planted her feet on the ground, and yanked up with all her strength. Following a sucking sound, a door wrenched open in the muddy soup. She strained to open it all the way, pushing it back on rusted hinges.

She didn't relish the idea of jumping down into the blackness.

She fished around her tool bag, pulled out her headlamp, and cinched it on. Flicking on the beam, she knelt over the darkness and peered inside. An old iron ladder led down to a cement conduit of some sort. It was dry down there, though the rain started to splatter through the open door.

Tucking the map back in her bag, she turned and descended the ladder, closing the door above her.

As she stepped off at the bottom, the reek of mildew greeted her. She was at the end of a tunnel. She walked in the only direction she could, the beam playing over smooth, curved concrete on both sides. The ceiling was low, so she had to duck to walk through it. She came to a T-intersection and decided to turn right. Moving cautiously, she remained alert for any sound of the things that liked the dark. She came to another intersection and bore right again, turning right at every crossing so she wouldn't get lost. Two more rights led her to a dead end, so she turned back and chose a different path.

Finally the tunnels opened into a spacious room. In its center, an old canvas tarp covered something large. A great iron double door stood at the other end.

She approached the tarp. Lifting one corner, she aimed her headlamp beneath it. Then she flung off the tarp altogether.

It was a vehicle like the ones out on the street. But some things were different. It still had four wheels, with a circular object protruding in front of the seat. But the clearance beneath was a lot higher, and the wheels were larger. Thick rubber rings encircled the metal ones, but they were flat where they touched the floor. Mounted on top of the vehicle were shiny black panels. They looked a little like the UV charger on her PRD and headlamp, but these were huge and bulky, more primitive, less sleek. They took up the entire top of the car.

She tried the door handle, lifting it to no avail. A small round metal piece with a slot was mounted just below it. She bent down, studying it. She'd seen this same thing on the vehicles outside.

She stuck her fingernail in the slot. Then she thought of the flat metal piece. She dug in her tool bag, closing her fingers around it. She slid it inside, and it fit perfectly. She tried the handle. No change. So she put it in again. Nothing. Then she tried twisting the serrated object, and heard a click. This time she pulled up on the handle and the door swung open. She sat down on the seat, placing her hands on the skeletal wheel before her. She gave it a turn and heard the flattened wheels squeaking on the cement.

Another slot lay just beneath the wheel. She stuck the metal piece in again and twisted. Nothing happened. Then she remembered the note on the map: *Allow five hours' charging time.*

She withdrew the metal piece. *It was a key.* A primitive metal key that worked mechanically rather than electronically. It was brilliant in its own way, so simplistic. You didn't have to worry about this kind of key losing its charge or going on the fritz like the TWRs always did. It would work every time. Genius.

She had to know how this vehicle worked. How would she get sunlight down here to charge it? If she could get this vehicle to start, even if the Rovers were across the country, she could make it to them so much faster.

She looked at the double door across the room. She climbed out of the vehicle and walked to it. It was held shut on her side by a series of bolts, so she threw them open and tugged on one of the doors. It came open with a deafening squeal and whine of rusted hinges. The car would fit through the egress. Beyond stood a corridor wider than the vehicle, angling up toward the surface at a gentle grade.

She ascended the slope until it ended at another set of great metal doors. A series of bolts locked it from the inside. She disengaged them and braced her back against the cold metal. Then she pushed, but they wouldn't budge at all. She strained and strained, looking for a bolt she must have missed. But she didn't see any. It hadn't been opened in a long time, and here the rain had seeped through, probably rusting the hinges tight. She'd have to retrace her footsteps, figure out where this door opened on the surface above, and use some kind of lever to pry it open. Then she could push the vehicle out and let it charge.

She reengaged the bolts and returned to the vehicle. She locked the double door too, then covered the machine with the tarp.

Eagerly she hurried back through the tunnels and climbed the ladder to the surface. She threw the trapdoor shut and hastened through the misty gray streets back toward the weather shelter, hoping she would find books on these vehicles so that she could figure out how they worked. Once again she stared up and down the street, but didn't see anything on the move.

Inside the shelter, the opossum had emerged from under the bed, munching happily on some grass she'd managed to scavenge the day before.

She went to the shelf and scanned the book bindings, looking for something that might describe how the vehicle worked. At first glance she didn't see anything.

Then she came across a thick tome with the word *Atlas* on its binding, and pulled it out, wondering what it was. It was full of maps. She'd been wondering how far she'd come from the city, but without any markings on her PRD's maps, she couldn't be sure. She read the coordinates off her PRD and looked up that location in the atlas. As she flipped to the pages, she was blown away by the beauty they contained. Color filled every page, offering so much useful information. Not just roads and landmarks, but rivers, city boundaries, locations of rest areas, historic sites, even old mines. She couldn't imagine why something like this would ever go out of use.

She picked up her PRD and swiped its map feature back to retrace the way she'd come since leaving the city. The location of the shelter went beyond the scope of her PRD. It showed only the glowing arrow with the location Rowan had entered for this place. She stared at the vector, marking a spot in a vast gray area, with no marked roads or structures. It was like the outside world didn't exist at all to this device. It made sense; people in her city had no reason to leave. Well, *most* people, she thought, with a pang of isolation. Anger welled in her at the memory of that midnight chase through the city, burying any notions of loneliness.

But at least where the city was concerned, Willoughby's PRD *was* loaded with detailed information, far more than what her own had held. Hers had included streets and buildings, so she could locate where she needed to remove a body. But Willoughby's showed how many people lived in each building, what each edifice's function was, even places where workers labored and which buildings had the most up-to-date media installations. She set her starting point as the place where she'd learned of the asteroid.

She clicked on the *show coordinates* button and looked them up in the atlas. She flipped to the correct page, but it didn't show her city at all. Instead there stood a building called *The University of New York.* An inset map showed the campus. She'd been walking around in the Earth and Planetary Sciences building. She stared down at the map, marveling at all the things that simply weren't there anymore. New Atlantic had been built on top of it.

She looked at another page that showed the area directly east of where her city now stood. Those buildings she'd seen out in the ocean had been etched in her mind. According to the old map, it was once called Manhattan, and the sea had been much farther east when this map was made.

She flipped through pages, measuring how far she'd walked using the scale bar. It had taken her three days, and she'd walked thirty-six miles.

She left the atlas open and returned to the bookshelf, resuming her search for a book about the vehicle she'd found. So many volumes had titles she didn't recognize, so she had to pull down nearly every book and examine its cover. At last she found one with a photo of a similar vehicle on the cover. It was called the *Automotive Repair Guide*. Inside were wiring diagrams, photos of machinery and tools. Helpful diagrams labeled what each part of the vehicle did—steering, brakes, electrical systems. The book described a car that ran on something called gasoline, with frequent warnings not to have an open flame around this fuel source.

Tucked inside the book were hand-drawn diagrams and instructions for the solar modifications that had been made to the car. It showed where extra batteries were stored, how to fill them with water, how to repair tires. It also diagrammed a wench system designed to pull the car up out of the storeroom and into the sunlight. She studied the pages until her eyes started to hurt. She ran her fingers through her tangled hair.

Now that she'd been dry a few days in a row, her hair was coated in grease. She had to get clean. But the shelter didn't have a disinfectant chamber. Instead it had a small space next to the toilet with a dial on the wall and a nozzle overhead. She wasn't sure what it did.

Taking a chance, she turned the dial in the small space, and water sprayed out of the nozzle. It smelled like rain, but as it jetted out it felt warm. She'd always wondered why some older workers called the disinfectant chamber a *shower*—then it hit her: At one point in time, it actually *was* a shower of water. Rather than treated air removing the oil from your hair and skin, a bin of slimy liquid mounted to the shower wall lathered up into bubbles. She stripped and got in. The slime took the oil right off her skin and hair. Ingenious. She basked in the warmth, never wanting to leave. But she didn't know the extent of the hot water supply, so at last she turned off the nozzle's stream. She got out and dried off.

It was nice to be able to take a shower without having to wait in a long line every sixth day. She had never known privacy like this, and she loved it.

And even though she hadn't seen another human in days, she was starting to feel a little less lonely. Being an anonymous cog in the machine, seeing other workers but not talking much to one another, felt far lonelier than being out here on her own, living this free day-to-day lifestyle. Though she was on a mission, her heart was swelling with possibility. *Anything could happen.* Every day had a new surprise in store. She had no idea what the next morning might bring, and it thrilled her. The message she waited for on her PRD was very different from the corpse cleanup messages she waited for in the city. The only thing that changed back then was who died and where, but the bleak task always played itself out in the same way.

Until last time, she thought grimly.

After she got dressed, she collapsed on the bed. At least now she felt caught up on her sleep. Despite being on the run, she felt more rested these last few days than she ever had before.

She lay in the dark, drifting off to the sounds of the opossum tottering around the shelter.

H124's PRD beeped. She sat up in bed, and it beeped again. Hurrying to the table where she'd set it down, she saw Willoughby's face flash on the floating display. She waved her hand through the image to complete the connection. He smiled when he saw her. Worry creased his face, but he managed a smile. "You're okay," he breathed.

She nodded. "Are you?"

He glanced around his office, then turned to her with a nervous smile. "Yes."

"Did you find them?"

"I did."

She watched him type in a few commands.

"I'm sending you the coordinates." He frowned.

"What is it?"

"They're farther away than I thought. *A lot farther.* Hundreds of miles from you. Scuttlebutt has it that they're packing up their camp in a few days, and there's no word on where they're moving to. You won't make it on foot."

She thought of the solar car. "I might have that one covered."

He raised his brow. "Really?"

She nodded. Her PRD beeped again, letting her know that Willoughby's coordinates had arrived. She waved her hand to another window in the floating display, bringing up the map. Her mouth fell open. He wasn't kidding. The Rovers lay eighteen hundred miles from where she was.

She looked at the time on the PRD. It was almost dawn. "I'll set out today. Just need to get this vehicle running."

"You have to be careful. The PPC hasn't given up its search for you. They've alerted other media-run cities. You've got to avoid those. I'll send you coordinates for those too. They figure you won't survive in the Badlands, and if you do, sooner or later, you'll end up in a city center again. And they'll get you there."

She leaned back in her chair with a sigh. "Why do they care? I'm just one person. A laborer, at that."

"They know you have copies of the information you found. They're worried that you could distract consumers from . . ."

"From what?"

"The order of things."

"I don't understand. Don't they want people to survive?"

Willoughby ran a hand over his face. He hadn't shaved. "They don't think there's a real threat. They think it's a hoax."

"A hoax? For what reason?"

Willoughby leaned closer to his PRD. She could see he hadn't slept. Dark circles clustered under his eyes. "Public Programming Control uses those who are plugged into the network for free labor. The PPC provides all the entertainment windows on the display, but there's a task window too. Every few minutes, sometimes seconds, you have to enter a code or press a button to keep the entertainment streaming in. What people don't know is that these commands keep the city's infrastructure running. Maybe your task window starts the food cube machine. Maybe it regulates one of the temperature control stations. Maybe it stabilizes the generators that provide electricity to the PPC tower.

"This way the media doesn't have to put any effort into maintaining the city themselves. Consumers don't even understand they're doing it. They're taught the code when they're little, so it's instinctive to them. But from time to time, we deal with hoaxes from those who want to funnel power away from the PPC and get the consumers to use their task windows to power some unsanctioned project. Other times hackers just want chaos, or feel like breaking down the media's control. If consumers spend time watching pirated programming from these hoaxers, the attention is routed away from their task windows, and the infrastructure starts failing. The PPC suffers every second the consumer is engaged elsewhere.

"It's easier for them just to kill you outright than to lose any power. They can't afford you to release that information in this city or any other. If people really started to open their eyes . . ."

"The PPC's hold would crumble," she finished. Her stomach turned.

"So keep your eye out. They're coming. They won't follow you into the Badlands, but they know you can't broadcast from out there anyway."

She couldn't believe this. A sour taste filled her mouth.

Willoughby glanced around, more uneasy than ever. "Someone's coming. I've got to go. I'll explain more later. I promise. Be safe."

Her display went blank. Suddenly she really did feel alone.

With the Rovers so far away, she had no time to waste. She had to get back to the vehicle hangar and start working. Cramming the automotive maintenance book into her bag, she donned her coat and headed out into the perpetual storm.

Chapter 14

Crouching on a stool in the vehicle hangar, H124 went over the auto book, studying the car. For one thing, the flat tires had to be inflated. She found a motorized pump against one wall and used it to fill them with air. She then threw the tarp off the car, revealing the hood. She opened it, staring down at the engine. It looked very clean. None of the wiring was corroded. She found an empty platform where the battery was supposed to be, with waiting wires running to the photovoltaic cells on the roof. She hoped the system still worked. This thing had been down here for ages.

She found the winch and a tow ring on the bottom side of the car, designed to pull the vehicle up the ramp and out into the daylight. The piece of paper described where to find a switch that would open the large double door. She flipped it, watching the sun's rays spill down the ramp.

On a nearby rusted metal shelf, she found the batteries that were described on the sheet tucked inside the automotive book. They'd been latched up in large, rusted boxes. Unlike their containers, the batteries within were immaculate.

In metal tins to the right of the boxes, she saw containers for water, so she filled them from a little spigot in the wall. She added it to the batteries, following the instructions carefully. She hoped they weren't too corroded. They'd been sealed and protected, and for that she was grateful. The terminals were clean.

She hauled one of the batteries over to the hood, opened it, and placed it inside. The other two she stashed in the trunk. She hoped to be able to keep one charged, or two if possible, so she wouldn't have to stop and reload them too often.

She pulled the winch hook back and attached it to the tow ring. Leaning inside the car, she switched a lever to *N*, following the instructions. Standing aside, she activated the winch, watching the cable pull the vehicle up the ramp and out into the daylight. She followed it out, catching a whiff of fresh air. A light drizzle rained down, obscuring the sun, but at least some UV radiation would get through to provide a charge. She watched the rivulets wash away the thin layer of dust on the cells. Now she just had to wait. Not wanting to leave the vehicle unattended, she sat down beneath a small overhang and leaned against a ruined brick wall, watching.

Hopefully, she'd be able to start the vehicle in five hours. That would leave a few hours of daylight to make some headway. She didn't like the thought of traveling at night, with the roads so choked with debris and laden with potholes.

She sat with the car for an hour, gazing up at the storm, listening to the rain patter on the roof. As time wore on, she decided to leave the car for a while. She had to go back to the shelter and pack up some things: few field guides, the atlas, more MREs. She thought of the opossum and felt a painful pang in her chest at the thought of leaving it. Its shoulder was healing nicely, though. It would probably be glad to be out in the world again.

She walked back to the shelter, imagining the journey ahead. She'd sleep for a couple hours, then pack up some food.

A few hours later, H124 arose from her nap and looked around groggily. She sat up, reaching for her PRD. This was it. The car had been charging for five hours. She'd read and reread the automotive book, familiarizing herself with the transmission, the pedals, giving herself a virtual driving lesson. It didn't look too difficult. At least she hoped it wouldn't be. She decided to take the book with her.

Then she'd filled her bag with MREs and grabbed a couple spare bottles with filters. From a hook near the door, she grabbed a warm-looking purple scarf. At the bookshelf, she selected the atlas, a couple of field guides on animals and weather. She scanned the shelves a little more and took a book with a story in it, something called *Boy's Life* by Robert McCammon.

Standing in front of the weather shelter map, she selected several locations that lay in the direction she had to take. She made sure she had their whereabouts on her PRD. Then she took the old PRD with Raven's recordings and placed it in her bag.

When she was ready, she approached the opossum, now sleeping under one of the beds. She stooped down, watching it breathe. A painful lump traveled down her throat. She looked at its cut, gently peeling away the bandage. Much better than before. She took off the bandage completely, waking up the opossum as she did so. It blinked up at her. She lifted it with care, pulling it to her chest. It didn't struggle or play dead this time.

She walked to the door, feeling the warm fur against her. She knew it belonged out there, with others of its kind, but she was reluctant to say goodbye. Taking one long, last look at the weather shelter, she exited, entering the code to lock it behind her. She climbed the stairs back to the ground floor, carrying the opossum with her. When she was outside, she set it down. It turned and looked at her, sniffing the air. The drizzle had stopped, and the sun shone down from gaps in the clouds. The opossum caught the scent of something and shuffled off.

"Goodbye," she whispered. "Good luck."

It hit her that humans weren't all that would be vaporized if she wasn't successful.

She readjusted her bag on her shoulder and returned to the charging car. Easing into the driver's seat, she inserted the key into the ignition. Closing her eyes and muttering a silent wish, she turned it. The car started. Lights dazzled across the dashboard. The battery meter was full. An old physical screen, similar to what she'd seen in the university building, winked on. It displayed a map, just like the colorful one she'd seen in the atlas, with a small car icon marking her position. The engine was so silent she couldn't hear it. She almost expected nothing to happen when she pressed he accelerator. She placed the transmission in *D*. As the car inched forward, she tested the brake. After pulling on the emergency brake and shifting the transmission back to *P*, she jumped out of the car, closing the great metal doors behind her.

Sliding back into the car, she looked at the road ahead, surveying the stalled cars and stone ruins that had spilled into the street. She'd have to move slowly, but not nearly as much as she'd been on foot. She wouldn't be as exhausted now either.

Turning onto the city's main street, she put her foot to the accelerator, weaving between piles of old bricks and rusted cars. She kept her eyes on the road, and turned on the windshield wipers to clear away the rain. This was it. For the first time since she'd left New Atlantic, she felt hope rise within her.

She sped up, heading into the unknown.

Chapter 15

Ahead of H124 stretched a sea of asphalt and ruined skyscrapers. The sky lay streaked with striped clouds, gleaming silver as they drifted across the deep blue.

She'd been driving for two days now. Her progress was slow, but not as bad as it had been on foot. She'd been using the car's screen to navigate toward the next shelter along her route, but many of the roads were impassable. As she wove between rusting cars and fallen buildings, she wondered if this human society had left any room at all for anything other than concrete. She encountered no open spaces, just building after building after building.

It had stormed solidly the first two days. Once, she had to take shelter under a bridge when another hailstorm threatened to damage the solar panel on top of the car.

The third day was proving to be blisteringly hot. The storm clouds had cleared in the morning, and the sun had been beating down relentlessly since then. She drove slowly through several decrepit towns, with broken asphalt linking them all, a sprawl of ancient cities that went on and on. Unlike the giant towers in New Atlantic, the tallest edifices in these places were only twelve or fourteen stories high. Most were long and squat, streaming by in an endless procession of ancient urban sprawl.

At first she'd rolled the windows down, trying to get a breeze, but found it suffocating. The thermometer in her car read 115 degrees F. At last she'd discovered a button called *AC* and turned that on, finding a welcome cold breeze blasting out of the vents in the dashboard. AC was the same as the climate control in her building. She rolled up the windows, continuing on, grateful for a break from the heat. But it meant that she went through the batteries faster and had to stop more often to recharge them.

Though she had to slow down numerous times to maneuver around abandoned cars and vast potholes that sometimes had left no street at all behind, she was making decent time, and her spirits were higher than she could ever remember. The sky stretched blue, with towering clouds starting to pillar in the west. Despite her dire quest, she found herself smiling at times.

As the storm clouds blew in, she discovered a raised road with crumbling ramps leading up to it. She drove alongside it for a bit until she found a ramp that remained intact. The screen in her car showed that this raised road was a very direct route to the next weather shelter. She decided to take it, climbing the ramp and stopping at the top.

Not as many cars lay scattered on this new road, which stretched straight into the horizon. The car's screen called it *Interstate 80W*. She paused, gazing down the road, letting the car idle for a few minutes. Along both sides of the interstate, rusted poles held up small platforms with metal frames. Some still held large rectangular shapes inside, and from some of these leaked ancient wiring and old lighting. She started to drive, wondering what they'd been for. This new road was incredible compared to the weathered way she'd come, and her time improved even more. Before she'd found this interstate, she'd encountered roads that had proven impassable. Others crossed rivers, but collapsed bridges had made it impossible to get over in the car, so she'd had to backtrack and sidetrack and find new ways past these obstacles. Now that she'd found this interstate, maybe she wouldn't have to skirt around anything. She wondered if she could stay on it until she reached her destination.

As she drove on, she spotted a broken and faded rectangle, still partially held up inside its metal frame. She could only make out a few words, and a smiling face, worn blank in numerous places, gazed out at her. It read *Upgrade from 16G!* and at the bottom something about "unlimited" and "fees."

She drove until she could no longer keep her eyes open, then decided to nap in the car for a while.

As it grew dark, she pulled over and curled up in the back seat. It rained at night, thrumming on the roof of the car. She found it reassuring and drifted off.

She awoke to strong winds buffeting the car in the darkness. The vehicle rocked back and forth, the gale howling through the vents in the dashboard. She sat up, grateful to find the inside of the car dry. She thought about what she'd parked near. Nothing tall. This new road she'd found wasn't lined with buildings like the other routes she'd taken. Everything was set back from it, so she couldn't think of anything that might break free in the high winds and come crashing down on her. Nearly falling back asleep, she suddenly worried she may have parked near one of the metal rectangles and climbed out to check, so groggy she left her headlamp in her bag. She couldn't see in the dark too well, so instead she walked in a widening circle around the car, trying to find tall shapes against the dark sky.

She heard the things in the dark before she saw them. They hissed, one on either side of her, also circling the car. She could only make out bent forms, walking somewhat upright, but mostly on all fours. One hissed again, closer this time, so close that a cold sweat broke down her back. To her left, the other one panted eagerly.

Her mouth went dry. She realized that the things had gotten between her and the car. She wondered how long they'd been out there while she slept, planning their attack. With such thick cloud cover, she couldn't make out anything around her, just the vague form of the car in the gloom. She'd never known pure darkness like this in the city. She started circling back toward the car, making it harder for them to close in on a moving target. As she stepped to the side she heard one hiss and saw a jet-black shape lunge just to the left of her. Fighting the urge to bolt, she kept a slow pace. She couldn't make out any shapes, just pieces of shadow come to life. The other one hissed, feet crunching on gravel. She leaped to the side as something caught in her shirt, tearing the fabric. Cold and clammy skin met her bare flesh. She wrenched the shirt out of its grasp.

The hiss became a strange, keening wail, and the hair on the back of her neck stood up. The other one made a grunting noise, then joined in the howl. She pinpointed its location in the dark, then dashed between it and the car. She ran with outstretched hands, slamming into the cold metal door. Yanking it open, she jumped into the driver's seat and tried to slam the door shut. Something held it fast, so she reached up along the doorframe. Her fingers came into contact with a leathery cold, and she pounded her fist against it until it retracted. Slamming the door shut, she turned the key in the ignition. A grating scratch ran down the glass, and she gritted her teeth. Then she was roaring out of the parking space, spraying dirt behind her. She switched on her headlights, and the right beam caught something on the side of the road, a dark, rain-soaked form, hunched over, eyes reflecting back green. It flashed by so fast she couldn't tell if it was human or some other kind of animal, but it was at least six feet tall.

She hadn't expected these things out here. When she didn't run into them on the first two nights driving, she'd thought they didn't like going near the car. Once she'd hit this interstate, she'd hoped that maybe they only hunted in the heart of the cities. From now on, she'd have to be careful when she stopped. Sleep only during the day. Maybe now that she'd found this relatively unobstructed road, she could travel more at night.

She drove on for the rest of the evening, eyes burning with exhaustion. At last, with the heavy clouds showing the glow of dawn, she pulled over and crawled into the back seat once more. But she couldn't fall asleep. She stared out of the window at the sky, waiting for it to brighten.

She pulled out Raven's old PRD and powered it up. She selected another entry. Raven appeared, this time sitting at the edge of a vast ocean. As before, she could make out the tops of buildings submerged some distance offshore. Raven pointed at them. "This was once a densely populated city. They built it right at the ocean's edge. Why is it underwater now, you might ask?" He tucked his hair behind his ear.

"As the earth continued to heat up, the loss of sea ice was staggering. Not only did ice cover hit record lows, but it melted much faster than anyone had anticipated. Huge shelves broke off and melted in the Arctic and the Antarctic. The sea level rose drastically as less of the earth's water was locked up in ice. Coastal cities like this one tried to fight back by raising levees and sandbagging, but it was a losing battle. Once thriving hubs of trade and commerce, these areas were quickly abandoned as floodwaters moved in with unexpected speed. The sea took them, forcing people to move farther inland. The cities were lost beneath the waves."

He pointed at the bizarre structures sticking up above the whitecaps. "I often wonder what it must have been like to live back then, to be in a city that wasn't atmospherically shielded, to have no idea of the doom that was about to befall you. The crazy thing is, they had advance warning. The climatologists told people that they'd experience unprecedented flooding. But instead of curbing greenhouse gas emissions, they used stopgap measures, like raising levees. It wasn't enough. It was too little too late, and these people paid for it with their homes and lives."

When the recording ended, it was still too dark to fall asleep, so she watched another entry.

Raven wasn't his usual cheery self in this one. His jaw was clenched, his eyes heavy with bags. Behind him she saw an unbroken vista of cement and toppled buildings. He centered the camera on himself. "Okay. This is a tough one. I'm calling it *Where Have All the Animals Gone?* You may have seen my previous entry about how ancient forests and landscapes were once teeming with wildlife. But if you've been traveling out here, you've probably noticed that's not the case anymore. What happened to all the magnificent creatures we used to share this planet with?

"Well, before humans evolved, there had been at least five mass extinction events in the history of our planet—events where a majority of species went extinct. These were due to megavolcanism, changing sea levels, asteroid impacts, and disease. Then humans came along, and a sixth mass extinction began to occur. Animals were overharvested for food. Their habitats were destroyed. Invasive species were introduced, both intentionally and inadvertently, and they killed off the native ones. Scientists in the late twentieth century stopped calling this the Sixth Extinction, but rather the Anthropocene Extinction, since humans were so clearly the cause. By then, humans were killing off anywhere from ten thousand to sixty thousand species a year. A *year*.

"The ancient extinction events had taken at least a million years to happen, often even longer. But this last one happened in only hundreds of years. There were some attempts to save bigger, iconic species whose appearance humans liked. Wolves, bears, giant tortoises . . . But their reintroduction attempts were largely unsuccessful, as the creatures were being brought back to fragmented and human-developed lands that could no longer sustain healthy populations. In other cases, there just weren't enough individuals reintroduced to keep up a healthy group. Back then, people ignored the interrelation of everything, doing little to save the necessary pollinator species like bees and bats. They weren't big, flashy, or cute, so they were left to die. Pesticides wreaked havoc on them.

"For the first time in the history of the planet, a single species was responsible for a mass extinction. And there weren't enough people willing to stand up and fight for wildlife.

"Of course, without these creatures, the planet was really in trouble. All of them had fulfilled a vital role in a vast web, each one doing something to regulate the planet. Maybe you've heard that old saying about how a butterfly could flap its wings in the Rocky Mountains and cause a hurricane over the tropics? Everything's connected in the natural world. Unsustainable development, endless pollution, a complete disregard for other species when money could be made . . . that's all my species practiced.

"So the animals slipped away, with little thought given to their disappearance." He looked into the camera for a long time, then gazed out at the broken landscape. He reached out and ended the recording.

H124 turned off the PRD. She wondered what it must have been like for people back then, as well as for the animals that once roamed this land.

Looking east, she watched the sun peek above the distant hills. When it finally streamed in through the windows, she allowed her eyes to close.

H124 sat up, peering sleepily out of the window. Twilight's glow faded in the west. Were those things back? It seemed like it was still too light out. She'd have to put her diurnal theory to a test. How long after sunset did she have before they came out? She kept her ears open. Then she heard something. Above the dull drumming of the rain droned some kind of engine way in the distance. She stared out. The sound shifted, and she looked the other way. Then it faded.

She pulled out her PRD, gaping at it. She'd been asleep for twelve hours. She'd been more exhausted than she thought.

Listening for a few more minutes, she waited for the sound to return, but it never did. She opened the back door and climbed out, stretching and yawning in the early evening hour. Another storm system was moving in. Lightning flashed, and she could smell the unmistakable scent of coming rain.

The sun had set, but the west still glowed gold and blue. She took some time to freshen up, always watchful for the prowlers. So far she'd only seen them well into darkness, so she felt a little at ease as she prepared for another long stint behind the wheel.

She climbed into the driver's seat, started up the car, and drove toward the fading twilight. As the dark deepened in the sky, she glanced up through the windshield and slammed on the brakes. Something had filled the sky with light. Her mouth hung open as she gazed up at a myriad of glimmering lights arcing from one horizon to the other. In the middle of the sky, so many twinkling bright points were clustered that it looked like a giant, glowing cloud.

Suddenly heedless of the night prowlers, she got out of the car, still gazing upward. Were all of these things stars? She'd seen a couple from inside the atmospheric shield, but never more than one or two. The entire sky was filled with them! As she watched, a light streaked by overhead, then vanished. The more she stared, the more she could see colors there, red and blue and more. An especially bright one burned steadily near the horizon. It was magical.

Growing more aware of her surroundings, she felt the shadows growing closer and decided to return to the car. She drove on, still glancing up at every chance she got. As the night wore on, she grew familiar with the stars, their arrangement and brightness most of all. She made up shapes among them when she could actually see them. Most of the time clouds obscured her view. But when they were out, she knew she was alive.

Being out here was like being in a constant maelstrom. Weather ruled all. She could see why they'd built the atmospheric dome, but she wondered what it was like when weather wasn't so violent, and people could walk about the earth with relative ease.

A storm blew in from the west. She drove along the interstate for hours, staring out at the lightning. At times it rained so much that her windshield wipers didn't even make a difference, and she had to pull over while rivers ran along the road.

She reached a flooded bridge and stopped, worried the car would wash away if she tried to cross it. The bridge stood about a foot underwater, so she turned the car off, deciding not to risk it. She stopped on the road for two hours, waiting for the rain to lessen. But even when it did taper off for a while, the river seemed to rise even higher, washing rain down from some other point. Finally she decided to drive across the bridge when the water level had lowered a little.

She crept onto it slowly, opening the driver's door to check the depth. Water gushed by just below the undercarriage of the car, her tires halfway submerged. She drove without stopping, closing the door as the current sprayed up on both sides. Gripping the wheel, she steered the car across the bridge, feeling the pressure of the water pushing against the car. She let out a "Whoop!" when she made it across. She couldn't remember feeling this accomplished before in New Atlantic. That life might have been safe until the day she left, but there was no thrill, no joy, no sense of greater purpose.

She drove on, at times feeling brave at the thought of what lay ahead, and others feeling lonelier than she ever thought possible. The night road went on and on, but the lightning kept her entertained. She wondered where the nearest human was. Or the nearest opossum, for that matter. She felt like she was the only living thing for miles . . .

The moon made a brief appearance, rising above a bank of storm clouds. It was full, a gleaming bright light, the clouds below it a magical shelf of silver. She was enchanted by the sight. Then she saw another flash of light some way down the road.

She squinted, trying to make out what it was. Then it vanished. A few seconds later it reappeared, flashing ahead of her. Two circles of white light, then two more, then two more. They disappeared, and she slowed down. Then they came back.

Three vehicles, speeding toward her.

Chapter 16

Spotting some bushes on the side of the road, she switched off her headlights and pulled over. She remembered what Rowan had said about how she didn't want to run into anyone out here. Moving off the road and onto a grassy area, she aimed for the bushes in the dark. She could barely make them out now.

Taking cover, she wondered if she should stay in the car or not. Finally she decided to. She could make a faster escape that way, even though she probably wouldn't get as good a look at whoever it was from behind the scrub.

The headlights were still a long way off down the road, but she hoped they hadn't seen her. Her heart thudded. If she'd seen their headlights . . .

She rolled down the window slightly, listening to the hum of their engines. Their cars certainly weren't electric. They buzzed loudly. Soon the lights grew brighter, illuminating the bushes. Her heart beat a little faster. Was she covered enough? She glanced around for a space of deeper cover, but couldn't make out anything. She couldn't risk turning the headlights on again, so she decided to stay put.

Now she could really hear their motors, droning toward her. The lights laid bare the section of road she'd just left. All three cars drew close. She could see dark forms inside, but couldn't make out any details.

The driver of the lead car stuck his head out, searching the side of the road. She held her breath. They passed her location, driving on slowly.

Relief flooded over her as she saw their taillights. But her blood froze again when the lead car stopped a short way down the road. The other two followed suit. She turned around in the driver's seat, kneeling so she could see over the back of it.

The driver of the first car got out, directing the car behind him to angle its headlights into the brush off-road.

"What do you see?" she heard a man ask from the second car.

"I'm not sure," the driver responded. He stepped closer to the shoulder, then held back. He waved for the third car to angle its lights, too. They stood backlit, and she couldn't tell what direction they were looking in. "It's a car," said the driver, and H124's breath caught in her chest.

Someone got out from the passenger side of the second car and joined the driver. He had long, greasy black hair. He bent down, peering into the bushes. "You're right! I knew I saw headlights!"

The long-haired man forged into the brush, the driver yelling after him, "Arch, are you crazy? This is prime night stalker territory! Get back to the road!"

She could see that the man named Arch was raking through the thick brush toward a dark shape there. As he parted some branches, she saw a reflection off a taillight. It was a car.

"We can come back in the day with more guys," the driver told him.

"The car I saw was moving. The driver could leave by then! We need another working vehicle." Arch pressed on, trying to reach the car in the dense bushes.

Broken-down cars littered the sides of this road, and she doubted they would have given this one a second look if they hadn't seen her headlights.

"It's old," Arch called back to his friend. "This couldn't have been the one I saw."

Suddenly three dark shapes came streaking through the bushes, and she heard the unmistakable hissing of the prowlers.

"Get back in the car!" shouted the driver. A couple of people who had gotten out to watch jumped back in. The driver started running back to his own car, then saw that his companion wasn't doing the same.

"I'm snagged!" Arch yelled from the bushes. H124 watched as the three shapes closed in on him. He broke branches and tried to thrash his way out, but two prowlers were already circling him. All three were nothing but dark shapes in the brush, hunched things that moved fast. She couldn't make out their details in the dark, but they seemed to stand upright, though one rested on its arms. Arch stopped, whirled around, then made a break for it between two of them. One leaped through the air, landing on his back, and he went down hard in the dirt.

"Arch!" shouted the driver. He rushed forward to help, and the two other prowlers turned on him, approaching, bodies poised to pounce. He backed up.

The man in the dirt screamed as the thing bit into his neck. A cloud of dust kicked up in the headlights. Two other people got out of the cars, but the driver yelled, "Get back in! He's gone! We've got to get out of here!" H124 saw more shapes snaking down the embankment. The driver saw them, too, and as his friend stopped screaming, he raced back to his car and slammed the door. The prowlers gave chase, but he got inside just in time.

The three cars roared off, speeding down the interstate. She whirled around, starting up her own car. She kept the headlights off, but even in the pitch-darkness she could see more figures streaking down the embankment, silhouetted against the open sky.

She backed up and accelerated toward the road as several closed in on her. She heard the thump of one striking the back of the car as she hurtled onto the road, speeding away. In her rearview mirror she saw a lone prowler standing on the shoulder. Then it loped back to where the dead man lay.

Night stalkers, they'd called them. What the hell were they?

She drove on, not wanting to turn her headlights on. Behind her she could see the vanishing red taillights of the other three cars. She drove slowly, keeping the car in motion in the center of the road, not going fast enough to damage it if she hit something. She imagined those things loping down the road after her, and as soon as the taillights vanished, she flipped on the headlights. Light flooded the road, and she floored it.

She crested a rise and came to an area where the road cut through small, rolling hills. She drove for hours across the undulating terrain. Briefly the moon peeked out from the clouds, and for a few minutes she caught glimpses of tall buildings in ruined cities along either side of the road. Desolation settled in on her. The only other humans she'd seen since Rowan and she'd had to flee from the city. She wondered what they would have done if they'd found her. Taken her car and left her there? Taken her too? Killed her? She remembered Rowan warning her to not let them know she was a worker, that they would torture her for her knowledge of PPC-run cities.

By the time she reached the coordinates for the next weather shelter, her eyes burned with exhaustion. The sun hung low in the west, lighting up some towering thunderheads in gold, red, and pink. She opened the car door, stepped out, and stretched. The X on the shelter map showed a spot she hoped was safe to stash the car. She pulled out her PRD, navigating toward the X. But when she got there, she stared out at a collapsed warehouse. She crawled into it, digging through the rubble, wondering if maybe a door led to an underground garage. But she didn't find anything. In the end, she dragged several huge pieces of sheet metal out of the warehouse and propped them up against two abandoned vehicles on the street. Then she drove her car beneath the sheets, getting it out of the weather, and hopefully out of sight of anyone driving along the roads.

She switched the PRD's coordinates to take her to the weather shelter, slinging her tool bag over her shoulder. She followed the blinking arrow, which brought her to a narrow alley cluttered with fallen mortar, bricks, and ancient rusted hulks of steel. She scrambled over the crumbling stonework, at last coming to a set of cement stairs that descended to a sunken doorway. She spotted the familiar weather shelter sign, the funnel next to the running man. She stepped over a rusted I-beam that lay across the top of the stairs, then half slid down a pile of disintegrating stonework that choked the stairwell. She heard the rumble of thunder in the distance.

At the bottom of the stairs, a metal door laden with holes blocked her way. She shoved all her weight against it, and it squeaked on rusted hinges. Finally, it creaked open just enough for her to slip through.

Darkness gathered in the next room, so she pulled out her headlamp and switched it on. She played the beam over the remains of the building. The ceiling had caved in, but someone had cleared a path through the rubble. At its far end, she spotted the familiar keypad. Sending the beam over the walls, wary of night stalkers, she hurried to the far end of the room. Bringing up the code Rowan had given her, she entered the numbers on the keypad, and the door slid open. She let out a sigh of relief.

She walked inside, and the door slid shut behind her. A quick circuit of the room revealed that no one else was inside. The layout was identical to the first shelter she'd been in. Books lined one wall, and she went to these first. True to what Rowan had said about the inventory differing, she didn't recognize any of the titles. It was a completely new set of books. She set her tool bag down on the small table. Then she scanned the book titles.

One caught her eye at once. It was a fragile volume, not hardbound like the others. *Sword Woman: Collected Stories* by Robert E. Howard. She pulled it down and opened it up. The smell of antiquity wafted up from its pages, a smell she found strangely comforting. She set it on the table, then returned to the books. She knelt down, scanning titles on the bottom shelf. She spotted a familiar-looking metal box and opened it. Inside lay a PRD identical to the one she'd found with the videos. She tried to turn it on, but the battery was dead. She placed it on the table, planning to recharge it and see if the contents were identical.

Another scan of the bookshelf rewarded her with four more volumes that caught her eye: *Fahrenheit 451* by Ray Bradbury, *The Sixth Extinction* by Elizabeth Kolbert, *The Scarlet Pimpernel* by Baroness Orczy, and *The Land That Time Forgot* by Edgar Rice Burroughs.

She took the depleted PRD and *The Land That Time Forgot* over to the small cot and stretched out. Her aching body thanked her, her muscles finally relaxing after a day of driving. She turned on the small lamp on the bedside table, then placed the PRD under it to recharge. Yawning, she opened the book. She'd read only the first page when her eyes closed, and she drifted into oblivion.

She woke from a nightmare. In it, the night stalkers had infiltrated the shelter, creeping along the floor toward her cot. She sat up, scanning the room. The small table light still burned brightly. She peered under her cot and the neighboring one. Then she made a circuit of the shelter, checking under the table, listening at the air vent, making sure the door was still locked. It was. Sighing, she drooped her head, rubbing the back of her sore neck.

She padded back to the cot and lay down again, taking off her boots and covering herself with the blanket. She lay there, staring up at the ceiling, unable to fall back asleep. She looked at the book next to her, then to the depleted PRD. It glowed softly, showing that it was fifty-six percent charged. She picked it up, scanning the contents, which were different from the one she'd found in the first shelter. She selected a new video.

Raven's face appeared, his long black hair waving in the wind.

"It's my second time on the restocking run, though last time I was only five and don't remember it too well. Can't believe what a wasteland it is out here. When you're brought up with books, you think the world is like they describe." He looked down, twisting the corner of his mouth. "But it's not." He looked behind him, where a crumbling road led into the distance. "We skirted around a Badlander camp today. I could tell my dad was pretty damn scared, but he tried to hide it." He held up three books. "We're putting more field guides in all the shelter libraries. Books on weather, animals, survival. Came across this score in an old burned-out library a few towns back." He held up a thick green volume. "It's called the *A Green Beret's Guide to Survival,* and it's chock full of great information. I'm leaving it here." He thumbed through the book, then set it down. "It's amazing we find any books at all now." He stared up at the sky as raindrops began to fall. One splashed on the lens. "Got to get inside." He reached over and switched off the camera. The file closed.

Still not tired, H124 got up and walked to the bookshelf. There she scanned the titles for the survival book, finding it on the bottom shelf. She pulled it out and brought it to the bed. Holding it in her hands just as

Raven had, she felt connected to him. Though they'd never met, she felt a strong sense of familiarity. For a while she flipped through the volume, seeing sections on what to do if you're dying of thirst or freezing to death, and how to build a temporary shelter. It was an amazing resource.

She picked up the old PRD. She selected another video from it. Raven stared back at her. He sat cross-legged outside a decaying building, on a dead street that looked like hundreds she'd passed herself.

She turned up the volume to hear his voice. "If you looked at any of the field guides we placed in the shelters, then you probably saw images of all the animals that used to live here. Pretty amazing, right?

"My family has handed down stories of huge bison herds roaming the western plains. Predators like bears and wolves hunted in the forests. Birds migrated across thousands of miles, back and forth from a whole other continent to the south."

He looked away from the camera. A collapsed building stood behind him, as broken cement and rebar stretched into the horizon.

"If you've been watching these, then you might have seen my previous entry on the Sixth Extinction. Thought I'd give more specifics. See, before humans held so much power over the earth, things were different. Back then, when climate changed on a global level, plants and animals could slowly move north and south, changing habitats so they could survive. There were times when huge ice sheets covered the area where I'm standing. Animals moved south to warmer areas, then moved back north again when the ice receded.

"But with this most recent climate change caused by humans, animals and plants couldn't do that. The change in climate happened way too fast. Cities and roads and fences had fragmented the land so much that animals couldn't move freely enough to save themselves. Plants couldn't grow in the asphalt of the cities. Animals were killed as they tried to cross roads and fenced lands. People shot them. Eventually, creatures like the bear and wolf survived only in patches of protected land called national parks. But they were separated from others of their species, and couldn't cross between the parks without being killed or starving to death. There was no food, after all, only human sprawl. The bears and wolves in these parks eventually mutated, becoming what my mom calls *genetically isolated,* as they didn't have a wide population to breed from. Ultimately, the few survivors grew sick and died off.

"The birds didn't fare much better. They need darkness to migrate, as many of them navigated using the stars. But the constant glow of the cities made this impossible. Habitat loss was staggering as humans sprawled across all the areas wildlife once inhabited. Many birds died from collisions with omnipresent plate glass, buildings, and vehicles. Food became scarce.

"Deforestation wiped out rainforests en masse, killing tens of thousands of species yearly. The only animals that survived were those who could coexist alongside humans, but these were often considered pests. Humans employed chemicals and traps to wipe them out. Mice, rats, roaches, raccoons, opossums . . . even their populations dwindled over time. My mom says that only roaches and bacteria will inherit the earth, when humanity has done its best to destroy it."

H124 could see a fire burning on the horizon, black smoke billowing up into the sky in a thick column of ash.

"Can you imagine what it must have been like to live back then, when things were still around? Green forests? Birds singing in their branches, packs of wolves howling? I would have loved to see a bear rooting around, digging up logs to find insects, or glimpse a long V of geese migrating north for the summer."

He looked down. "What can we do now? It hurts to live in this time. Everything's gone wrong; I can feel it in my bones. It's not supposed to be this way, but the devastation just keeps mounting. It's as if an ancient war machine were trundling on, trampling everything underfoot, leaving behind only broken cement in its wake. A lifeless wasteland, stripped of all beauty and value.

"We don't even live out in these ruined places. We wouldn't be able to survive out here."

He picked up a handful of rubble, which crumbled as he closed his fingers. Then he reached down and ended the recording. She set the PRD down. Had it really all been so different? She tried to imagine standing on the ruined street above her when it was a grassy field, or a forest of trees. She tried to imagine the sound the birds might have made as they sung in the branches, or what a deer would have looked like stepping gracefully over logs to drink by a clear stream.

She closed her eyes, imagining that time, and fell asleep.

* * * *

At dusk she showered, tucked away the new books she'd found, and ate a quick meal of an MRE that was called *Meat Substitute Salisbury Steak*. Then she tucked more rations into her tool bag, took one long look at the weather shelter, and locked it up.

Her car waited for her beneath the debris she'd covered it in. She got in and drove it out from under the sheet metal. Rain fell, pummeling its roof. At least it wasn't hailing. Yet.

She drove for two hours in the darkness, then felt her throat constrict when she saw headlights in the distance. Again she shut her lights off and pulled over next to one of the numerous ramps she'd seen along the road. They typically led up an embankment, crossing a bridge over the road. Many of the bridges had long since collapsed, but a few still stood. This was one of them. She'd explored a couple, looking for places to sleep, and usually found a series of buildings nearby, their window frames bereft of glass. They all looked similar, though she didn't know what they'd been used for. They had tall overhangs jutting out, and upright rectangular contraptions with rotted hoses spaced evenly under the overhangs. Any markings on the rectangles had long since been weathered away, but she could tell they'd once been electronic. She'd slept next to one of these buildings more than once.

As the headlights grew closer, she decided to drive up the ramp and see if she could find one of those buildings to park behind. She maneuvered up the slope and crossed the old bridge, hoping that it would hold. It did. To her relief, a little way down this smaller road, she saw one of those buildings with the overhangs. Other structures stood nearby, with tall signs that had toppled over. They were probably once visible from the interstate. She'd seen the same fallen signs all along her travels. They were hollow and shattered, and looked like they'd once held lighting. This turnout still had one intact sign. It leaned against its building, covered in mold and dust. She could still make out the symbol, a giant yellow M set against a red background.

She glanced over her shoulder and back at the interstate, seeing the approaching lights. She thought she must be nearing some center of activity for these people. She hadn't seen anyone else for days.

She pulled between the buildings, careful not to drive over anything sharp. Behind them lay a crumbled space of asphalt, and she pulled in flush with one of the walls. She debated whether or not to get out of the car, then decided she would run over to the interstate and see if they drove by without pulling in.

On the watch for night stalkers, she ran.

Chapter 17

She knelt down behind one of the railing supports at the cross bridge and watched. The headlights were about a mile away. Two cars. They started to slow as they approached the exit. There was every chance they'd seen her headlights when she'd seen theirs, but maybe they'd think she was one of their own. She wondered if they had some way to communicate between cars. If so, and they'd tried to communicate with her, they'd know she wasn't one of them. Now the two cars slowed even more as they pulled off toward the ramp. She ran back to her car, boots thumping on the broken pavement. She raced between the two buildings and jumped into the driver's seat, shutting and locking the door.

She wasn't sure what to do. They'd see her if she drove. She decided to stay put. Next to her lay several pieces of rusted sheet metal. She jumped out, hefting one up and leaning it against the car. Maybe they'd think it was an abandoned vehicle. She slid back inside.

For several agonizing minutes she waited. Had they turned the other way? She didn't see any headlights. And then she saw them, flashing on the buildings around her as they drove down the street.

They shone their lights down between the two buildings. One car had turned her way. She reached for the ignition, ready to start it up. Just as the headlights pierced the darkness behind her, the second car appeared in front, exploring the next street up.

But they still hadn't seen her. As long as they didn't spot the solar panel on the roof, they might think it was a derelict car. Maybe they wouldn't notice it in the dark. She waited. The car behind her pulled past, down the little lane. The other car joined it a block away. The drivers stopped, talking to each other. Cracking her window, she caught snips of conversation.

". . . couldn't have been them . . ."

". . . said those things killed Arch."

". . . didn't see another car?"

She wanted to bolt, to swing the car out and make for another section of town. But they were too close. As they revved their engines, so much louder than her silent car, she smelled the scent of something rotten.

They pulled back around, each one taking another street this time. But as one of them turned, its headlights played over her car. She ducked down in time, but if they were familiar with this area, they'd remember there'd been no car there.

She heard one of them shout, "There!"

And that was all she needed.

She started up the car and shot out of her hiding place, the sheet metal crashing to the ground. She careened around the corner and back to the main drag.

All she could hope for now was that her car was faster than theirs.

She turned quickly onto the road, hoping she could lose them among the maze of streets. If she could get far enough ahead of them . . .

But the two cars worked in tandem, cutting her off at every turn. They could definitely communicate with each other. She flipped a U-turn and sped back toward the interstate, trying to outpace them. She veered onto the entrance ramp, gunning her motor. The car shot forward as she raced around an old wreck on the side of the street and sped onto the highway, pushing the car faster than she ever had before.

She was almost half a mile away before the two vehicles got onto the entrance ramp. She felt both terrified and giddy. She was faster than they were!

She pushed the needle on the speedometer higher and higher, reaching over ninety miles an hour along the interstate, veering around stalled cars when she saw them. Up ahead she saw a hill. If she could get over it, then cut her lights and veer off somewhere, they'd have a hard time pinpointing her location.

She saw that the two cars were falling behind in the distance. She crested the hill so fast that for a moment she was airborne; then the car hit the asphalt with a bang. She held fast to the steering wheel and gazed at the road ahead, looking for a place to pull off. Then her blood froze. Headlights flashed in the distance, at least six more cars. She didn't dare turn her lights off going this fast. She saw a dirt turnaround in the median and whipped around on it, heading back the way she'd come. She'd been watching that side of the highway since she got back on, and hadn't seen any wrecks. It was a risk, but she had to take it. She turned off her headlights and sped forward in absolute dark, keeping the car as straight as possible. She used the headlights of the two approaching cars to let her know where the road was. This stretch was very straight, so she used it to her advantage. Just before the two cars were about to pass her, she spotted some derelict vehicles on the side of the highway. She slammed on her brakes and slid off the road, pulling in next to them.

Sweat beading down her back, she waited. The two cars sped by. She thought of staying where she was, but when they met with the other six cars, it wouldn't take them long to figure out that she'd turned off somewhere. So she pulled back onto the interstate, keeping her lights off. She reached the ramp, considering whether she should continue on the interstate. She hadn't traveled this stretch, though, and with her lights off, she could plow into a stalled car. She got off at the ramp again, hoping they would think she had in fact moved onto the interstate. Driving as fast as she could, she sped through the desolate town, past the ruined M sign, and the initial place she'd parked.

When she was out of view of the highway, she dared a flash of her headlights to get her bearings. The road stretched for miles, up a little hill. She then switched off her lights and headed down the road cautiously. If she wrecked her car, it was over. She maneuvered past some potholes, switching on the dim yellow parking lights when she needed to navigate past an obstacle. She wove around some stalled cars, then debris from buildings that had long since collapsed into the street, mostly bricks and masonry stones, old lumber.

She ascended the little hill, atop which the crumbled road became little more than dirt. She crested the zenith, looking behind her. Her heart moved into her mouth when she saw headlights piercing the darkness behind her. But they were far away, passing the exit, speeding down the highway. She swallowed hard. She hit the emergency brake so the rear brake lights wouldn't show. She couldn't see anything. Finally she dared another flash of her headlights. It illuminated the desolate stretch of dirt, as well as some long-collapsed structures and scattered wire and posts from fallen fences. She turned off her lights and coasted down the hill, looking for a place where she could stash her vehicle.

She looked at the car's screen, which told her this was the "farming community of Fort Meriwether." Part of a building still stood, and she thought it might give her enough cover. At the same time, if they came this way, it looked too obvious a hiding place. Panic welled up in her gut. Once again she was being hunted.

Lights cut through the darkness ahead. Three more cars appeared over a hill a quarter of a mile away. She flipped around, heading back, hearing their strange engines gunning after her. She knew they'd seen her. A cold wave of fear swept over her. She raced back down the little hill toward the interstate. But already the six cars had exited the interstate and formed a roadblock. She stifled a cry and looked for places to turn out, but the cars moved quickly to intercept her. They closed in, the three from behind, forming a tighter and tighter circle.

She turned down the last open side street, where they cut her off. Trapped, she locked all her doors. When they saw that she was cornered, they got out of their vehicles, rough-looking men and women who regarded her with cold, calculating eyes. Their clothes were ragged and torn, stitched together from a dozen different fabrics. Many wore red-and-black paint on their faces and bodies, designs she didn't recognize. They came over, leering down at her. One tried the door, and when he found it locked, he pulled out a long, thin piece of metal and slid it down inside the door. The lock popped open.

He was tall, with brown hair cascading down his shoulders. His face was rough and whiskered, and his pale green eyes gazed down shrewdly. He opened the door and grabbed her by the arm, wrenching her out of the car. He shoved her into the crowd, where someone punched her so hard in the stomach that she doubled over, falling to her knees. Then they moved past her, most taking no notice, instead gazing at the car, at its solar panel and high clearance modifications. She managed to stand up. Two of them held her in place, one with his hand on the back of her neck, and a woman holding her arm so tightly that she could feel it bruising.

"That's some ride," the long-haired man said to her.

She didn't say anything. She remembered Rowan's warning to not let them know anything about her.

"I think we'll be taking it." As he started to slide into the driver's seat, she threw her head back, twisting free of the man's grip, then turned and shoved the woman to the side.

H124 rushed to grab the long-haired man's arm. "I need it," she told him.

"So do we," he said.

"You don't understand. I have to reach my destination."

"So do we all."

She glanced around. The two who had been holding her had so much hatred in their eyes that their gaze burned. The leader paused. Instead of getting in the car, he lingered on her. She looked back at him, trying not to betray her terror. Suddenly her life felt worth as much as a rusted car.

"If I don't reach my destination, we're all going to die." She craned her neck, making sure no one was getting too close. "All of us."

The leader gave her a wry smile. "Some of us sooner than others."

"You don't understand," she said, masking the plea in her voice. She had the feeling that the moment she showed any kind of weakness, they'd descend on her like a pack of night stalkers.

He started to slide back into the driver's seat, but this time she gripped him forcibly. She wasn't going to give up now. The car was her best chance of reaching the Rovers, of having a shot at stopping this asteroid. She wasn't going to lose that because some greedy jerks wanted her car.

"I can't let you take it," she insisted.

He snatched her hand, his skin rough against hers. "I don't think you have a choice. We need a solar car. And you've got one." A curious look swept across his face. "Where did you come from?"

She stared back at him, her jaw set.

"What's your name?"

She narrowed her eyes. She didn't have a name. Just a designation.

Rather than climb into the driver's seat, he bent into the car and pulled out her tool bag. He dug through it, finding the books and Willoughby's PRD. He gave a long, low whistle. "Wow. Will you look at that? That's city center tech." He turned back to her. "You a thief?"

"No," she said.

"You from a city center?"

She thought quickly. "Of course not. Does it look like I'm one of those jacked-in deadbeats?"

He really took her in then, scanning her up and down. "No, you don't," he said finally. He yanked her elbow. "You look like a city worker. And I think you're going to ride with me. Get in the car."

He manhandled her around the side of her vehicle. Anger flooded through her, and she grew hot. She wanted to wheel on him and pound him with her fists, but with all his companions around, she knew she wouldn't stand a chance.

Maybe if she rode with him a little while, she could convince him to let her go, tell him of the asteroid. At least that way the car wouldn't be out of her sight.

He shoved her around to the passenger side and stuffed her in.

"Let's get back to base," he said to the others. "If the night stalkers aren't here yet, they soon will be. We've stood around for too long already. Let's go!"

They all returned to their cars. Doors slammed, and as he crossed back to the driver's side, she thought of making a run for it. But that would leave her alone out there, back where she started, on foot, making slow progress. And the more west she'd headed, the more these thugs had started showing up, not to mention the night stalkers.

She stayed put as he got into the driver's seat. He started the car, then settled his eyes upon her. "Now you can tell me all about yourself," he said, pulling away with the others.

She watched him drive, fighting a sudden territorial urge. She'd been the one to find the car. She'd been the one to get it working again and winch it up into the daylight. She didn't want some violent stranger driving *her* car. That's how it felt to her now. It was *her* car. Who was this guy anyway?

"Who are you people?" she asked.

"I get to ask the questions."

She stared forward. "Can't we just converse?" She tried to make her voice sound even, reasonable, when what she really wanted to do was slam his head against the glass, kick him out of the car, and get as far away from him and his posse as possible.

She looked back at him, considering it. He had a tough look about him, like he'd had a hard life. He was in his late twenties, she guessed, and his lean, muscular frame looked like it had been in a scrape or two over the years.

"What's your name?" he asked again.

She grew silent.

"Did you come from a city center?"

She crossed her arms, fixing her gaze straight ahead as he drove.

"You know," he said, looking at her, "you'll probably find answering my questions a lot more palatable than if I left you to the others. Some of them don't have my charm and patience."

She said nothing. At least he was going west. After a few minutes of silence, she asked, "How far are we going?"

"About twenty miles." The dashboard lit up his face.

"So you just drive around, looking for people to steal cars from?"

He readjusted his seat belt. "Something like that. We were just going to steal your supplies, but when we saw that you had a solar-powered car, that changed."

"But why take it? You have plenty of other vehicles." She surveyed the throng of cars before her.

"Hear that?" he asked her. "Their engines?"

She didn't answer.

"They're internal combustion engines."

She raised a brow. She decided the less ignorance she showed of the outside world, the better. She didn't want him to know he was right, that she was from a city center.

When she didn't say anything, he went on. "It's old tech, but it works. Also loud as hell, and our enemies can hear us coming." He ran his hand affectionately over the steering wheel of her car. "But this? Solar power? Quiet. And from the size of that panel, I'd say this is pretty old tech too. But it works like a beaut."

She had no idea what a *beaut* was, but she knew there was no way she was going to let this guy keep her car. She wanted to ask him how he lived out here, how they all got by, what they ate, how they survived the storms, but she kept silent.

"Even got one that runs on steam," he said. "You should see it. And then there's the Big Worm. Glorious."

She finally lent him her eyes. "What's that?"

"A steam train. Fixed the track from here to Delta City, and that thing runs like a blade on ice. But we have to find stuff to burn, which can be hard. But when it goes, it goes."

She had no idea what he was talking about, but tried not to let on. "So what's the point in taking me? Why not leave me to the night stalkers?"

"Fun devils, aren't they?" he said, grinning slyly.

"Yeah. Real fun."

Something sad overtook his face, an old hurt. She watched his expression change. A second later, he came back to the present. "I took you because you intrigue me."

She decided to go for it. "Look—I really do need to be somewhere. It's incredibly important."

"I'm sure it is."

"You don't understand." She turned in her seat to face him. "Something bad is coming. Something that could kill us all."

"And you alone can stop it?" he asked, with a half smirk.

"I'm going to try."

He let out a laugh, and she rankled at the sound. "Well, hell," he said, and she realized the laugh wasn't entirely derisive. "Maybe we can fix you up with a methane-powered car later." She didn't know what methane was, but she believed that about as much as she believed he'd stop right now and let her have her own car back.

"I need *this* car," she insisted. "I have a very long way to go, and won't be able to get any . . . methane . . . on my way. I need the sun. It's the perfect power source, right over our heads."

"When you can actually see it." He regarded her, then looked back at the road. "Listen. You're determined, I'll give you that. But you don't seem to grasp a vital component of the situation here."

"What's that?" she asked, her wrath stealing up inside her again.

"You're our prisoner."

"What possible use could I be to you?"

He suddenly looked serious. "Information." He pulled Willoughby's PRD out of her tool bag again. "I'm no idiot. I know you're not from around here. Where did you get tech like this?"

She just stared back.

"Did you kill whoever this belonged to?"

"Of course not!"

"See? If you were a Badlander, you'd brag about it. You've got an innocence about you, a kind of naïveté. That stands out. You did come from a city center." When she didn't answer, he slowed down, letting the others get ahead of him. "Which one?"

She decided to try to bluff him, thinking of how Rowan got in and out of New Atlantic. She hadn't even known there was more than one shielded city until Willoughby had mentioned it during her escape. "I've been to a city center before, but I'm not from one of them," she lied.

"Which one?"

"That's where I got that PRD."

"Which city center?" he said again.

She decided not to answer. "I'm not sure. I was just a kid."

"You've been breaking in and out of city centers since you were a kid? How?"

"I didn't say I'd been breaking into them. I went to one once. I found that PRD."

He turned it over in his hands. "This looks brand-new, not years old. This is new tech."

She thought quickly. "It was a prototype back then."

"How did you get into the city?"

"Some guy got me in. It was a long time ago."

He turned the PRD over in his hand. Steering with his knee, he popped open the back of it. "It doesn't have a tracking chip. Doesn't even have a place for one."

He reached over and closed his hand on the back of her neck. He forced her head down, fingers feeling along her scalp.

"What are you doing?" she asked, batting his hand away.

"No head jack."

"I told you that."

"What's a chinook?

"Excuse me?"

"Or a Death Rider? If you can tell me that right now, I'll leave you alone."

She had no idea what a chinook or a Death Rider was. Never heard of them.

"What's your name?" he asked again.

She tried to think of a name. "Bowen," she answered at last, thinking of a character in *The Land That Time Forgot* book she'd found at the shelter.

He watched her out of the corner of his eye. "That's an unusual name. I'm Byron. But what's your real name? Your designation?"

"What do you mean?"

"You're a worker, aren't you?"

"A worker?" she asked, trying to sound ignorant. She could tell he wasn't buying it at all.

"And you can get us in."

"I have no idea what you're talking about."

"You can get us into Delta City, through the atmospheric shield."

"I have no idea how to do that. Besides, like I said, I have somewhere very important to be."

"And we have something very important to sabotage," he said grimly.

"I can't help you," she insisted. She decided to take a chance. "Listen. An asteroid is coming. It's on a collision course with Earth. A long time ago it was being mined in outer space, and a disaster happened, altering its course. It fragmented, and some if it has already hit, causing massive damage on impact. There are still three more chunks that haven't hit, but they're about to. The first will hit in less than two months, followed by two more. They'll wipe out whole regions. But that's not even the worst part. The main asteroid is going to destroy us all."

He was silent.

"We won't survive. Nothing will. Unless we can find a way to stop it."

"What's an asteroid?"

She frowned. "It's a huge rock out in space. They can devastate life on a planet if they're big enough, and this one certainly is."

"How do you even know about this?"

She looked over at him. "I found an ancient laboratory, a place that studied that kind of thing. I saw the diagrams of how these things are going to strike the earth."

"Ancient? How do you know what you saw wasn't malfunctioning?"

Rage flared in her eyes. "I looked at the equipment. It was running. I saw images of how much destruction the smaller chunks had caused in the past."

He lifted his brow. "And you know how to stop this thing?"

"I've got a lead."

He gave a wry smile. "I've heard a lot of stories to get away from the Badlanders before, but that one is the craziest. How could anyone know about this, anyway? No one knows what's out there."

"They used to." She reached into her bag to get her PRD, so she could show him the videos.

He caught her hand. "Not so fast."

"But I can show you!"

"Yeah, I'll bet. And stab me while you're at it."

"I just need my PRD."

He slid her bag over to his side of the car, tucking it between his body and the door. "I'll hold onto it for now."

"Please just let me show you."

He stared at her in silence, then sped up to catch up with the others.

"Please let me go," she begged. "Believe me, the world is about to be destroyed."

He met her gaze in the glow of the dashboard, his eyes softening a bit. "Sorry, but you're along for the ride."

They turned off the highway and took an exit ramp toward a glow on the horizon. Firelight flickered in the distance, illuminating old, ramshackle buildings. A thick haze of smoke hung near the ground, and as they drove through it, she stifled a cough. Then the glow grew brighter, and they pulled into the Badlander camp. She looked out in wonder. About a hundred people huddled around small fires, cooking and talking.

As they pulled into a large lot full of cars, she stared out, frightened, as five Badlanders savagely beat someone lying on the ground. She gaped as the man tried to get away. She turned to Byron. "Shouldn't we do something?"

He looked at her and laughed. "Sure, if you want to get killed. Wow. You're really not from around here." Parking the car, he glanced over at the fight, then leaned back toward her. "Stay put. You do not want to go out there."

He climbed out of the car, then shut and locked the door. Already the car had attracted attention, as a couple of people—and soon a dozen others—gathered around it, staring at the solar panel.

"Who the hell's that?" a woman asked, gesturing at H124. Her bright red hair stood in sharp spikes, and a labyrinthine tattoo covered the sides of her face.

"Who cares? Look at the car!" her friend replied, a thin man with greasy blond hair braided down his back. Every inch of his skinny arms was covered in tattoos. Behind them, the man who was being beaten ran away.

H124 glanced around, wondering where Byron had gone to. "Okay, okay," she heard his voice saying. He pushed through the onlookers, back toward the car. "Look all you want, but don't touch. Where's Firehawk?"

The skinny man spoke up. "Still gone."

"Damn."

"Why, what's wrong?" the man asked Byron.

"Never mind," Byron said curtly, then opened the passenger door. He grabbed her arm and pulled her out, his fingers gripping her like a wrench

"Fresh meat?" asked the woman.

"Not quite," said Byron, dragging H124 past them. "Stick with me," he told her under his breath.

As they walked away from the crowd growing around the car, he called back, "If Firehawk comes back, somebody get me." He pushed her through a cluster of tents and lean-tos, makeshift shelters set up against the few remaining walls of whatever long-forgotten town this was.

She wrenched her arm from his grip. "Where are we going?"

"To my tent. I've got to keep you safe until Firehawk gets back. If I'm right, you're going to be crucial to our plan. You're just what we were waiting for."

She shook her head. "I don't see how . . ." She met his gaze firmly. "I can't help you with your plan. I have more vital things to do. Please try to understand." It felt strange for her to beg, but at this point, short of running away into the night to be killed by night stalkers or trying to fight the Badlanders to get back to her car, she didn't have many options. If he didn't listen to her, she'd have to wait for a chance when she was left alone, to somehow sneak back to her car.

"This is important too," was all he said, then pointed in the direction of his tent. "C'mon."

She walked a few more paces with him before she stopped. "Who's Firehawk?"

"He's the leader of another Badlander group. We work together sometimes."

"Is he a better listener?"

Byron managed a smile. "Maybe. I'm sure he'll hear your story and instantly give you a methane car and send you on your way."

"I have to try," she said. "I want to talk to him."

"Well, he's not here." He placed a hand on her back, hurrying her along as three cruel-looking Badlanders came up to them. Their clothes hung in rags, stitched together and torn. Hatred wafted off them. Two men had facial tattoos, abstract designs that curled around their eyes. The men hadn't shaved in weeks, and the woman's eyes were so narrowed and shrewd that she gave H124 the chills.

"What do you want?" asked Byron.

"Come to see our deliverer," growled one of the men, and the others laughed.

"Word gets around." Byron pulled H124 closer to him. "So you've seen her. Now we're passing by."

He pulled her along once more. She glanced at them as they passed, catching their sneers. What had made these people like this?

"Don't look at them," Byron whispered. "Just keep moving." As they walked through the encampment, she memorized every turn and step back to her car.

They got to his tent, a run-down collection of tarps slung over a rusted metal frame. He pulled a flap aside and pushed her in. A large cot stood in one corner, and a workbench cluttered with tools and devices she didn't recognize took up space at the back. A solitary leaning stool stood before it. In another corner stood a chipped washbasin and some ragged towels.

"Home, sweet home. At least for the last couple months." He grabbed some rope off the workbench. "Turn around."

She stared back at him. "No way."

"Do it."

He turned her around, grabbing her arms and binding them together. She thought of striking out and running. But with all of them out there, still active and awake, she wouldn't last long. Her best bet was to wait until everyone was sleeping and sneak out then.

He moved her to a metal pole in the center of the tent and tied her to it, then bound her feet together. Begrudgingly she let him, hoping he would hurry up and go to sleep. She didn't say anything else, just sat in silence as he slung her bag next to the washbasin, then splashed water on his face. With an exhausted sigh, he collapsed onto his cot. "Sorry about the accommodations," he said, peering back at her.

She didn't respond. She didn't even ask what was next, what would happen tomorrow, because she didn't plan on being around.

Readjusting his position, he put one hand over his face, and in a few minutes, she could hear the soft sounds of his breathing. He was asleep.

Outside was a different story. She could hear people shouting, taunting each other, sounds of fights, and then something made such a loud bang that she jumped and hit her head on the pole. It woke Byron. "Just a gun," he told her, then turned and went back to sleep.

She had no idea what a gun was, nor could she see the purpose in a device that made such a loud noise. She sat listening, working the ropes that bound her hands. He hadn't tied them very tight, probably counting on her fear to keep her in the tent. She managed to get one hand free, then twisted it around to loosen the rope on the other one. She listened to his even breathing, heard him murmur in a dream.

Things started to quiet down outside. She still heard the occasional shout, and another gun exploded in the night. She got up into a crouch, straining against the ropes, forcing them to loosen. Every few minutes she paused, listening to the sounds of Byron sleeping. He stirred once, talking in his sleep, then shouted out loud, sitting straight up. "Damn," he said in the dark. "You still here?"

She felt lucky this had happened before she left. "Unfortunately."

"Good."

Then she heard him roll over, and a few minutes later, the soft sounds of him returning to his slumber.

She strained against the ropes, finally getting both hands free. She went to work on her feet, and at last they were loose enough for her to step out of the rope.

Now the world outside had grown much quieter. She still heard some people milling around, talking in low voices. But they would probably do so all night long; she had a feeling this camp had sentries. Getting past them would not be easy.

Listening one more time to Byron, she satisfied herself that he was asleep and crept to the tent flap. Opening it just a crack, she peered out. No one stood around in the immediate vicinity. In the distance, she could still see a few bonfires burning, the light bouncing off the parked cars and makeshift tents.

She slid out quickly, throwing the flap back over the tent opening. She ran in a crouch, sticking to the shadows. She paused at every corner of an old building to check for movement. She spotted a group of four people standing around a small fire. One punched another in the arm, and he responded with a violent sock to the face. She sprinted past while they were distracted.

She skirted around the back of the next row of tents, past a group of at least six or seven men and women sitting around in collapsible chairs, drinking and talking. She ran around the backside of the lean-tos, staying on the outskirts as much as possible. She didn't want to go too far outside the encampment's perimeter, though, as she figured that would alert the sentries or attract night stalkers.

She thought of merely strolling brazenly along, trying to blend in, but with her plain hair, ordinary clothes, and lack of tattoos, she didn't think she'd have a chance of fitting in. She weaved around part of a collapsed building, at last coming to the final stretch of vehicles where her solar car was parked.

Two sentries, a man and a woman, stood guarding the vehicles, talking to each other a few feet from her car. She was trying to figure out a way around them when she heard movement in the dark behind her. She spun, and two men came into view. They'd been sitting inside one of the cars she'd passed. They stood up, closing the doors behind them.

One looked to be about fifty, with a downturned mouth and a scar that ran from his right ear down beneath the collar of his frayed shirt. The other one was younger, maybe in his thirties, with a blue Mohawk. His face was inked with elaborate swirls and geometric shapes.

"Hey," said the older one. "You're the one Byron brought into camp. The one with the car." He narrowed his eyes, peering at her in the faint firelight. "You're one of them."

"Them?" she asked, confused.

"From one of the cities."

She shook her head. "No. I'm not one of them."

"Then why did you have city tech on you?"

She tried to sound tough. "I stole it."

The blue-haired one stepped closer. "And that car! Where did you get that car?"

"I'm a wanderer out here just like you. I found the car along the way."

The older one laughed, a mirthless, airy sound from a throat that had probably been slit when he got his scar. "Fat chance." He moved closer to her, and she took a few steps back. "What are you doing out here?"

She struggled for an answer. "I'm supposed to check on the car. Byron doesn't know how to set it up to charge overnight."

They both frowned, weighing her reply. She thought Blue Hair was buying it, so she started moving toward the car. The two sentries, when they spotted her, would be a different story.

Suddenly the one with the scar lunged forward. She staggered back, and he barely missed grabbing her, snagging her sleeve instead. She wrenched it out of his grasp. "What the hell do you want?" she asked.

"Your blood," said Scar.

"Your guts," said Blue Hair.

She glanced around, not sure where to go. They advanced quickly, and when one grabbed her shoulder, she shrugged him off. He cursed, and the two sentries heard. They rushed forward, surrounding her.

"What do we have here?" sneered one of the guards, a tall, lean man with a hawk nose and cold eyes.

The other sentry grinned joylessly, drawing a knife from her belt. "It's Byron's little captive."

"Too bad she died trying to escape," said the first sentry.

They all laughed, closing in on her. Scar got so close she could smell his putrid breath. As he reached out, she ducked down and ran under his grasping arm. Then she was racing into the shadows, trying to put some distance between herself and her assailants.

As she rounded a corner, Blue Hair vaulted over a parked car, landing in front of her. He pulled out his own knife, a huge, wicked-looking blade that flashed in the distant firelight. She backed up, almost running into Scar, who had moved in to corner her. Once again she turned and sped away, snaking between them.

The two sentries whooped in the darkness, abandoning their post in order to get a piece of her. She ran, banging her shin on something solid in the shadows. She could hear them gaining on her. Blue Hair cut her off again, zipping between two tents. They knew their way around much better than she did. She looked ahead, finding that she'd cornered herself, and spun around, racing past the female sentry with the knife. The blade came flashing down in the dark, catching H124's hair. She felt a shallow cut zing down the back of her neck, so she ducked and rolled, managing to dart away.

She sped for the deepest shadows she could find, a narrow row between two lines of tents. She raced down it, hoping they hadn't seen where she went. She walked slowly, stealthily, keeping an ear out for them. She was almost at the end of the row when someone slid up behind and grabbed her. He slapped a hand over her mouth and turned her around. It was Byron. He removed his hand and held a finger to his lips. Her pursuers ran down the opposite side of the tents. She could see their looming shadows on the tarp material.

Byron held her fast. She could smell him now, the scent of rain, the way the wind smelled when it came from the west. The attackers passed by.

"They'll double back now," he whispered. "Why the hell did you try to make a break for it?"

"I have to get out of here," she insisted, keeping her voice low.

"You're going to get killed out here. Those guys don't care that I'm trying to keep you alive. They can't see the bigger picture. You're not safe."

"You're the one who doesn't see the bigger picture," she whispered harshly.

The pursuers did double back, hunting along the sides of the tent row. If she'd run out there, if Byron hadn't stopped her, they would have seen her when they returned.

They passed by as she and Byron stood in the darkness. She became aware of his proximity, his chest pressed against her, the strength of his arms around her in the narrow space, the warmth of his body. She'd never been this close to someone for this long. It made her feel odd and slightly dizzy. His hand rested on the back of her neck, pressing her face into the crook of his neck, and she could smell his warm skin.

"I think they'll go back to their post now."

She looked in that direction, but saw only the narrow aisle between the tents. "And the two other guys?"

"Probably get drunker and forget everything five minutes." He looked down at her. She could see his eyes gleaming in the firelight. "Now are you going to come back with me?"

"I have to get back on the road."

He slapped a hand to his forehead. "You're so goddamn stubborn!" He gripped her shoulders with both hands, and gave her a stern look. "Look. I'm sorry I've ruined your day and taken your car. But you have to help us. It's important."

"I don't see how it can be more important than saving the planet from imminent destruction."

He exhaled. "How about doing both?"

"What do you mean?"

"Maybe we can figure out a way to do both. I just need your skills right now."

She rolled the thought over in her head. "If I help you, do I have your word you'll send me on my way after?"

He looked away, then ran a hand over his face. "That wouldn't really be entirely up to me."

"Then who else is it up to?"

"Firehawk," he said gravely. "He might need you for more work."

"Then help me get out of here now." She knew she was taking a chance, but she felt a strange understanding with him.

"I can't. I just can't." His eyes looked genuinely regretful. "If it wasn't so important . . ."

"*What's* so important?" she demanded, still whispering.

"Lives are at stake. Our people are being decimated by PPC troops. We need your help to stop them."

"Is that before or after I get flayed alive on a spit over a fire?"

He grinned. "I'll do my best to prevent that." He took her arm, gently this time. "C'mon. Let's get back to my tent. They won't mess with you in there. We have our own codes, and that's part of it. Our tents are our homes. No barging in."

She let him lead her back that way. When they got to his tent, he held open the flap for her, and she bent to pass under his arm. Damn. Back again. He'd lit a dim UV lantern, and she could see the rope on the ground where she'd left it.

He walked in behind her. "You're bleeding."

She could feel the sting where the sentry's blade had cut her on the neck.

He walked over to the washstand, pulling out a clean cloth. Then he returned and softly cleaned the blood off her neck. "It's not bad." His hands felt warm on her neck. She'd never felt someone touch her hair like that. It sent a pleasant shiver of chills down her back.

When he was done, he placed the cloth on the nightstand and turned to her. "This time I'm tying you to me in the bed."

She gave a small laugh.

He didn't smile back. "I'm not kidding." He picked up the rope and took her elbow, leading her over to the bed. He tied one end around his hips, the other end to her waist. When he got close, she smelled a hint of rain once more.

He stripped off his top shirt, leaving on his well-worn pair of jeans and black tank top. "C'mon," he said, motioning her toward the bed.

She pulled against the rope. "This is ridiculous."

"Only because you made it so." He pulled her over to the cot and lay down on it. She reluctantly let him pull her down beside him.

The cot turned up at the edges, forcing them to lie flush together. She'd never lain next to someone before. He turned off the lantern and moved his arms around, at last draping one over her. "Sorry," he said. "Don't want you to make another great escape."

He shifted to his side, turning toward her. She could sense the proximity of his face, his *mouth,* tried not to think about it. A wave of new emotion swept over her; she became all too aware of the length of his body, of the feel of his strong legs next to hers, of the scent of his warm breath on her neck. She could feel the rise and fall of his chest and stomach as he breathed next to her. She'd had dreams of this kind of thing before, but hadn't known what to make of them, so she tried to just forget them. They'd only filled her with an empty ache when she awoke to her real life. Now she tried to shut off her senses, to tune out everything about him. He was her captor, she told herself, a disgusting individual who'd taken her freedom, her car, and had put her in the middle of this dangerous encampment with no thought of the bigger picture. He was completely disgusting, she assured herself.

Whoever this Firehawk was, he had better listen to her. Nothing they needed her to do could possibly be more important than her mission, not even saving a few lives. Not when every life on the planet was in danger. She had to make them understand.

She listened to Byron breathe in the darkness, waiting for that soft, even sound of sleep. But it didn't come. And she had the acute sense that he was every bit aware of her closeness as she was of his. As he shifted, she felt the whiskers of his cheek brush against her face. She fought off a strange, aching desire for him to close the distance.

"Asleep?" he whispered.

"Not much chance of that." She caught herself and rolled her eyes the other way. "Being in this strange place where people are waiting to cut my throat."

"Can't blame you for that. Well, I for one won't cut your throat."

She blinked in the dark. "That's good to know."

They lay in silence until he whispered, "Sorry. I'll try to get you in and out of Delta City as quickly as possible."

She said nothing, just lay next to him, and finally tried to close her eyes. They stung with fatigue.

She awoke to shouts in the camp, feeling as if she'd only just dozed off. She guessed she'd gotten about fifteen minutes of sleep. Byron had done only slightly better. Though they hadn't spoken for most of the night, she could sense he'd remained awake for much of the evening. Sunlight streamed in through the tent opening.

She heard snippets of shouted conversation. "We have to move!"—"Firehawk's not back yet."—". . . got the device!"

Byron stirred, his opening eyes meeting hers. Their green intensity struck her. She'd never been so close to someone before, at least no one who was alive. He watched her for a long moment, and she could feel something passing between them, some unspoken communication, but she didn't know what it was. Then he turned, shifting his weight. He untied the rope. It had been uncomfortable as hell to sleep like that. Getting up and stretching, he moved to the opening of the tent.

He stuck his head through the flap, and H124 squinted in the sudden brightness. "Astoria, what's going on?" he asked as someone rushed by.

"Firehawk's got the prototype," she heard a woman answer. As the newcomer stopped outside the tent, H124 got a glimpse of a black Mohawk and dark, piercing eyes. Spiral tattoos covered a sepia face. "But we've got to move today. They're mobilizing, but we don't know to where."

"What about Firehawk? Where is he?"

"He's fallen under fire outside the city. Someone managed to get out to tell us we should leave now, but Firehawk stayed behind with the rest of his team. He says we're supposed to meet him there."

"At the tower?" Byron sounded incredulous.

The woman nodded.

"How the hell is he going to get in the city?"

"He found a worker." She looked through the tent flap at H124. "Another one. I'll get Dirk and meet you at the car." She turned and rushed off. Byron turned in the tent doorway.

"What's happening?" she asked.

"Change of plans. We're leaving today. Now."

"Who's coming? What did she mean?"

"The death squad." He hurried about the tent, shoving gear into an old, worn duffel. She watched him stuff in climbing rope, carabiners, a belt full of tools, a portable laser torch, and some water.

"Who is the death squad?"

"The PPC sends them to wipe us out. It's why I need your help. They've already killed too many of our people."

"Can't you fight them?"

"They have the numbers, and the advanced tech. And they keep finding us. We can't stay in a single place for long. Firehawk thinks that if we carry off this mission, we'll know their movements before they can reach us." He looked away, that haunted expression returning to his face. "We want to end their operation for good."

She saw now why he'd been so insistent. "Where do we have to go?"

"Delta City."

She tilted her head.

"I'm guessing you're not from that one."

She gave him a blank stare.

"Delta City," he elaborated. "AKA Murder City."

"Murder City?"

"Sadly. You'll see what I mean when we get there."

"How far is it?"

"It's right here. Damn thing stretches from east of Lake Michigan all the way down to the Mississippi delta. It's everywhere. We're on the eastern border." He stuffed a jacket into his bag and then turned to her. "But we don't have to worry about all that. We're concentrating on a specific section of the city: the PPC Tower."

H124 thought of the one in New Atlantic, and how heavily guarded it was. "How do you expect to get in?"

"Simple," he said, grabbing her hand. "You're going to get us in."

She let him pull her to the door. "Are we taking my car?"

He nodded. "It's quiet. We'll take it to the edge of the atmospheric shield."

She frowned, watching him as he packed the last of his supplies. Maybe she could slip away somehow after they were done. Maybe he wouldn't be keeping so close an eye on her after he got what he needed in the city. And the media communications tower presented an interesting opportunity. Could she somehow carry off a pirate broadcast? Warn people of the imminent danger? Tell them to break away from the networks and seek shelter? She didn't know where those people could hide . . . maybe underground somewhere. She could broadcast some contingency plan in case she didn't find the Rovers.

And in case the Rovers didn't know what to do, even if she did locate them.

They moved quickly through the camp, stopping at the solar car. Two others approached, both giants in their mid-twenties, she guessed. The woman had been the one to peek into Byron's tent earlier. Red streaks ran through her black Mohawk, and the man's hair hung in long black dreadlocks around his rich umber face. A few of the dreads were a vibrant blue.

"These are Astoria and Dirk."

Dirk offered a quick nod, while Astoria stared her down as if thinking how best to gut H124 so she could eat her for dinner later.

"Be nice," Byron told Astoria.

The brawny woman relaxed her shoulders. "Always." Her chestnut eyes narrowed on H124. Again it gave her the shivers.

"Twins who couldn't be more unalike," Byron told her. "Astoria will shiv you in the gut for your shoes, and Dirk will weep over a swatted fly."

Indignation flashed in Dirk's eyes. "That's not entirely true."

Byron smiled ruefully. "Yeah. Not entirely." He patted Dirk on the arm. "But he knows his way around tech, and can sneak into anything."

"Glad I can be of some use," Dirk huffed.

Byron gestured toward the car. "Pile in." He handed back H124's bag, sans the knife and Willoughby's PRD. But it still had her MREs, books, and water bottle, now empty.

Astoria and Dirk got in the back, as Byron opened the door for H124. He closed and locked the door, and got in.

He pulled away from the encampment, weaving between randomly parked cars. They pulled out onto a main road, H124 staring out at the desolation. She leaned forward, looking up at the sky. The asteroid was out there, and she was losing precious time every minute she was with them.

She turned to Byron. "Please," she said. "I have to finish my mission."

"Our people are getting killed."

"I know, but a hell of a lot more are going to suffer the same fate if I don't get out of here."

Dirk leaned forward from the back seat. "What's she talking about?"

Byron waved him off. "Nothing."

"Nothing!" H124 yelled. "*Nothing?*"

Byron gave her a soft gaze. "Tell you what. You get us in, you'll have an opportunity to warn people."

"How? You know how to do some kind of pirate broadcast?"

Astoria chuckled in the back seat, as if that were the stupidest question she'd ever heard.

"I see you already thought of that option," Byron told H124. "I'll show you when we get there."

"And then?" she asked, raising a brow.

"We let you go."

The back seat erupted in laughter. "Yeah, we'll let you go," repeated Astoria.

Dirk was still leaning toward the front seat. "Warn them about what?"

H124 turned to face him. "An asteroid."

"An aster what?"

"It's a space rock," Byron chimed in, "and supposedly it's going to slam into the planet."

Dirk's eyes widened. "And you didn't think to tell us?"

Byron closed his eyes and shook his head, waving it off. "We don't even know if it's really coming." He looked to H124. "You said that lab you found was ancient. It could have been malfunctioning."

She turned to him. "Is it worth taking the risk?"

Byron pressed his lips together. "You'll have the chance to warn people in Delta City," he assured her. "That's all I can do."

"And then let me go," she added.

"Yeah," he said. "And then let you go."

She didn't believe him at all.

Chapter18

Long before they reached the city, H124 could smell it. "What *is* that?" Byron wrinkled his nose. "Methane."

She fought the urge to gag. "Where is it coming from?"

"The infrastructure of Delta City can't handle the population. A long time ago, they started pumping the sewage outside the city. They have sewers within, but outside . . ."

"It just runs off like rivers?"

"Rivers of shit," Astoria said from the back seat.

H124 pulled her shirt up over her nose. It didn't help. She could feel the back of her mouth start to water, a precursor of what was to come. Digging around in her bag, she pulled out the scarf she'd found in the weather shelter. She tied it around her face, covering her nose and mouth. It didn't help much.

"It works well for us," Dirk said.

She looked back at him incredulously. "What do you mean?"

"It's where we bottle all the methane that powers our cars."

She looked away in disgust. "Ugh."

Byron wrinkled his nose. "It's dangerous, though. The methane runners can get blown sky-high sometimes. The gas is extremely volatile. Just a spark. and *whamo!* You're bottling methane for the angelic choir."

"The angelic choir? Who are they?"

Byron looked at her. "You know. Checking in at the pearly gates?"

She gave him a blank stare.

"Wow. You really don't get out much."

They drove on, storm clouds gathering above. Late afternoon changed into evening. Soon it grew so dark she could see the dim glow of the distant city.

All around them the ground glistened and squished as far out as she could see. The scent of urine stung the inside of her nose. She tried to breathe through her mouth and think about something else.

The radiance grew brighter and brighter. She could see a wall looming before them, the same orange glow that her own city let off, the same bright pinpoints from the floating lights. But the atmospheric shield was different. It rose straight up, stretching across the horizon. She leaned forward in the passenger seat, trying to gauge the top of it, but couldn't. "Is that a wall?" she asked.

He shook his head. "A dome. So big it just looks like a wall."

Her mouth fell open. "How big is this city?" She didn't know what Lake Michigan or the Mississippi delta were.

"More than seven hundred miles long, if you can picture that."

She tried to imagine how big that was and how many people lived there. He gauged her astonishment. "I'm guessing you might be from New Atlantic. This place isn't tucked away and orderly like your city. This is going to be rough."

Just out the window, waves of fecal matter flew up from the wheels. She was sickened that this was her car plowing through the muck. It wouldn't take long for the panels to get caked.

Still they drove on. The dome kept growing. She kept thinking they'd reach the edge at any moment, but instead it just loomed larger. Soon it filled the whole night sky, and the light was so bright she could barely see beyond a squint.

Then, along the ancient concrete base, she spied enormous carbon dioxide ports, identical to the ones she and Rowan had escaped through.

"Are we heading for those?"

Byron nodded. "Yep."

She spun toward him. "But we can't get in from this direction. We'll be incinerated."

"Not if you turn it off."

"Does it even have a TWR for that?"

He gave another nod, slower this time.

She stared back at the colossal shield. "I'll try. I'll also have to open that environmental barrier in the middle too."

His brow rose. "So you have done this before."

"Once." It felt like a long time ago now. "What happens once I open it?"

"We enter the city."

"But won't they try to stop us the moment we go through?"

He laughed. "You definitely didn't come from this city center. "

He stopped near the entrance to one of the CO_2 vents and switched off the engine. "We're about to enter utter chaos. You won't have just the PPC death squads trying to kill us. Badlanders have a price on their heads."

"You mean ordinary citizens might have it out for us?"

"Not the ones who are plugged in. They don't notice anything. But the rest? They're the dangerous ones."

"The rest?" she asked.

He didn't answer. Instead he pulled out an antique metal device she didn't recognize. Reaching into his pocket, he produced a handful of cylinders.

"What's that?"

He loaded the cylinders into a round barrel. "A gun."

"What does it do?"

"Punches holes in anyone who stands in our way." She gazed at it as he put it in his pocket. "And it makes a hell of a bang." He climbed out of the car. She got out too, followed by Dirk and Astoria. "Ready?" he asked them.

They nodded, but H124 was far from ready. She still wanted nothing more than to get back to her car and speed west. They walked to the outtake of the vent. The air was horrible and stale, and they couldn't stop coughing. H124 turned on her headlamp, and they followed suit.

Byron stood next to her. "Let's see if it's even on first." He kicked a reeking rock coated in excrement toward the vent. A wall of fire flamed down, sizzling the rock's coating. "That's a yes."

H124 peered into the dark vent. She spied the TWR, but it was on the other side of the incineration field. She didn't know if she could send it a message from this far away. She closed her eyes, concentrating. She sent the message for the TWR to turn off the detection shield. She felt it click in her mind and said, "I think it's off."

Astoria marched forward, and H124 grabbed her hand. "Wait. I'd throw something else in first."

Astoria narrowed her eyes at H124, then spotted another rock on the ground. It glistened in a layer of sewage. Then she kicked it in, and it landed safely on the other side.

H124 took a long look at them. "I don't understand why you couldn't just do this yourselves."

Astoria's mouth fell open. "Are you serious?" She gave H124 a disgusted look. "Because our brains haven't been fuc—"

Byron brushed past her and clasped H124 on the shoulder. "Good work. Let's go."

They entered the dank, cool vent, heading toward the city. H124's heart quickened. She thought of her late-night escape from New Atlantic and of the Repurposers. Now she was walking back into that world. Her legs slowed, and her hands shook. She felt Byron come up beside her, heard his every breath. If she could warn people, if she could get a broadcast out, she had to risk it. She also knew that if the PPC wanted her repurposed before, they'd want her dead after this.

She trudged on in the dark.

Chapter 19

At the transition zone before the central semipermeable membrane, the air was so thick with carbon dioxide that she could barely breathe. All of them hacked and coughed in the confines of the tunnel. She thought of Rowan's words, that it was only designed to let the CO_2 out. She had to use her theta waves to temporarily disable the membrane, allowing them access.

In the dim light, she approached the theta wave sensor and got within operating range. She closed her eyes, feeling her way to the sensor with her mind. She felt the connection slide into place, then sent an off signal. Instantly the membrane went down, and oxygen flooded the tunnel.

She gasped for fresh air. Gathering themselves, they walked on, past the transition zone. H124 moved to the receiver on the other side. She sent an on signal, and the air pressure changed. She swallowed, popping her ears. "We're in," she whispered to Byron.

They proceeded cautiously.

When they reached the mouth of the tunnel, H124 gazed out into absolute chaos.

High above, amber lights floated, giving everything the same sickly orange glow that she'd grown so used to at home. But this place was not the clean, ordered space that New Atlantic had been. There she'd run through empty streets, no chance of anyone noticing or helping her. At the end of the tunnel, she disengaged the shielded membrane, and they emerged into a seething throng of people. She replaced the shield on the other side.

The air reeked with sweating, dirty human bodies. The stench of sewage had been bad outside, but here it was just as noxious, mixed with strong waves of body odor and decomposition. Gagging, eyes streaming, she pulled her scarf back up over her nose and mouth.

Thin, dirty people crowded every foot of the street. They squatted against buildings, lay on the ground, huddled in doorways. Byron pushed his way through with the casual indifference of someone who'd done it a thousand times.

Above them, a floating sign shimmered: *It's Time.*

H124 lingered on it, wondering what it meant. Then she got behind Byron as he cut through the crowd. People grabbed her shirt, arms, ankles, asking her if she had food. She handed out MREs, and the people scurried away with them without a second glance back at her.

Behind her Astoria pushed over a begging woman, while Dirk mumbled an apology.

They passed another floating sign: *It's Your Civic Duty.*

An old man grabbed Astoria by the shoulder. She whirled on him, knocking him down with a fist to the head. H124 rushed over and helped him up. "You didn't have to do that!" she shouted at Astoria.

Astoria narrowed her eyes. "These people don't have to live like this. They choose to." She regarded the old man with contempt. He clung to H124, asking her if she had any water.

"I don't. I'm sorry." The old man shambled off.

"They could leave if they wanted to," Astoria grumbled. "Fucking sheep. It may be hell here, but it's what they've grown up in, and they're too afraid to leave. The hell is familiar, and that's all they care about."

Frowning, H124 pushed past her and caught up with Byron, who was halfway down the block. It was then she saw the PPC tower, looming so high she had to crane her neck to see the top. She'd never seen a building so tall. He'd picked a good place for them to enter the city. They were close to the communications tower.

She glanced around as she pushed through the teeming elbows, hands, and pleading faces.

Byron gazed up at the tower. "Reaching it will be comparatively easy."

"To what?"

"Getting inside." She remembered pounding on the glass of the PPC building in her home city. In New Atlantic, a person on the street was a novelty. The guard had been shocked and let her in. But in this place—she studied the swarming masses—there would be no way a guard would just let them in. "And that's where I come in?" she asked.

He nodded.

"Any ideas?"

"I've got a plan." He put out his hands, parting his way through the crowd. She got in behind him again. Glancing down the alleys as they passed, she asked, "Do Repurposers wander around?"

"Not out here. Too dangerous. They'd get torn apart."

A large group of curious bystanders was now following them. Then came a voice, twisted and desperate: "Look! Badlanders! We can exchange them for food!"

A murmur swept through the crowd, and H124 felt a flash of fear. The crowd pressed closer, and someone grabbed her arm. She flung them off.

"Just keep moving," Byron urged softly.

The murmur grew louder, then someone started shouting.

"Where do you think you're going?" shrieked a woman.

"Stop! Get them!" cried another.

All around people started to stand, advancing on them.

"Stop them!" someone shouted. "Alive or dead, they're worth tons of food!"

The crowd ahead seethed forward, their mad faces filling H124's view. One pushed through the group. His clothes hung in dirty rags around his scrawny shoulders. "You have food?"

"No," she said. "I gave it all away."

He gritted his teeth, and his eyes flashed with rage. "To who? I'll kill the son of bitch. WHO HAS FOOD?" He pushed past her, wading into the mounting crowd behind her.

"Who cares who has that scrap of food?" called out a barely clad old woman. "If we bring them in, the PPC will give us enough for two days!" Then a fight erupted, the man in rags punching in every direction, knocking others to the asphalt.

Byron gripped H124's arm. "We have to get out of here."

But already the crowd ahead had closed ranks. A rabbling mob encircled them. H124 felt someone seize her hair, as hands pulled at her garments. Shrugging them off, she clutched her bag to her side as someone tried to rip it off her shoulder. There was no way she was going to let it out of her possession again.

"Get off!" she yelled, tugging it free.

"She's got food in there!" a woman screeched.

"I don't!" H124 insisted. "Get away!"

Byron grabbed her again, but she didn't need the cue. She was already darting through the crowd next to Astoria, who violently shoved anyone who stood in their way. Someone hit H124 in the back of her head, and another tripped her. She staggered back to her feet, feeling the weight of dozens trying to rip at her and pull her down again.

She threw punches and kicks, but the desperate sea kept rising. She elbowed someone in the ribs but realized it was futile. Greedy hands grabbed her ankles and arms as she thrashed helplessly.

A burly man grabbed her by the throat. She felt the life oozing out of her. Then a fist collided with his face, shattering his cheekbone.

Byron took her hand. "Run!"

"I'm trying!" she shouted, twisting free. She gave a final kick to her last assailant, and sprinted onward. She was free. Nothing could stop her now. She thought of the broadcast. Of the asteroid.

Chapter 20

Byron pulled her down an alley through a break in the crowd and descended a long staircase below street level, Astoria and Dirk racing behind. The throng tried to follow them, but they were so emaciated and exhausted that they quickly gave up.

Byron ran down, farther and farther, the others in tow, until even the orange glow from the floating lights barely penetrated the dark stairwell.

H124 clicked on her headlamp. "What is this?"

"There's an entrance to the tunnels down here. Delta was built on top of an older city, which was built on one older yet. No one uses these tunnels anymore. They sealed them up long ago."

Astoria caught up. "Fortunately we've opened one of the entrances, and put our own lock on it."

H124 jogged down the steps. "Where do they lead?"

"Straight to the underbelly of the PPC tower."

They caught their breath at the bottom of the stairs. Byron stopped in front of an antiquated door. He pulled out his PRD and entered a code. The lock clicked open. H124 could see where they'd cut through ancient welds around a rusted doorframe. It was the oldest-looking door she'd ever seen, more rust than door. Like some of the old doors in New Atlantic, it too had a manual handle. As Byron turned it, a musty smell blossomed out. Dirk choked. H124 aimed her beam through the doorway, where a cement-lined hallway led away into darkness. Dust motes drifted in the air.

Byron tilted his head. "C'mon." He led the way. When they all filed in, he locked the door behind him. They all switched on their lamps, and she could see more of the neglected space. The reek of mold and mildew was strong, even through her scarf.

Byron was already hurrying down the hallway, so she followed. As they descended more steps, the cement gave way to old stones, each mortared in place. They passed through elaborate arched doorways. The floor became uneven.

"What was this place?" H124 asked.

Byron gazed up at the stone ceiling. "No one knows. Someplace old."

She could see that. The floor sloped, and an earthen smell overtook the trace of mold. They headed down the steep grade. She could smell water, as stones glistened everywhere. The four of them ascended a series of staircases, all made of individual stones. The ceilings arched high above her, another marvel of stonework. Soon the bare floor sloped upward. She felt an empty expanse overhead. She shone her beam up, to a cavern whose top vanished into obscurity. Humidity hung heavy in the air, while somewhere nearby she heard the dripping of water. The sides of the tunnel were smooth and wet and made of white rock. The space narrowed as they moved on, and H124's moist breath plumed in the air.

They passed through a narrow aperture of wet rock, emerging into a colossal room, the likes of which she'd never seen. High overhead hung massive columns of rock, tapered off at their dripping ends. On the floor rose similar pointed spires, while in some places columns linked the ceiling to the floor. Water trickled everywhere.

She slowed, scanning the cavern.

Byron dulled his pace too. "We don't know what this is, either."

"Someone built this?" she asked.

"If so, we don't see why," he answered. "Some think it might be natural."

She creased her brow. "Natural?"

"You know . . . not made by humans."

"Oh." She took in the sight under a new lens. "It's beautiful."

He stopped, gazing up. "Yes."

Then he hurried on, and she forced herself to stop staring. Soon the floor grew even stranger as they came to an area with a metal railing. Byron hopped over it, as did she. It ran alongside an even cement walkway. They rushed along, Byron checking the clock on his PRD. "We don't have much time to meet Firehawk in the building. We're running behind."

"Damn crowd out there," Astoria muttered, venom in her voice.

Dirk moved in silence, glancing back at the rooms of dripping rock.

They followed the walkway until they came to a door filled with mold-encrusted glass. They passed through into a smaller room with another glass door at the other end. H124 felt her ears pop. Byron moved through the second door, beyond which lay a set of stairs between two narrow walls of rock. They took them two at a time.

At the top of the stairs a third door waited. Entering a room with an old desk and some hanging displays, she saw on them images of some of the formations they'd passed, with long descriptive passages underneath. She yearned to stop and look at them, but Byron was already walking through another door at the far end of the room. As she caught up with him, she spied an image of a winged black creature. She stopped in spite of herself. The faded description below said it was called a bat, and that they used to live in caverns like the one she'd just been in. Though there had once been more than a thousand of species of them that kept insect populations in check, they'd gone extinct as a result of habitat loss, white nose syndrome, and the use of something called *pesticides.* She looked up at the image again, studying its incredible wings and huge ears.

"Let's go!" Astoria croaked from the far door.

H124 ran to catch up.

Through the next door, it was back to cement walls and floors, a utilitarian tunnel leading steadily upward. They rushed along, Byron checking his PRD once more.

"How is Firehawk getting into the city?" H124 asked.

"He's got a worker helping him from within. I thought they had a methane car, but I didn't see one when we parked. Maybe they're running behind too."

Byron stopped in front of a modern door with a theta wave receiver. "This is it. The sub-subbasement of the PPC tower."

She glanced at the others. Dirk looked sick, as if he were about to throw up. He didn't have the hardened temperament of the other Badlanders. Sweat glistened on his face as he stood there shifting from one foot to the other.

She stepped close to the receiver and concentrated, sending an off signal to the door's lock. She heard it disengage and sent the open signal to the door. It slid open. She saw that look of disgust on Astoria's face again. "Why can't you use the TWRs?"

Byron passed through the door.

"Because they do something to workers like you," Astoria said. "They mess with your brains when you're babies."

A chill coursed through H124. *They did?* After seeing what the Repurposers had done to people, she believed it. But her own brain? What had they done?

When they had all piled inside, she locked the door behind them, then thought better of it. She unlocked it and slid it open a crack.

"What are you doing?" asked Byron.

She met his grim gaze. "In case I don't make it out with you all." She pushed past them. "Where do we go next?

Byron motioned with his chin. "Up."

They moved toward a ramp and came to a set of stairs, as well as two elevators—a fancy one for executives and a basic one for maintenance workers like her.

"Can you run that thing?" Dirk asked, pointing to the worker one.

H124 nodded. "But they might notice if there's no scheduled maintenance."

Byron turned. "Stairs then."

Astoria groaned.

Dirk shook, the sweat still beading on his brow. H124 wondered if this was the first time he'd broken into a city center. He wiped the perspiration off his forehead with his sleeve.

They hurried, taking the stairs two at a time. By the tenth floor, H124 was feeling her lack of sleep.

"What floor is Firehawk going to be on?" Astoria asked from behind.

"You really want me to tell you?" Byron said.

"Tell me, or I'll throw you off this damn staircase."

"Three hundred thirty-four."

"Damn it! I shouldn't have asked!"

Progress was slow. They fell into a rhythm, taking twenty floors before resting.

"You sure they'd detect us in that elevator?" Astoria wondered, as they sat on the stairs.

"Not necessarily," replied H124. "It's not a routine check or anything, if it's like my city. But if someone was watching and noticed a maintenance worker and three other people who look like you all do . . ."

Astoria looked disappointed. "Gotcha."

They continued up. H124's burning legs slowly morphed into rubber. Halfway up, at floor 174, Dirk finally retched over the railing. He wiped his mouth and lingered there for a moment. H124 watched Astoria place an unexpected hand on his back. She then moved past her brother. He took up the rear, looking wretched.

H124 lost track of how many times they rested. She just kept seeing Byron glancing at his PRD. The tension hung in the air, as all of them knew how late they were. Climbing the stairs took far longer than any of them had expected.

Finally they reached the designated floor, legs trembling. Byron waited by the stairwell door, and H124 unlocked it, more weary than ever. They slipped inside, Byron leading the way. He pulled out his gun, aiming it both ways down the hall. They were clear.

"We need to find the surveillance room." He brought up a floating map on his PRD. H124 looked over his shoulder while he checked it. "This way." He nodded to the left, and they followed him down the quiet corridor.

H124 felt eyes everywhere. She was sure they had cameras in all the corridors and only hoped no one was looking at this hall at this particular time.

They hastened to a door halfway down, and Byron gave her the signal to open it. She approached the theta wave receiver and commanded it to open. Nothing happened.

"What's wrong?" asked Astoria, wielding her gun.

"It's locked. I don't have access."

"Now what?" Dirk asked, glancing back down the corridor with the same queasy look.

"I can do a work-around, but it might take a few minutes." H124 concentrated, sending the unlock signal to the receiver. It didn't obey. She thought *open* and *close* in the same instant, then imagined the door stuck halfway. She envisioned it locked and unlocked at the same time—an image of the bolts secured, double-exposed over one of them open. The door made a series of clicks, then locked and unlocked, slid open a little way, then closed.

She heard Astoria gasp. "Damn," she whispered. "That's creepy."

H124 sent the door more conflicting images of it being in two states at once: open and closed, locked and unlocked. It clicked through a series of settings, and with a hiss and acrid smell of burning electronics, the door slid open.

"Let's go," Byron said.

They entered a small room in which a variety of servers whirred. H124's breath frosted in the air.

Byron did a quick circuit of the room, his gun level. He returned to the others. "Firehawk's not here yet."

Dirk licked his lips, then manually slid the door shut. Second-guessing himself, he opened it just a crack. "Where can he be?"

Byron shrugged.

"Damn!" Astoria lowered her gun.

"Maybe we should bail, try this again a different time. All go in together," Dirk suggested.

Byron shook his head. "He'll be here."

"Unless he's dead," Astoria countered.

Byron remained adamant. "We have to wait. The death squad is moving on us, and if we can find out when and where, we can be one step ahead of them. It's worth the risk."

Dirk shifted from one foot to the other, a full-blown nervous wreck. "And if they realize we're in here? If they already *know* we're in here?"

"Just cool it," Byron told him.

Silence fell over the group. Over the next few minutes Dirk kept peeking through the small crack in the door.

H124 toured the room, surveying the vast array of servers. The PPC certainly had a staggering amount of room for information collecting.

She returned to the door, and Dirk hissed through his teeth. "Someone's coming."

They pressed against the wall, guns at the ready. The footsteps came nearer, then stopped outside the door. Fingers laced through the opening and pushed slightly. A familiar face peered into the room. "Byron?" it whispered.

Rowan. She couldn't believe it.

Byron hurried to the door and wrenched it open. "Firehawk! You made it!"

"Thank the gods you're here," Rowan laughed, grasping his shoulder. "I didn't know how the hell I was going to get in." His eyes fell on H124, and his jaw fell agape. "You?"

She felt herself smile. "*You're* Firehawk?"

He took her in his arms. At once she felt relief steal over her. She wasn't as scared. "How the hell are you here? I didn't think I'd ever see you again," he admitted.

Byron raised his eyebrows. "You two know each other?"

"Are you kidding me?" Rowan said, grinning. "If it weren't for her, I wouldn't even have the prototype. She saved my life."

Astoria looked at H124, impressed.

"And when we parted," Rowan added, "I told her to stay the hell away from the likes of you all." He clasped hands with Astoria and Dirk. Even Dirk looked a little less nervous. "You're alone?" Dirk asked Rowan. "How did you get in here?"

He looked down with pursed lips. "The worker I was with got killed in the firefight. But a PPC exec I've been talking to did some work-arounds to get me into the city. She was sympathetic to our cause. But they . . . they killed her after we got into the building. It won't be long before they find us in here. We've got to move fast."

He met H124's gaze again. With a brisk smile he moved past her, and she felt that familiar buzz of electricity. He pulled out the same device she'd seen him steal in New Atlantic. He approached one of the servers and opened a panel. Gently he pulled out one of the control crystals and slid the device in behind it. Then he replaced everything and stood back. "That should be it." Rowan pulled out his modified PRD and took it out of hibernation mode. A stream of data flowed over the display. He grinned. "It's working! We're patched in to their communication."

Dirk looked over his shoulder. "Won't they find the device?"

"Not if they don't know to look for it. It's untraceable." He glanced once more at his display. "C'mon. Let's get out of here."

After leaving the room, H124 took out her multitool and fixed the door, bringing the lock back online and leaving the door just as they'd found it.

"Did you come in through the tunnels?" Rowan asked.

Dirk nodded.

"Let's hurry back there," Rowan decided, taking the lead.

H124 stopped. "Wait. I can't leave. I've got to get out my message." She turned to Byron. "Please. Help me."

Rowan approached her. "Is this about the asteroid? You want to warn people?"

"I've got to."

Rowan looked thoughtful. "This would be your only chance to do it, I suppose." Rowan turned to the others. "Byron, get them out. We'll join you back at Rocky Basin Camp." He turned to H124. "You guys arrived in the solar-powered car?"

"Yes."

"I left my car right next to it. I assume that's a new find?"

H124 crossed her arms. "That's one way to put it. They stole it from me."

Rowan turned to Byron. "Just leave us a car. You get the hell out of here. I'll see to this."

Byron hesitated. "No. I'll go with her. We can't risk losing you. You know this tech better than anyone."

Rowan shook his head. "We can't risk losing *anyone*. Just go!"

They all hurried to the stairwell, but Rowan took her hand and started up instead of down. "We have to patch into the antenna manually. Unfortunately, that means going up," he told her, giving her hand a squeeze.

Byron and the others started down. Then Byron paused on the stairs and looked up at her. "You going to be okay?"

She met his eyes. "No one can stop me now."

He smiled. "I admire your resolve." He ran back to her and handed her Willoughby's PRD. "Just in case you need it." He glanced at Rowan. "You watch after her, or I'll kick your ass." With a smack on Rowan's arm he returned to the others and raced down the stairs.

When she looked back at Rowan, he had a puzzled expression. "What was that all about?"

"Might feel guilty for kidnapping me."

"That must be it," he said with a sly smile. "Guilt." He started up the stairs with her. "You don't get out much, do you?"

"So everyone keeps telling me."

As they rushed upward, her legs felt as if they'd give out at any second. Her feet were starting to numb, and all her muscles quivered. But she thought of getting the word out, of saving lives, and it was enough to make one foot follow the other.

They went up ten more floors, where he came to a halt outside another stairwell door. She opened it quickly, and they slipped inside a hallway. It was empty, with only the humming of distant machinery to be heard. "This is about as high as you can go in this building. The antenna's above us. I hope you're not afraid of heights."

He pointed to another TWR next to an iron door. She opened it, gasping as the door slid open to admit a draught of fresh air and a stunning view. The city stretched out beneath them, little specks of buildings reaching as far as she could see. Millions of lights twinkled below.

"Will they catch us up here?" she asked.

"We choose Delta City for our pirate broadcasts because the PPC troopers are stretched too thin here. It isn't as protected as New Atlantic."

Rowan stepped out onto a narrow metal walkway. The wind whipped around him, tossing his hair. She joined him, looking down. She was instantly dizzy. She'd never been this high up. She could see the roofs of skyscrapers far, far below. And overhead, she could see the curve of the shimmering atmospheric shield.

All about the tops of the buildings she saw green gardens. She pointed to one. "What are those?"

"It's where the media elite grow their food."

She thought of the giant food-producing warehouses in New Atlantic. She'd even peered inside them a few times. They used plants that were grown there to make the food cubes that fed the citizens. But it was nothing compared to the gardens she looked out on now. "So many!"

"Still not enough to feed all the people in the streets." He pointed ahead. "The antenna's over here." He walked along the platform, and she noticed she could see right through the holes in the grating, down thousands of feet below. She forced herself to look up.

He placed a hand on her shoulder and shouted over the wind. "It's a bit overwhelming the first time!"

"Yeah!" she managed to say. "A bit!"

They followed the walkway around a corner, and the antenna came into view. It was a massive protrusion sitting at the very top of the building. She craned her neck but couldn't see its peak.

He pulled out his PRD, entered a few commands, and held it up next to the base of the antenna. The wind whipped around, forcing his hand to waver. "This'll take a few minutes. It has to lock on to the right frequency. They change it constantly, and it'll probably switch up a few times as you get out your message."

She got out Willoughby's PRD and pulled up the videos she'd recorded, showcasing the damage wrought by the asteroid's smaller chunks. "Can we sync this to your PRD and patch in these images?"

He took it from her. "No problem. Just point at me when you want me to play the video." He pulled up the imager on his PRD and focused it on her. "Do you know what you're going to say?"

Her mouth went dry. She hadn't thought about that. Part of her hadn't been sure they'd make it this far. Now that she was here, she had to say something. She had to persuade *everybody.*

"When you do this, I'm going to cut all the PPC's programming that's being transmitted out. So when you're talking, you'll be the only thing these people see or hear."

She swallowed. No pressure.

He glanced at his display. "Okay. It's locked on to the frequency. You ready?"

"Not really." Maybe the Rovers could access the PPC's programming. Maybe they'd hear her. Maybe they'd start on a solution even if she didn't make it to them in person.

"In three, two, one . . . *you're on.*"

H124 stared straight into the imager's eye. She was frozen. She swallowed again, then began, "Please listen carefully to what I'm about to say." She felt her stomach churn. "Disaster is about to strike us all. Right now, an immense asteroid, a nine-kilometer rock in space, is on a collision course with our planet, along with several fragments. The first will strike the earth in less than two months, followed by two more. The main asteroid will collide with us in just over a year. If anyone knows a way to stop this from happening, I urge you to do all that you can. If you don't know how to stop it, it's imperative that you seek cover. Go underground and stay there. Bring supplies."

Rowan held up his hand, then entered some commands on his PRD. "Frequency's changing again. Hold on a sec." While he fiddled with it, she gazed out over the city. It sprawled endlessly, toward every horizon, a sea of concrete and steel and glass and lights. Suddenly, in the far distance, some of those lights went out. Then more blinked on the other side of the city, and fell into darkness. She watched as block after block went out. "Okay," Rowan called out. "You're on again."

She stared into the imager again. She felt braver now. "The following images were recorded after smaller chunks of the asteroid broke off and crashed into the earth." She pointed at Rowan. He played the video of Chicago's devastation. People screamed, fires raged, and buildings fell. Everything came crashing down.

When it was over, he pointed back at her. "You're on," he mouthed.

She stared into the camera. "The pieces that are going to hit this time are far bigger than the ones you just saw. And the primary asteroid will cause a global catastrophe. Life as we know it will come to an end. This isn't a stunt, this isn't fiction. This is really happening, and if you want to live, you've got to act. And again, if anyone can prevent this, please, for all of our sakes, know that the fate of the world rests in your hands." She went silent. All around the PPC tower the city plummeted into darkness. Rowan mouthed, "Are you done?"

She nodded. He cut the transmission and took her hand. "That was great. Now we have to get the hell out of here." He pointed to the darkened streets below. "See all that? All those lights that just went out? You got people's attention."

She followed him back down the catwalk. "How do you know?"

"Jacked-in people, the ones you just talked to, keep up the infrastructure of the city. They don't know it, but they do. To keep their entertainment going twenty-four-seven, they enter a series of commands into windows in their consoles."

She thought back to what Willoughby had said about this, then remembered the floating console she'd seen in that living pod when she went to take care of her last corpse. She'd seen the man entering commands into the window.

"All those lights going out? That was them listening to you. They stopped typing in commands. The PPC doesn't like distractions. They keep the masses tuned in to what they want them to watch, the games they create, the shows they make. In return, each citizen performs a task that keeps the city running. They regulate water, gas, electricity . . . *everything.* Right now, I guarantee you some pressure valve didn't get released, and water is spewing all over the place. But . . . the important thing is that they *listened.*"

She agreed. Taking his hand, she got them back through the door, grateful to be out of the howling wind. She could hear him a lot better

as he said, "I wonder what the scuttlebutt is on the inside PPC channel."
They started down the stairs, and he checked his PRD. "Thanks to that
device I picked up in New Atlantic, we can eavesdrop for the first time."
He started reading, then froze.

She stared at him. "What is it?"

"They're on to us all right. The soldiers are moving to surround us."

"Let's go!" She took his hand again, and they dashed down the stairs.

Chapter 21

They tore down the stairs, using the railing at the landings to career around the corners. H124's legs had forgotten their exhaustion. Above them she heard soldiers filing into the stairwell. "Down there!" one of them yelled, and her blood froze.

They raced to the next landing, where she jolted to a halt as she heard soldiers entering the stairwell below. Rowan stopped too.

She stared up. The soldiers were descending. She thought of exiting at the current level, making for the maintenance elevator, and going down. But the soldiers could easily cut the power, and then they'd be trapped.

Rowan reached into his bag and pulled out a coiled rope. "We'll have to take the fast way down." He quickly secured it to the railing, tested the knot, then pulled out a pair of gloves. He handed them to her, and she put them on. Then he tore a sleeve from his shirt and sliced it in half with his knife. He wrapped the two pieces around his hands and gripped the rope. "You ready? I'll go first."

Before she could answer, he leaped over the railing and went sailing down the rope, dropping past the soldiers coming up. One discharged a blast of energy, but was too slow on the draw, missing Rowan completely. The men started up again and would soon be at her landing. Clutching the rope, she held her breath and leaped over the railing. Immediately her hands started to burn, and she could smell the gloves heating up. As she zipped past the soldiers in the stairwell, one fired his flash burster at her, but again was too slow. A searing pain erupted through her fingers. With Rowan's weight on the rope, she descended much more quickly than he had. Then his weight disappeared, and the rope twisted wildly. She craned her neck to see the bottom. Rowan was staring up at her. She was almost there. She braced herself as she came in fast, squeezing the rope even tighter. Then she felt Rowan's hands on her hips, and he caught her in his arms. Her cheek brushed his as he set her down.

Reaching up, he yanked hard on the rope. "Watch out."

They both stepped to the side as the rope came crashing down, coiling at their feet. "Just in case they wanted to follow us." He grabbed the line and raced to the door she'd passed through earlier. She unlocked it, then sealed it behind them. They ran down the cement hall and through the metal door to the area that held images of the stone spires. They ran through the series of glass doors, her ears popping as they did, and soon they were back in the natural stone caverns. Her breath plumed in the air as she switched on her headlamp.

She listened for their pursuers above the echoes of dripping and running water. "Will they follow us down here?"

"They haven't before. I think they're too afraid to leave the building."

She thought of the swarming mass of desperate people outside and could see why. She didn't doubt that anyone associated with the PPC would be torn apart if they went out there.

They reached the outer door and stairs, and they ascended them two at a time. At the top, they emerged onto the city street. Hovering in the air was another sign: *It Doesn't Matter How. It Doesn't Matter Who.*

For now the little alley by the stairs was deserted, but she could see a swarm of people milling around in the main street.

Rowan took her hand, and they ducked down the side alleys. Another sign hovered in the shadows: *Murder Is Your Civic Duty. Know the Meaning of Sacrifice.*

They moved quietly down the narrow backstreets, smelling something rotten. She knew the odor all too well. It was a decomposing body. But this stench was infinitely more pungent. She pulled her scarf up over her face as they rounded another corner. Here a tight alley emptied out on the far side into the main street. But there was no way they could use it.

Hundreds of dead bodies lay piled in a staggering heap, stretching all the way to the main road, which lay a hundred feet away. Arms and legs jutted out, black and slick with decay, piled more than twenty feet deep and spilling out into the neighboring alley where they stood.

A sign shimmered above: *Before They Get You, Get Them.*

She gasped, eyes streaming at the rank smell. "What is this?"

"A murder alley," Rowan confirmed. He pulled her away from it, ushering her toward the next lane. It was stacked even higher with the dead. She saw a corpse close to the edge, fresher than most. Blood caked around the man's throat, which had been slashed open with a jagged weapon. A ragged hole yawned in his chest. Rowan pulled her forward. A woman's body stuck out at the edge of the pile, skull shattered, eyes glassed over. She too had a gaping hole in her chest.

"They were all murdered?" she asked, unsure how this could happen.

Rowan kept leading her away, trying to find an alley they could take back to the main street that led to the CO_2 vents.

"Delta City never enacted the population controls that your city did. The city couldn't handle the massive explosion. Not enough resources to support people. They starved here. So the PPC sanctioned a different kind of population control." He stared down a few more alleys, one choked with bodies, another a haven for a large group of people who were leaning against the walls and sleeping on the ground. There was no way they'd make it to the end of the alley without being attacked again. And this time it was just the two of them.

"There are kiosks all over town. If you bring them a human heart, they give you food cubes."

Her mouth fell open. "What?"

He nodded. "And it's not much food either. Maybe a day's worth. But if you kill enough people . . ."

"The population goes down . . ."

"And the PPC doesn't have to worry so much about the masses besieging their tower."

She shook her head, trying to understand.

"Here," Rowan said, reaching the next alley. Only five or so people milled around it, talking to one another. Clothing hung in rags on their skeletal shoulders, and dark circles gathered in the hollows beneath their eyes. "Just walk casually." He put his arm around her, then pulled hers around his waist. "Let's just talk quietly to each other, and try to blend in." She saw a couple at the far end of the alley. The woman's head rested on the man's chest. She did the same to Rowan. They moved slowly, passing the first person, who sat against the wall, bony legs kicked out. They stepped over him. He didn't even look up.

They bypassed two others, and began to approach the couple. The woman lifted her head and stared.

H124 knew there was no way they'd blend in. If anyone really looked at them, even for a second, it was over.

"Hey," said the woman. "You're not from here." She pulled on her companion's shoulder. "Look at them! They've been eating well, wherever they're from!"

The man sized up Rowan. "Looks like a Badlander."

The couple moved forward, blocking their way. "You a Badlander?" the man asked.

Rowan shook his head. H124 pulled away from him, tensing for a confrontation. "I'm just like you, trying to survive," he said.

The woman plucked at her own filthy sweater, nudging her friend with hunger in her eyes. "We can get a lot of food for them."

"Yeah," the man said, licking his lips. He lunged for Rowan's arm.

Rowan dodged to the side, slamming his elbow down on the back of the man's head. "I don't want to fight you!" he hissed through his teeth. "Just let us leave."

The woman watched her companion collapse to the floor, rage sweeping over her face. "I'll kill you!" she screamed, charging forward. She plowed Rowan in the chest, sending him backward. H124 wheeled on her, swinging her around. Then she brought her fist into the woman's throat. The latter gasped, falling to her knees, clutching at her neck.

Rowan grabbed H124's hand. "C'mon!"

They burst from the alley into the street, then slowed, once more trying to blend in. A throng of people shambled around the center of the road, and Rowan kept to the edges, not so far where they'd stand out, yet not close enough to get dragged down.

They moved toward the edge of the dome. She could see the atmospheric shield stretching straight into the sky.

"Hey!" a man shouted to their left. "Hey, you!"

She glanced in his direction, spotting a tall man with gray skin pulled taut over his bony, shrewd features. "I know you! You came in earlier! With a group of Badlanders!" The people around him stopped moving. They saw their prize. Ravenous, they darted forward, desperate hands grasping.

"Run!" Rowan yelled to H124.

And she did.

Chapter 22

Hands snatched at her hair, and she heard her shirt rip. Someone grabbed the waistline of her pants and jerked her back. She went down hard on her back, kicking out violently. As a woman held onto her pants, H124 twisted around and punched her in the face as hard as she could. The woman screamed out a spray of blood as H124 leaped to her feet and ran toward the CO_2 vent. She saw a tangle of people ahead and Rowan's boot sticking out. He was down. She sped up, driving her shoulder into the gathering of skeletons. Two of them went sprawling, allowing Rowan to slug two more of them and get back on his feet. The vent wasn't far off now, but they had more pursuers, bare feet slapping on the asphalt.

"You get in front!" Rowan yelled. "I'll hold them off while you activate the TWR on the lock."

She dashed ahead of him, slipping past a phalanx of desperate people running to their left. She shrugged off frantic hands as they snaked out to grab her. People tripped over one another in their desperation and were trampled.

Two hundred feet.

An alley opened up to their right, and a stream of dirty faces poured out. The horde would cut them off and reach the vent first. Hundreds of jeering faces blocked their way.

Then a gentle hand clasped her arm, and a voice said in her ear, "Come with us." She saw that an elderly man and woman had fallen in beside her, struggling to keep up. They were gaunt and wrinkled, but their eyes were kind. "You won't make it to the vent. We can help you."

The throng ahead blocked their view of the vent. They couldn't fight all of them, weak and thin as the people were.

"We'll get enough food for *four* days!" someone in the crowd shrieked.

The old man tugged H124 off to the left as she flung off yet another, who grabbed her opposite arm. Suddenly Rowan was next to her.

"Please," the woman said to them. "Come this way! You can escape through the tunnels." She opened a hatch in the ground. "Hurry!"

Rowan pushed H124 toward it. "Do it!"

She ran for the hatch, finding a ladder leading down. She grabbed the sides and slid down, Rowan trailing behind. The old couple descended just as the crushing mass grabbed the hatch door, trying to follow. The old man was the last in, slamming down the hatch before they could enter. He drew a bolt across, leaving them in darkness.

H124 switched on her headlamp, revealing round tunnels leading off in three directions. The old woman climbed to the bottom and gripped her arm. "We saw your broadcast on our display and had to come find you. I think you'll want to see this." She smiled weakly, her long white hair hanging in greasy strands around a pale, sunken face. Her sad blue eyes stared out, wide and watery. "I'm Tessa."

The elderly man reached the bottom of the ladder and held out his hand. "And I'm Rory." H124 shook it, feeling a hand so thin that it seemed as if a page from one of her books was all that blanketed his bones. His eyes were a milky brown, and his ivory hair stood in stark contrast to his brown face. Both of them were so gaunt she didn't see how they were alive.

The couple turned to Rowan. He introduced himself.

"We have something you should see," Tessa told them. "You *must* see." She tottered away in the dark.

Rory gestured for them to follow.

Rowan leaned over and whispered in H124's ear. "I hope they're not luring us to a cannibal cookout. We do have a lot of meat on our bones."

H124 widened her eyes.

"I'm kidding. Kind of. They seem nice."

"*Seem* nice?"

"Yeah. Just in case they really are planning to eat us."

They followed the old couple in the pitch, and she watched as they held hands. She wondered how long they'd known each other, and what it would be like to know another human for so long that you could grow old together.

They passed through a series of old hatchways, taking ladders down deeper and deeper. Finally they came to a door that looked just like the ones to the weather shelters. A glowing keypad was mounted on the wall beside it. "Rory and I found this place years ago," she told them. "We hide down here during the purges."

"The purges?" H124 asked.

Rory looked up at her, his mouth set in a grim slash. "Every few months the media troops sweep through the streets and take hundreds of people."

H124 frowned. "Where do they take them?"

"We're not sure. But we never see them again," Rory told her.

Rowan met her gaze. "But after a purge, there's always a surplus of food cubes."

H124 didn't get his meaning right away. "As compensation for taking their friends?"

Rowan shook his head. "No. Remember when I said on the roof of the PPC tower that there wasn't enough food grown in the gardens to feed everyone? Rumor has it there's not even enough to feed the citizens who are plugged in and maintaining the city's infrastructure. The media elite gets food from the plants, and everyone else gets . . . other food cubes."

Her eyes went wide. "So you're saying . . ."

"Afraid so."

She couldn't believe it. "So the new food cubes are made from . . ." She swallowed. "And that's why they don't wipe out everyone in the streets? Because they need them for . . ."

Rowan nodded. "That's the rumor."

Rory gestured toward the door and its glowing keypad. "Tessa and I have survived dozens of purges thanks to the tunnels. And now this bunker. No one else knows it's down here."

He entered a code, and the door hissed open. He turned and waved them in.

As they stepped inside, Rowan gave a long, low whistle. The area beyond was huge. H124 took it in. It certainly wasn't a weather shelter. They walked into a cavern of floating displays and servers like the ones in the PPC towers, but much older. It didn't have the sleek appearance of new tech. Shelves lined with books stood in the center of the room.

"Come look at this," Rory told them, leading them into the next room. This one was even bigger than the first, with a ceiling at least fifty feet high. On the floor lay a huge silver bag attached to a complex machine with readouts and transmitters. She had no idea what it was.

"What is this place?" Rowan asked.

"We weren't sure at first, either," Tessa told him. "But look at this." She led them back to the anteroom and sat down in front of one of the hovering displays. She waved her hand through it, bringing up a video of the silver thing, now fully inflated and floating up into the sky.

Rory stepped forward to lean over Tessa. Then he turned to them. "We figured out that this thing took off into the sky and sent back information. Not sure why, though."

"What kind of information?" Rowan asked.

Tessa pulled up a series of text and numbers. "This kind." It read:

TEST: 1456.3
APOLLO ENGINEERED PARTICLES: detected
PERCENTAGE REMAINING: 92%

H124 remembered Raven's video about the Apollo project. "Wait—I know about this."

Rowan looked astounded. "You do? How?"

"I found this old PRD in one of the weather shelters. On it this guy said that a long time ago they sent these sulfate aerosol particles into the air in hopes of reversing the damage humans did to the climate. But it all backfired. It didn't act the way they'd hoped. Instead of it reflecting heat, a lot of it became trapped. Then one day it came crashing down and made everything worse. So they sent up a different engineered particle, one designed to stay up longer. And it never came back down." She looked back to the deflated silver object in the other room. "They must have sent that thing up to see if the particles were still up there."

Rowan looked around. "It's no artifact. This is relatively new tech. This has got to be Rover."

She waved her hand through the display, moving between what looked like different projects. One read *General Climate Model (GCM),* listing a number of different factors beneath it:

Enter Variables:

Methane (CH_4) content: 3000 ppm
Carbon Dioxide (CO_2) content: 600 ppm
Nitrous Oxide (N_2O) content: 450 ppm
Sea Surface Temperature (SST) Increase: 3°F per century

Prediction: ~7°F temp increase over next 100 years

She noticed she could enter new numbers for any of the variables. "This looks like a way to predict what's going to happen to the climate in the future. You put in a possible scenario, and it gives you an end result. So they've been studying this . . ."

Tessa turned to her. "That's why we thought of you. If they've been sending these sensors up, maybe they could also send one of those things up into the air to divert the space rock."

H124 didn't know how it would all work, if it was even possible. She stepped closer to the display, seeing a small line at the bottom. It read: *NASA Langley Stratospheric Aerosol and Gas Experiment VI Satellite: offline.*

NASA. She knew that word. Pulling out her PRD, she brought up the videos she'd taken back in New Atlantic. "I know this word too," she told them. "It was some kind of organization that dealt with the asteroid pieces." Hope welled within her. "If this terminal is somehow linked to it . . ."

Rory gestured for her to come closer. "I've heard of them too. Take a look at this." He walked over to the shelves of books and pulled down a volume. It was called *A History of NASA.* In it, the NASA Langley Stratospheric Aerosol and Gas Experiment—or SAGE VI project—was mentioned. It was a *satellite* that orbited the earth, sending back data. It had been designed to study the effects of the artificial sulfate particles, the later engineered particles, as well as something called *ozone.* It lamented that no one knew who had launched the particles into the atmosphere, and that everyone was suffering because of it. The end of the book addressed the disbanding of NASA.

The hope fell inside H124. So NASA was no more. Apparently it hadn't been around since the time books were still being printed.

Rowan stared over her shoulder. "They've been gone a long time." He walked back to the floating display, reading that it was offline. "I wonder if their tech is still up there, or if it came crashing down too." He brought up a floating keyboard and typed a few commands. Then he sat down, typing in more. He cursed. "I can't figure this out! We need a Rover."

"But where are they?" Tessa asked. "This place has been abandoned a long time. Rory and I had to clean it up quite a bit when we moved in down here. It was dusty and filled with mildew. Folks hadn't been here in years."

Rory crossed his arms. "Our guess is that this used to be a Rover bunker on the outskirts of Delta City. Then when the metropolis sprawled past it, they abandoned their outpost."

"We've got to find them," H124 said. "I found these old PRDs in the weather shelters. This guy recorded a history of what happened to the planet. The Rovers are still out there. He must be one of them."

Rowan held out his hand. "Let me see one of these PRDs." She pulled one out and gave it to him. He frowned. "All this tech's old. Decades old. How do we know these people are still around? They could have been wiped out."

"I can't believe that. On the video, the Rover—Raven—says that it's his mom's old PRD. That could explain the age of the device. He could have made those videos recently."

Rowan met her eyes. "Or he could be dead by now."

She shook her head. "No. I have to find them. I have to believe there's a chance." She gestured around at the bunker. "This proves they held on to science. If they were in touch with that NASA satellite, then they have the ability to reach out into space."

The room fell silent. Tessa and Rory looked at each other, then the old woman walked over and took H124's hands. "You've got to try," she told her.

"I will. I'll find them." She held up the NASA book. "Can I take this? There might be information in here about a lost technology that could help us."

Tessa gave a reassuring nod. "Of course."

Rowan's PRD beeped. He pulled it out, bringing up its hovering display. "It's the device we stashed in the PPC tower. It's letting me know what the PPC is planning." The color drained from his face.

"What is it?" H124 asked.

"It's Rocky Basin Camp. The PPC's moving on it right now. It's under attack."

"Where's Rocky Basin Camp?"

"It's where I sent Byron and the others to meet us."

"They're going to walk right into that?"

He nodded. "From what I'm reading, it's a slaughter. We've got to reach them."

Tessa motioned toward the bunker door. "I know a way you can get out quickly."

"Let's go," H124 said, joining her.

The four of them left the bunker, climbing ladders and braving the tunnels once again. H124 was astounded at the couple's ability to keep up despite their malnourishment.

Finally they paused at the bottom of a ladder. "This is it," Tessa told them. "Climb up here, and you'll be right in front of one of the CO_2 vents."

Rowan shook her hand, then Rory's. "Thank you so much." He started to climb.

H124 shook their hands too. "What you've shown us is amazing. The Rovers are out there, and this makes me think they can definitely help us."

"As will you," said Rory.

She gave an awkward smile, and climbed.

When they reached the top, Rowan braced his shoulder against a hatch. "You ready for this? We could emerge into a crowd of hostiles."

"I'm ready."

He unbolted the hatch and cracked it open, peering out. "There's a crowd, but I see the vent. The way is almost clear. Let's go!" He hurried out with her in tow.

At first they walked slowly, trying to blend in, but the crowd must have been pacing, waiting for them to reappear. "There they are!" cried a man.

"We'll get to eat!" shouted someone else.

A pair of groups closed in from both sides. H124 and Rowan made a break for it.

Then the phalanx on the left picked up speed, colliding with that on the right. As people fell in front of her she leaped over them, nearly tripping as someone grabbed her ankles. She landed unevenly, but she quickly regained her balance and kept running.

Fifty feet to the vent.

She glanced back to see Rowan slamming a fist into a man's face.

Twenty feet.

She started to slow, already thinking at the TWR to bring down the membrane. She felt it click in her mind, and she sailed through the vent's opening. Rowan followed, but was nearly stopped by a man grabbing his shoulders. He shrugged him off, and H124 thought *Membrane up* at the TWR and felt it switch back on.

The crowd seethed before the egress, piling up, crushing one another against the wall.

They'd made it.

She leaned over, catching her breath. Rowan did the same. Then she straightened up and stared out at the dirty, starving mass, sunken eyes fixed on them in pity.

She gripped her tool bag close to her. "I'm sorry," she said. "I'm so sorry."

Rowan took her hand and turned her away. Together they walked into the dark tunnel. They made their way in silence for a few minutes, and she met his eyes in the shadows. "Earlier today I thought this place was called Murder City because the Badlanders had a price on their heads."

Rowan shook his own. "When you're desperate, killing someone for a little bit of food starts to look more and more tempting." They kept on at an even pace. "But they don't rely solely on people murdering one another."

"What do you mean?" She switched her headlamp on.

"They send out their own death squads. Most people they kill, but then there are the slavers too."

She raised her eyebrows. "Slavers?"

Rowan moved stealthily in the dark, glancing behind to make sure no one had followed them. "The PPC doesn't just need jacked-in people to maintain the infrastructure. They also need menial laborers."

Menials. She remembered them from the dank tunnels under New Atlantic, vacantly pressing a button or pulling a lever, eyes staring into infinity, mouths parted lightly, expressions blank. "They had those where I came from."

Rowan donned a grim face as he kept ahead of her. "The PPC modifies their brains."

"You mean like what they did to me? So I'd be able to interact with theta wave receivers?"

Rowan slowed as they approached the middle barrier. "No." He turned to meet her eyes in the gloom. "They lobotomize them. Give them a simple task to carry out."

She stood there, unable to move. "What?"

"They give them water every couple of days, some food once a week, and they have a never-ending supply of job applicants."

She remained frozen. She felt like someone had punched her in the gut. Repurposers. That's what they'd been trying to do to that last corpse she'd been sent to clean up. Only things had gone wrong. They must have known she'd notice the foul play. And she'd taken too long in the apartment. They knew she knew. And they were going to Repurpose her.

Numbly, she walked up to the TWR but couldn't get her mind to concentrate on opening the barrier. She closed her eyes tightly, then balled her fists. Nothing.

She felt Rowan's hand on her shoulder, a warm comfort. "It's okay," he said. "Take your time." She knew she couldn't take her time. His people were dying right this very minute. Maybe even Byron and the others.

She forced her mind to focus, to open up. She sent the off signal, and instantly the air became unbreathable with carbon dioxide. "It's down," she coughed. He hurried through and she followed, then sealed the barrier again.

They jogged through the dark, her beam bouncing off the tunnel walls. She felt sick inside. When they got past the area so thick with carbon dioxide she couldn't stop coughing, she tried to breathe a little deeper.

They reached the end of the tunnel, the smell of urine and fecal matter so strong it made her gag. They raced outside, and to her surprise, she saw that Byron had left the solar car for them. Rowan ducked into the driver's seat, then stood back up with the keys. He threw them to her. "You know this car a hell of a lot better than I do. You drive."

They piled in, and she started it up, grateful to be back in the driver's seat. It was like meeting an old friend again. She spun the car around and rocketed away from the oozing sewage.

Rowan watched her as she drove. "Anyone who interrupts the infrastructure maintenance with a pirate broadcast like we just did gets targeted. The system breaks down, and even if it's just for a few minutes, it damages their power structure. If enough people wake up repeatedly, or for a long stretch of time, the PPC would be in huge trouble. The city would grind to a halt. The citizens don't know it, but they have the power to take down the whole system."

A second wind of hope flooded through her. "Do you think that's what will happen after my message?"

"No, unfortunately. You saw the lights go out for a few minutes. But soon people will be back to watching what they always watch. Mindless 'reality' shows that aren't based in reality at all. The people in those shows aren't even real. It's all generated by a central computer, a random group of CG people doing randomly generated acts. The images will flash in the citizens' minds, dull their thoughts, and by tomorrow, they probably won't even remember there was a pirate broadcast, or they'll have decided it was a joke. All they need is right in front of them. They don't need to leave their living pods. All they have to do is consume. They won't unplug and think."

She felt rage swell within her. "But . . ." She'd always been a little envious of the clean, spacious, luxurious living pods of the citizens compared to her own tiny, sweltering room. But now she was grateful she'd never been plugged into the network.

The smell of sewage finally abated as they got far enough away from the viscous brown rivers pouring out of the city. She pushed the car as fast as it could go, following Rowan's directions to Rocky Basin Camp, rocketing at almost ninety miles an hour down the old battered road. When they got closer, they saw a flaming glow on the horizon.

"Damn!" Rowan cursed. "The camp's on fire."

Chapter 23

As she mounted a small rise above the camp, Rowan pointed to a worn dirt track leading to the top of the hill. "Take this side road here!" She maneuvered the car over the bumpy ground. "Okay. Stop here." He jumped out and pulled out his diginocs. She watched him scan the burning camp. She climbed out too, and he handed her the diginocs. "It's completely destroyed!"

She raised them to her eyes and surveyed the camp. She saw an area where tents had been, where cars had been parked. Now only burning tarps and old buildings met her eyes, alongside burned-out husks of vehicles. Strange black lumps littered the ground. She pressed the zoom button on the nocs and realized that they were corpses, their black hands more like gnarled claws reaching out, as if grasping for air.

He took back the nocs and switched on the thermal setting, then quickly lowered them. "Too bright. The fire will mask any signs of life." He tried the bioscan to pick up any traces of heartbeats or breathing. For a long moment he scanned the camp and surrounding areas. Then he lowered them slowly. "Nothing. No survivors."

"What?" She grabbed the nocs from him and tried too. She searched for any sign of movement, but the flickering flames were all she could see.

Rowan's PRD beeped. He read it quickly. She recognized the fast scroll of the PPC comm channel that he'd tapped into with the prototype listening device. "The troops have moved on to Black Canyon Camp. They're about to strike! We only have a few minutes to reach them!"

She tossed him the keys, figuring if he knew the way, they could get there that much faster. He caught them in midair, then swung into the driver's seat. She slid into the passenger side.

"I won't let them take Black Canyon Camp," Rowan swore. He hit the accelerator, and she slammed back into her seat.

They mowed over a number of dirt tracks, catching some air as they crested the hills. They could see the fires in Black Canyon Camp long before they reached it. It burned brightly on the horizon.

H124 held onto the armrest as he sped across dirt and broken roads.

Before long they parked the car on a rise and continued on foot, approaching the camp in darkness. When it came into view, H124 merely stared. Like the other site, dozens of tents and vehicles formed a makeshift encampment. But the scene was utter chaos. Badlanders had retreated to the edges of the bivouac, some taking shelter behind cars, others running for cover in the barren landscape beyond.

PPC troopers closed ranks, moving as one, an impenetrable line of black-clad soldiers wearing shock trooper gear. She slapped her hands over her ears as the Badlanders fired an impressively huge gun mounted in the back of a rugged vehicle. A pulse of light split the night sky, blinding flashes followed by cacophonous booms. Some of the shock troopers fell, and the line broke.

The death squad fired back, focusing their weapons on the Badlanders hiding behind the vehicles. The car with the mounted gun tumbled backward, the gunman screaming in agony as he rolled on the ground.

"What was that?" she gasped. There had been no flash this time.

"Sonic weapon," Rowan said. "We've been unable to duplicate it." He started running down the hill, drawing his own small handgun.

She didn't know what she could do to help, but she couldn't just stand by. She raced after him, taking shelter behind a burning vehicle on the perimeter of the fighting. Rowan started firing, taking out two death squad soldiers.

She pressed her back against the tire of the car, the rubber hot through her shirt. Cautiously she peered out, gauging the situation. If a lone PPC trooper was out there, maybe she could take him by surprise.

About twenty feet away, a dead trooper lay, his energy discharge weapon on the ground beside him. It was the same kind carried by the Repurposers. She ran over at a crouch and picked it up. Then she hurried to a jeep that had escaped the fires. She crawled under the car on her knees and elbows, barely emerging on the other side. Then she fired the flash burster into the line of soldiers, taking down the two on the end. They fell hard into the dirt, twitching. One of them turned to her, lifting his sonic weapon. She scrambled out from under the car and took off just as a blast came barreling past. The jeep tumbled sideways, and she dove. He spun to hit her again, but he was taken out by the Badlanders, who had resurrected the mounted gun.

She ran back to the overturned jeep, taking refuge on the far side of the skirmish. Catching her breath, she shinnied around the front of it, taking another look at whom she could hit next.

One of the soldiers had broken away from the rest and fired his sonic gun at a lone man. The victim screamed, falling to his knees. As the trooper stepped to one side, she recognized the fallen man at once. Byron. She jumped and ran toward the trooper, hitting him in the back with the flash burster. His body spasmed as he met the dirt. Racing forward, she skirted around the back of the advancing line, coming at Byron from the side. He struggled in the dirt, trying to stand up. She rushed to him, throwing an arm around him. Blood streamed from his ears, and he gasped for breath as she helped him up.

Already the trooper she'd hit was on his feet, shaking his helmeted head, trying to get his bearings. He lifted his weapon, focusing on her. She hit him again with the flash burster, and he staggered forward. But he wasn't going down. As the electricity flashed through his armor, she realized it was shock-resistant. He raised the sonic gun, but she zapped him once more, trying to drag Byron to safety.

Between her and the trooper lay a dead Badlander, hand still curled around a gun. As the trooper brought up his firearm again, she let go of Byron and dove for the weapon, fingers closing around the cold metal. She took aim and pulled the trigger, firing point-blank through the faceplate of the trooper's helmet. He listed forward, then fell to his knees. Then his arm sagged, and he fell face first, landing in a heap.

She stood over the trooper, hand trembling.

"Thank you," Byron breathed behind her. She turned, helping him up once more. "Thank you."

She lugged him over to a group of cars and gazed out at the battle. Her hands wouldn't stop shaking. The gun felt cold in her grip, and her mouth had gone dry. Her heart hammered. She looked out at the man she'd killed. She'd *killed* him. Now only four PPC soldiers still advanced, with more than a dozen Badlanders firing on them. As two more troopers went down, the remaining ones scattered, running for cover in separate directions.

"We're winning," Byron whispered, bringing his hands to his ears. "Ugh. I feel like a ten-year-old MRE that someone spat out."

H124 watched from a distance as Rowan advanced on one of the last two soldiers, ducking and rolling as he fired off a shot that hit one squarely in the chest. She saw Astoria running along the perimeter of the camp. Leaping on the car the last soldier hid behind, Astoria brandished a vicious-looking knife with a serrated edge and crashed down on him. The car blocked what happened next, but H124 saw the blade appear again, slashing downward.

A round of cheers roared up from the Badlanders. They all rose and came back down from their remote positions, raising their firearms in the air. Byron slumped down on the ground, grinning. "Can't believe we sent them packing."

She heard Astoria calling out in the darkness. "Dirk?"

"Here!" came a voice. Her brother staggered out of the shadows into the firelight, face battered and bleeding. Shrapnel protruded from both of his legs, and he collapsed. She rushed over to him, hugging him and rubbing an affectionate fist on his dreadlocks. "Where the hell have you been?"

"Fighting!" he replied.

She went to work on his wounds at once.

Rowan came into the clearing, holstering his gun. "H!"

She stood up. "Here! I'm with Byron."

Rowan jogged over to her. "You okay?"

"I'm fine."

"Saved my ass," Byron said.

Rowan grinned. "She does have a habit of doing that."

As everyone gathered in the center of camp, H124 heard something in the air. At first it was a dull, throbbing sound, a distant thunder she couldn't quite place. It grew louder. "What is that?" she asked.

Everyone quieted to listen.

The thrumming grew, so low and powerful she could feel it vibrating in her chest.

"What the—" Byron began.

Then Rowan pointed to the sky. "Airship!"

Everyone scattered into the darkness.

"Take cover!" Rowan yelled. He pulled her with him, heading back toward the solar car. "C'mon, Byron! Move your ass!"

Byron ran alongside them, leaping over mounds of dirt and smoking debris much to his discomfort. "What is it?" she asked between gasps.

"We're dead if that thing sees us."

Strange lights appeared on the horizon behind them. Beams flashed out, piercing the night.

"It's coming!" Byron screamed.

At last they reached the car. Rowan wrenched open the driver's door, sliding in. Byron hurried into the back, and she was the last to enter. As she closed the passenger door, she stared up into the sky. A massive airship appeared, a metal monstrosity thundering across the sky. Tremendous exhaust ports in its underbelly shot out columns of heated gusts, making the air shimmer. The engines thrummed so loudly now that it rattled her ears.

Rowan peeled out, keeping the headlights off. Dazzling searchlights trolled the ground, finding the dead PPC soldiers and the overturned cars of the Badlanders.

As they sped away, the airship gyred in a wider circle. She watched in horror as the light fell on a group of fleeing Badlanders. The low thrumming started to climb in tone, and then a brilliant flash erupted from the ship's bow. The light took out half the hillside, incinerating the three Badlanders; one second they'd been there, running, and the next they were columns of ash blowing in the wind.

H124 covered her mouth with her hand.

"Oh, gods," Byron said, staring out.

Another blinding flash from the ship lit up a different patch of landscape, instantly vaporizing two more Badlanders who had been escaping in a jeep.

"Get us the hell out of here, man," Byron shouted from the back seat. Rowan whipped the car around. Then Byron spun in his seat. "No, wait! I see Dirk. He's not going to make it!" Before either of them could say anything, Byron threw open the back door and rolled out.

She watched him race away, limping slightly.

"Are you crazy?" Rowan shouted after him.

H124 couldn't even see Dirk in the chaos.

"Just get her the hell out of here!" Byron yelled back over his shoulder. Suddenly she saw Dirk just as Byron reached him. He was crawling on his belly, trying to make it up a hill.

"Damn it!" Rowan cursed. He spun the car around, tearing off in their direction.

Byron grabbed Dirk's arms, half dragging him up the rise. Above them the airship wheeled in the sky, heading toward them. As Byron and Dirk crested the rise, almost near the car, a deafening boom cracked through the sky. H124 slapped her hands to her ears as the whole hill lit up, the white searing into her eyes. Rowan screeched the car to a halt.

The light faded, and she stared out, her retinas so burned she could only see a bright circle. She blinked, and the circle turned from silver to blue to green. Then all she could see were the silhouettes of Byron and Dirk, the latter hanging off his friend's shoulder, seemingly unconscious. They were still too far away. Rowan threw the car in gear, ready to close the distance.

From the other side of the rise, a jeep roared up. "Get in!" the driver yelled to Byron. H124 recognized Astoria at the wheel. Byron hefted Dirk into the back seat of the jeep, then jumped in himself. And like that, they were roaring off in another direction.

Keeping the headlights off, Rowan turned the car and sped back down the hill, weaving it over an old, dirt-packed road. They jostled and bumped along, hitting rocks so hard she expected the axle to crack in half.

The ship turned slowly, sending the beams of light in their direction. If it saw them, one blast would end their lives, their mission, and the world. For a brief second, she thought of that immense asteroid out there, hurtling toward them in the dark of space, and of the devastating impact it would have on the entire planet. Then she thought on the trifling war the PPC waged quietly on its citizens, as well as the overt one it waged on the Badlanders. If only they knew, if only they could all see the big picture, work together—

A blast from the airship hit the ground in front of them.

Chapter 24

The solar car swerved as the ground before them turned to molten rock and fire. Rowan almost rolled the vehicle, righting it at the last second as he veered out of the blast's way.

He slid to a stop, changing direction. The beams followed them.

"What are we going to do?" she asked, gripping the armrest as he spun into a U-turn.

He straightened the wheel and hit the accelerator. "Part of why this site was picked for a camp," he said, skittering around a boulder, "is that there are old mine tunnels."

He pointed into the darkness. In the side of the hill, she saw a black aperture. He sped for it, and another blinding flash scorched the ground behind them. Her teeth clacked together as they sailed over a bump and slammed down hard on the other side.

As the ship's beam searched for them, they reached the mine opening and rocketed through. Rowan slammed on the brakes, then leaped out and ran back to the entrance, where he hit a button. A door slammed down. She got out. "These mine entrances are disguised," Rowan told her. "Hopefully the airship didn't see us enter."

She could hear the distant hum of the ship. It seemed to be moving away. "Will they land and try to find us on foot?"

Rowan shook his head. "Airships usually have only have a few people on board—the pilot is also the gunner. They won't risk coming down here, where they'd be outnumbered."

They could hear the ship moving off.

"It's searching for the other Badlanders," Rowan whispered. "I hope they made it to the mines."

"Are there more openings like this one?"

He gave a grim nod.

She hoped Byron and the others were safe.

The timbers at the entrance continued to burn. Rowan walked toward it, stopping a few feet away. "If we go out there, we're dead." He slumped down, exhausted. "We'll have to wait it out."

"Won't they send more troopers?"

"Not immediately. They'll have to regroup, figure out their losses." His shoulders slumped. "I can't believe this. We lost so many." He collapsed down against the wall, and looked up at her. "Come sit by me. Tell me where you've been."

She walked over, staring at the sealed entrance, then sat down next to him.

"Did you like the weather shelters?"

She nodded.

"And the Rovers? Any leads?"

"Only that they were last seen about a thousand miles from here." She couldn't hide her disappointment.

"Did you get a sense of them in the weather shelters, at least? Did you look at the books?"

Again she nodded. "I can't believe all the things in those books. All the animals!"

"Amazing, isn't it?" He turned to face her, cross-legged. The light from the fires illuminated half his face, casting the other half in shadow. His eyes were soft and blue and deep. He looked toward the mine entrance, his gaze now far away, a frown on his face.

She felt the desire to reach out and take his hand, but didn't. "I'm sorry about your people."

He picked at a patch of caked mud on his pants and bit his lip. "So am I."

She watched as his body shook. He quickly wiped his palm across his eyes and turned away. Now she did reach out, touching his shoulder. He kept averting his gaze, but he brought a hand up, lacing his fingers through hers.

Her stomach flip-flopped at his touch. When he faced her again, his eyes flared with such intensity that she could barely hold his gaze. She didn't know what to do or what this feeling was. Then he leaned in. She could feel his warm breath on her skin, as well as an intense pull, a desire to melt into one. His lips brushed against her cheek. She closed her eyes at the pleasant roughness of his whiskers, and when she caught the scent of his skin, the primal urge overtook her. Finally his lips joined with hers, and her whole body trembled with desire. She leaned into him, giving into the sensation. He moved closer, pulling her to him as he kissed her.

Sparks jolted through her as their bodies touched, her stomach against his. She kissed him deeply, arms wrapped around his back, pulling him even closer. Fire consumed her. Time ceased, and the world stopped. Only his warmth, his touch, his scent existed. She ran her fingers through his short hair, and she felt the contours of his back. She was breathless.

Gently he leaned her back, laying her on the ground. He lowered himself onto her, and a delicious sensation surged through every part of her being. He kissed her neck, hips against hers; she'd never felt anything so exquisite. She gripped his back once more, feeling his muscles move sinuously. Their eyes met, and she felt a powerful connection with him, something that reached right down into her soul and met his head-on.

He blinked at her, then pulled away suddenly. "Holy hell."

She sat up too. "Are you okay?"

"What was that?"

She wasn't sure what he meant. The whole thing had been amazing and new for her.

"That whole . . . thing . . . that . . ." He swept his hands through the air, indicating back and forth between them.

"I don't know," she confessed. She couldn't seem to catch her breath. Her body ached in a way she'd never felt before.

"You're . . ." His intense blue eyes bore through her, doing nothing to help her breathe any easier.

All she wanted was to feel him again. She sat up. "I . . ."

He rose to his feet and straightened his jacket. "Wow." He paced away, then stopped and looked down at her. "Have you ever been . . .?" He shook his head, pacing again. "Of course not. Of course you haven't been. You're a worker."

"Haven't been what?" Her whole body was trembling now, in a pleasant way. She wanted him to come back.

He stopped. "I don't think I'm the person who should . . ." He resumed his pacing. "I mean, I'm just a no-good Badlander and you're so . . . otherwise."

"I don't think I'm following you."

"I just can't be your first . . . not in good conscience."

She waited for him to clarify. "My first what?"

He ran a hand over his face. "I think you should have more time in your new, free life to choose exactly who you want . . ."

She wasn't sure what he meant. "Who I want?"

He sat back down next to her. "Never mind. I'm okay now. Sorry about that." His eyes met hers, and she could feel the same visceral link pass between them. Her lips ached to feel his again. He snapped his gaze away, staring out. Taking a few deep breaths, he flexed his hands, curling and uncurling his fingers. Then he bent his head forward, exhaling. "Listen," he said. "If you're going to catch up with the Rovers, and if they really are a thousand miles away, you're going to need something much faster than a car." He met her eyes. "You need to fly."

"Fly? Like in an airship?" She thought of the massive ship that had rained fire down on them.

"Not exactly. There's an old airfield not far from here. It used to be a gathering place for pilots, but there aren't many left now. Though I've heard that one landed there a few days ago. He might still be there. And he might help you. It'll be a hell of a lot easier to fly over Delta City than to try to cross it on foot. You can't skirt around it. It reaches south into the gulf, and all the way up to the Great Lakes. You'd have to go through the city itself to make it out west, or journey either very far south or north to get a boat. Flying is your best bet."

She didn't relish the thought of going back into Murder City. "Can you tell me where the airfield is?"

"Better yet, I'll take you there."

He stood up to open up the door and peer outside. She followed him. Parts of the terrain around them still burned. Rowan stepped out carefully, gazing up at the sky. "Looks clear. We need to leave before they come back with more troopers."

He moved back to the car, H124 at his rear. Climbing in the passenger seat, she looked across at him. "What about the others?"

"They'll have moved on to the other camps by now, scattered, as we're about to do." He pulled out his PRD, checking their secret channel. "No chatter. No one needing help."

She leaned over, looking at the display. "Anything about Byron?"

He scrolled through a few pages. "Taking refuge in Rusted Knife Camp with Dirk and Astoria. All is well."

"Where's Rusted Knife Camp?"

"South of here."

"And this airfield?"

"North."

She sighed, glad they were okay. She leaned back in the seat. Flying. She was going to fly.

Rowan backed the car through the mine entrance and flipped around, starting down a steep embankment. He left the headlights off. In the distance, a faint light glowed in the east. Her eyes stung with fatigue.

"Why don't you try to catch some Z's?" he asked her.

"Catch some Z's?"

"Sleep."

She didn't understand the connection, but settled into her seat all the same. Rowan took off his jacket and bundled it up, making a pillow, then handed it to her.

"Thank you," she said, propping the jacket up against the glass. She let her eyes close.

Two hours later she struggled to wake, feeling stiff and cramped. "Aren't you tired?" she asked. The sun had risen, revealing a bleak landscape of broken cement and burned-out buildings.

"Just a bit. But I need to get you to the airfield and then regroup with everyone at Rusted Knife Camp."

"How far are we?"

He slowed the car. "This is it now."

She peered out at a vast flatland with a few small rusted buildings that lacked walls and, in some places, roofs. Two paved roads stretched parallel into the horizon, pitted and potholed.

"This is an airfield?"

"Not much to look at, I know. Hardly anyone flies anymore. Not many planes left."

"What's a plane?"

"An airship of sorts. With wings." Rowan scanned the airfield. "Hopefully, the pilot is still there. Hard to tell. He usually stashes his plane out of sight in that building." He pointed at a shed with several pieces of rusted metal propped against it, covering an ingress.

"Should we go see?"

He looked at her regretfully. "This is as far as I better go."

She contorted her face.

"I think you'll have better luck convincing him to take you if I'm not there."

"Why?" She found herself reluctant to go alone, yet chastised herself for it. She'd been alone since Rowan left her outside New Atlantic until the Badlanders had picked her up outside Delta City. But now she felt the pang of not wanting to leave him. She'd never needed anyone before, so she shoved the feeling away. She was out to save the world, wasn't she? Not take comfort in people she met along the way, however different they might be from those she'd been raised among.

"The Badlanders haven't always been kind to this place. He might shoot me on sight."

"That's reassuring."

"I don't think he'll shoot you. No one would mistake you for a Badlander. Don't worry. He can be trusted."

"So he can be trusted as long as he doesn't shoot me?" She started to get out of the car. Then he took her hand. She felt the heat of his fingers as he raised her hand to his lips and kissed it. "Take care out there, H." Their eyes locked. Then he pulled her back into the car and brushed her face. His lips met hers, and that familiar shock zinged through her. She kissed him back. Then he let her go. "I expect to see you again," he said. "Somewhere. I'll stay here until you're safely off."

A painful lump formed in her throat. Then she grabbed her bag and got out of the car. "Take care of my car, okay?" she asked. She wanted to say something else, something more, but couldn't find words for her feelings. Instead she leaned into the window and gripped his shoulder affectionately.

She set off toward the long rows of steel buildings. He remained idle as she walked toward them, and a couple times she stole glances back over her shoulder. Dust drifted in hypnotizing patterns across the dry ground, and each step kicked up fine brown dirt. She was almost to the first building, a shed that had once been painted red, when she heard the unmistakable cocking of a gun, a sound she'd become all too familiar with.

"Stay right there," came a gruff voice from around the corner. She came to a halt, and a man walked into view holding a huge firearm with a double barrel.

He was the oldest person she'd ever seen. He walked slightly bent, and wore dusty overalls over a blue button-down shirt so worn she could see his bony elbows through the fabric. The knees had also worn through, and he wore some kind of red thermal layer underneath. A tuft of white hair stood up atop his head, while his red-rimmed blue eyes blinked at her in the bright sun. He stared at her with a face so pale it looked like parchment stretched over bone. She held out her hands, showing she was unarmed.

"I need your help."

"Is that so?" He took her in, cocking his head to the side.

"I was told you might be able to fly me somewhere."

"Firehawk told you that?" He looked toward the solar car, where Rowan waited.

"You know him?"

"In a way. Know his kind."

She remembered what Rowan had said about the rough history with the Badlanders. "I really need your help."

"Why's that?"

"I'm trying to save the world."

He cracked a smirk, and lowered his gun a bit. "The world, eh?"

She nodded. "That's right."

"No small task."

Now she cracked a slight smile. "No, sir."

"Sir!" He lowered the gun some more. "Haven't been called that in well . . . ever."

He surveyed her tool bag and dirty clothes. "What do you want to save the world from?"

She looked up at the sky, a cloudless blue slate overhead, from which the sun beat down on them. "An asteroid."

He lowered the gun all the way. "How's that?"

"A giant space rock is headed this way."

"And how do you propose to save the world from a giant space rock?"

"I don't know. But I'm trying to find the people who might. "

He arched his eyebrows. "The Rovers?"

Hope blossomed within her. "Yes."

"Don't know where they are."

"I've got a lead," she said, "if you'd be kind enough to take me. They're leaving in a couple days, and I won't make it by car."

He lifted his gun, this time resting the barrel on his shoulder, holding the stock in the crook of his arm. "Well, I guess I've flown for less."

She beamed, "So you'll help me?"

He scratched his head. "Oh, hell. I don't see why not. Bored out of my mind. Where they at?"

She pulled out her PRD and approached. He eyed her suspiciously but didn't back away. She brought up the map, the arrow blinking where Willoughby had said the Rovers would be.

He ran his hand over the rough stubble on his cheek. "That's a fair distance. Have to refuel. More than once, at that."

"But you can do it?"

He took the PRD into his arthritic hands, waving his finger over the floating display to see more of the map. "I think so."

Her hope was now a garden. She might actually have a chance at meeting with the Rovers before they moved to some unknown destination. They'd know what to do about the asteroid, and her journey would be complete. She couldn't believe it. It felt like another life, another her, who had crawled down into that dark basement and discovered the ancient lab down there.

He handed back the PRD. "How long we got?"

"Until what?"

He looked up. "Until it hits?"

The thought brought her back to the present. "Two months before the first fragment hits, followed by two more. A year until the big one arrives, and it's a planet killer."

"Not much time."

"The Rovers will know what to do."

"How do even you know about this?"

"I found an old building laden with ancient information. The data predicted when it would hit. Pieces of it already have."

"And did they stop it back then?"

She shook her head. "No. It did a lot of damage. But the imminent chunks are much bigger. They'll wipe out everything."

"And you think the Rovers can do now what people back then couldn't?"

"I have to believe that."

He licked his finger and held it up in the wind. Cupping his hands over his eyes, he gazed to the end of the runway. "Storm's coming. I think we can beat it if you're ready to go now."

"I am." She looked back to where Rowan had parked. He was still there. Her stomach gnawed on itself.

"Let me do some preflight stuff. Got some hot chocolate if you want."

"Hot chocolate?" She'd never heard of it.

"Best kind east of the Mississippi." He held out his hand. "I'm Gordon, by the way."

She shook it, thinking of Rowan's nickname for her. "H."

He eyed her. "Just H'?"

She nodded.

Then he turned and approached the shed. She followed. She was so close to the Rovers that every molecule in her being thrummed. She had to reach them. Everything depended on it.

Inside the shed she saw a big, beautiful red machine resting in its center. Two wings reached out from either side, and a long blade was mounted on its nose. Gordon walked over to a small cabinet above a workbench and pulled down two chipped ceramic mugs. He spooned some dark brown powder into each.

A pot of water boiled on a small hot plate. He poured some into each cup. Reaching in with a spoon, he stirred both, then smiled. "Here you go. Hot chocolate."

She walked over and took the proffered cup, smelling it first. It was hands-down the best thing she'd smelled in her entire life. She smiled. "Wow."

"Tastes even better." He sipped his, then set his cup down and walked over to the plane. "Have a seat," he called over his shoulder, pointing to a worn stool near her. "Can I have a look at those coordinates again?"

She handed him her PRD, and he pulled out a white plastic-and-aluminum dial with varying increments of measurement on it. The thing looked ancient. "Gotta run this by the old whiz wheel," he said.

"Whiz wheel?"

"The E6B. It's a flight computer. Helps me plot the course we'll take."

She stared at it. "Computer? But it doesn't even have power."

He smiled and pointed to his head. "It's all up here." He started moving the dial around.

She sipped the hot chocolate and watched him work, relishing both. While she perched on the stool, he finished his calculations and checked over his plane, holding up his own PRD, which projected a checklist. After she finished her drink, he came back and drank his down in three long gulps. "We're about ready." He pointed at her tool bag. "That all your gear?" He gave her back her PRD.

She nodded.

"Well, welcome aboard." He walked her over to the passenger side and opened the door for her. She hoisted herself up using a grab bar and settled down into the seat.

Walking around to the other side, he gazed outside. It still looked sunny and calm. Swinging himself into the plane, he landed in the pilot seat. "Take that buckle there and strap it in the middle of your chest," he told her.

She reached down, finding two black straps that went over her shoulders and lap, and latched them in the middle with an antique metal buckle. She felt a reassuring click.

He started up the engine. The blade on the nose of the plane began whirring, so fast it blurred. Then he eased the plane out of the storage shed and into the daylight. Angling it out onto the runway, he looked over at her. "Ready?"

She bowed her head.

"Then here we go." He eased the plane forward, gaining more speed on the runway. Suddenly she could feel the wind buffeting the wings. "Winds are always a little high this time of year, but we'll make it," he reassured her.

They zipped down the airstrip, traveling faster than she ever had before. The end of the strip loomed up before them, beyond which lay rocks and a small rise. She gripped the seat as the rise grew impossibly close, and then the nose of the plane tilted up. She felt the plane rock to the right, lifting slightly as the wheels left the ground.

And then they were airborne. She let go of the seat and gripped the doorframe, staring down as the airport buildings shrunk beneath them. She could see the dusty road she'd driven on with Rowan and, glinting in the distance, a tiny square she imagined was the solar panel on the roof of her car. Rowan was just now pulling away, heading south toward the other camp.

Then they drew higher, and she took in a vast landscape, the likes of which she'd never seen before. All of Delta City lay before them. As they rose in altitude, she could see the gleaming of the atmospheric shield, stretching across horizons. All along the base she saw carbon dioxide ports like the one she'd entered. Soon they passed the perimeter, flying over the shield itself. She could see the PPC tower where she'd made her pirate broadcast. Around it, millions of gray buildings bristled upward. Long, dirty streets that had been so insufferably crowded on the ground now looked like dark little ribbons winding among the buildings.

Soaring over the tops of buildings, she peered down through the shield into the teeming chaos.

They flew for more than two hours like that, the view of clustered buildings and narrow streets all blending together. At last they reached the far edge of the shield, and the entire scene changed.

She could see the shapes of hills, dried riverbeds, and brown dust extending endlessly. The wind caught the plane again, and the craft dipped. She gripped the seat, her heart crawling up into her throat. She looked over at Gordon.

He grinned. "We'll be okay. See this?" he said, pointing at a dial that floated in some kind of oily liquid. She read *270° W* on the bobbing device inside. "That tells us which way we're heading." He pointed at the icon of a little plane, titled slightly above a flat line. "This tells us how level we are." He pointed at another dial. "And this is our air speed." She blinked at it: 140 mph? Could that be right? If so, she was elated. No cracked roads to drive over, no potholes that could destroy a car's axle. No night stalkers. No flooded streets. Her body started to relax. She felt like the birds she had read about. She gazed out at the clouds nestled in the blue sky and felt a freedom she'd never known.

He caught her expression and smiled. "Great, isn't it?" He pushed back in his seat, relaxing his shoulders.

"How long can we fly before we have to refuel?"

He looked at the gauge. "About five and a half hours if the methane tank is full. Of course, just crossing Delta City eats up a chunk of that."

She studied him for a while, the way he turned the controls with the ease of experience. "How long have you been a pilot?"

"Sixty-five years. My parents taught me when I was fifteen. They were both pilots too."

She looked down at her lap, then turned to the window. "What was that like?"

"Hell, the best feeling in the world! They were both crackerjack pilots. They could do all the stunts. They had a sweet little red biplane with yellow on the wings. I love that plane. Still got it in storage. My grandfather was also a pilot, and before that, his mom. A whole family of aviators going way back."

She looked at him awkwardly. "I mean . . . what was it like to have parents?"

He met her eyes, and his face dropped. "You didn't know your folks?"

She pursed her lips. "It wasn't like that where I grew up . . . parents didn't raise their kids."

He squinted in the sunlight. "I see. You're from one of the city centers?"

She thought about how Rowan said he could be trusted. "Yes."

"Rough break. Of course, it's no picnic out here either."

"Picnic?"

He smiled. "It's when you eat outside."

"Oh. I see." She didn't see.

"Anyway, I'd say having parents is one of the most comforting feelings in the world. You always have a home to go to, no matter what. You have people who love you unconditionally. When I was young, I struck out on my own to open my first airfield. Back in those days, more people lived outside the city centers, and I actually made a decent living at it. But I always knew that if I failed, I could go back to my parents, and they would welcome me. It's a damn shame you didn't know that feeling growing up."

She remained silent.

"So who raised you?" he asked.

She stared out at a scattering of clouds, imagining that they were a family of opossums. "Different people. We call them caregivers. They're workers like me, only with different assignments. They were always changing shifts, and I didn't know any of them too well. When I was six, they put me up in a living pod and gave me my first job."

"Not much of a childhood. What was your job?"

"Cleaning places, mainly. Toilets, sinks, that kind of thing."

"Doesn't sound like a very fun life for a little kid."

Fun? She'd never thought about that before. "No, it wasn't, but it was a lot better than my later job."

"And what was that?"

She stared down at the parched ground, watching waves of dust flowing over the surface like gauzy sheets. "I, uh . . . removed corpses from buildings and incinerated them."

He whistled. "Wow." He went quiet then, stealing looks at her now and again. She felt awkward about her upbringing, so she just kept staring out.

As they flew, the clouds grew menacing. Billowing gray soon gave way to strange green, balls of fluff. They flew under the thick cloud layer, beyond which the blue sky was completely obscured.

"Cotton ball clouds," Gordon said.

"What are those?"

"Dangerous. That's a tornado sky."

"What's a tornado?"

"Let's hope you don't find out." He looked at his fuel gauge. "Unfortunately, we need to land soon. We're going to have to put down in this."

They started to descend, the now-familiar dip making her a little sick. The wind pushed the plane from side to side, but Gordon did his best to keep it righted. "Strong winds," he said, pursing his lips. It was the most worried she'd seen him.

Another gust hit them so powerfully that they surged down. Her stomach dipped wildly, and for a moment she hovered weightlessly above her seat. Then he regained control, and her butt met the seat again. She seized the grab bar.

"This is going to be rough." He glanced over at her. "You're still buckled in, right?"

"Yes." Another sickening drop.

Sudden rain poured from the clouds, pummeling the plane. The downpour slapped against the windows, drowning out the sound of the propeller. The plane swept back and forth, lurching up and down in violent gusts that robbed the breath from her chest. As a fresh wind pushed the plane to the left, she slammed against the door, slapping her hand to the glass as she tried to stay in her seat. The belt dug into her shoulders.

"Hold on."

Lightning flashed around them, while the thunder boomed and rumbled. Before them, a portion of the cloud started to funnel downward. She was fascinated by its spiral, twisting in midair, dipping ever lower. Then another cloud funneled up from the ground, arcing toward its earthbound twin. "Let's just hope those two don't touch," Gordon said. He veered the plane off to the right, giving the strange clouds a wide berth.

It looked like the clouds might vanish back where they'd come from. The one on the ground wound down and vanished, as the one in the sky lifted back toward the parent cloud. Then suddenly both returned with renewed strength, meeting in the middle. They churned and danced, growing thicker and stronger. She could see dirt and other objects rising from the ground, spiraling within the funnel.

"Damn it!" Gordon cursed. He looked back at the fuel gauge. "We're going to have to take our chances on the ground. We can't stay up in this, and we can't turn back. We'd be stranded with no fuel and a hell of a long way to walk through some dangerous country."

She gripped her seat. "So we put down?"

"We put down." He banked sharply to the north, steering away from the funnel cloud. "We're about twenty miles from the fuel outpost. I think we can skirt around this thing a little and still make it."

She stared out at the raging storm, the lightning flashes burning her retina. She had to trust in Gordon, trust that he knew what he was doing.

She held on tight and gritted her teeth.

Chapter 25

The tornado changed directions, shifting northward toward them. They'd almost skirted around it now, dipping low toward the ground. The plane whipped around in the gale-force winds, and H124 felt so sick she didn't think she'd ever be able to eat again. Below them the ground raced past, the plane plunging so low she felt as if she could stick her legs out of its bottom and run along the dirt.

"Almost there." Gordon gripped the controls, leaning forward as he made adjustments.

Then an old airfield came into view, its ancient markings barely visible on the cracked pavement. A tattered flag hung from a rusted pole, and a few collapsed hangars lay in piles along the northern side of the runway.

She craned her neck to the south, seeing the monstrous tornado gyrating in a furious storm of dust, rain and other things churning in its dark depths. Then the wheels hit hard, and she bit her tongue. They slowed, jostling along the weathered runway. Gordon's lips pressed together so tightly that all the color had drained from them.

He looked over his shoulder as the plane came to a stop next to the fuel pumps. "Can you see if that thing's changed directions?"

She looked through his window at the funneling black cloud. She watched it wind and spit its way across the terrain, trying to judge its distance and course. Using a small hill in the backdrop as a frame of reference, she realized with a sinking feeling that it had shifted north. "It's headed this way."

Gordon jumped out of the plane. "We have to be quick. Can you help me?"

"Of course!" She unbuckled her belt and climbed out, instantly feeling the heat rising in waves off the old runway. The air hung heavy and humid, blistering around her. Sweat beaded on her back and forehead as she hurried around to the fuel pumps. The rain soaked her. Gordon opened the plane's tank, and she pulled off the hose, hurrying toward him. But when he tried to fill the tank, nothing happened. He pressed the lever again. Nothing. "It's empty," he said.

She had a delayed reaction. "What?"

He hurried back to the plane. "We have to try the airfield's backup tank!" The wind picked up speed. "Get back in!"

She ran around to the other side of the plane, and he started it up again. They taxied down the runway, stopping in front of the last collapsed building. Jumping out, he raced over to the ruined edifice, got down on all fours, and shimmied through a hole in the rubble. She watched his legs and boots disappear, then she climbed out of the plane. The wind whipped around her, plastering her hair to her face. She brushed it back, and gazed into the horror of the funnel cloud. Churning ever nearer, it plowed toward them, kicking up debris. A low rumble sounded forth.

She ran over to the hole in the rubble and knelt down, staring into the dark. She couldn't see him. "Gordon?" She could barely hear herself above the roar of the approaching tornado. "Gordon!"

His face appeared then, framed in the dim filtering light of the afternoon. He crawled back through the debris, and she stood to aside as he got out. He held up a small key, then jogged over to a rectangle in the runway. "Give me a hand!"

He pulled up a chunk of pavement, which flipped open on a set of groaning hinges, revealing a metal door with a lock. He slid the key in, then pulled up on the handle. Beneath lay a series of secondary tanks. She allowed herself to breathe again. "Are they full?"

He reached inside, pulling out a hose. "We're about to find out!"

She rushed over to the plane's tank and opened the fuel door for him. Behind them the tornado chugged inexorably closer. Now she could really see the debris cloud around it, a revolving mass of heavy objects that would kill them instantly if it got close enough.

"That thing still headed our way?" he asked as he filled the tank.

She watched the monstrous funnel tear up the terrain. "Yep!"

"Figured! Wouldn't want the trip to be too easy!"

She laughed in spite of the situation, and that made him chuckle. A gust of wind hit her so hard she lost her balance and knocked against the side of the plane.

"Now don't get blown away!" he said. "I'm starting to get attached!"

She braced herself against the tail of the plane. "I'll do my best!" The tornado was deadly close now.

"Halfway there!" Gordon said, but she didn't think they'd make it. The pump was filling the tank too slowly.

"Can we take off with what we have and fill it up somewhere else?" she yelled.

He shook his head. "There is nowhere else! It's this or nothing!"

"We could go back!"

"Not with half a tank, we can't!"

She bit her lip.

As he kept the hose in the plane, she watched the black cloud fill her view. She could hear its cacophonous roar.

Three-fourths full.

The howling wind tore off the roof of a building at the end of the runway. "Time to go!" Gordon shouted above the din. He unhooked the hose, and they jumped back in the plane.

Not bothering to strap in, he started it up and gunned down the runway. Wind tore at the wings, shuddering the plane. She gripped her seat, her teeth clenched. The little plane jerked side to side, and suddenly they were airborne, speeding away from the funnel cloud. He banked the plane sharply away from the storm. "You got nerves of steel," he told her as they rose higher and higher.

The plane dipped beneath the heavy cloud layer, toward a section of sky that now shone clear in a few patches.

"Do we have enough fuel?" She leaned toward the fuel gauge. It was a little over three-fourths.

Gordon grimaced. "Not to get to the airfield I wanted to reach."

"What do we do?"

"There's another one, but . . ." His voice trailed off as he chanced a look back at the storm. The plane stopped shaking so violently. "Should be smoother now."

"But?" she prompted.

He glanced over at her with worried eyes. "It's a bad place. Bad people. It's dangerous, and I wanted to avoid it."

"PPC?"

"Badlanders. And not the ones like Firehawk belongs to. Dirty bastards who like to kill, who live for it. They'd tear us apart if we landed there. They're called the Death Riders. I've heard stories . . ."

"About what?"

His eyes looked haunted. "I'd rather not say. Not to a young thing like you."

"I can take it."

"I'm sure you can, but I can't. I have no interest in robbing you of any more innocence than you've already lost."

"Can we land somewhere else?"

He shook his head. "Not with this little fuel. When we get there, we'll have to fuel up fast."

She tilted her head. "Faster than we just did?"

He bit his lip. "Faster."

Before long the air cleared, showing long patches of sapphire. As the hours passed, they talked about weather, and he taught her more about flying. The sun beat down through the windows, heating up the cabin. The ground was brown in every direction. In some places, the ancient paths of rivers, now long dried up, were still visible. She saw charred patches and strange spires dotting the landscape.

"What are those?"

Gordon looked down. "Trees. Old ones. Burned a long time ago. Whole forests of them. Now they just stand there, blackened sentinels of a bygone age."

This was what Raven had been talking about. The scorched forests.

They flew over a dense patch of dead trees, then rolling hills, brown in most places, and black from grass fires in others. Soon a giant column of ash and smoke appeared on the horizon. It billowed upward, filling the distant sky.

"Fire," Gordon said.

"Natural or humans?"

"Don't know. Could be natural, all this lightning we've been having. But it could also be the Death Riders. They burn the camps of other Badlanders. I've even heard that when they're running low on food they . . ."

She looked over at him, but he didn't finish.

"We'll have to land soon. The fuel stop's just on the other side of that fire."

They flew on, veering to the right of the smoke column. She watched it tower upward as they passed. The air in the plane grew acrid and unbreathable, so she pulled out her scarf and covered her mouth.

Gordon started coughing uncontrollably.

Soon they were past the fire, and he pointed out a small runway in the distance. "Let's just hope we can land." He started the descent. H124 searched the ground for any sign of the Death Riders. She didn't see any vehicles moving, nor any encampments spread out below them. Just the old runway.

Gordon steered the plane down. It jittered and shimmied, and she watched his brow wrinkle. "It's the heat. The air is so light it makes it hard to land." Heat waves shimmered off the broken runway, distorting the air in front of the plane. "Don't worry. I deal with this all the time."

She gripped the door handle as the wheels touched down with a screech. They jostled and bumped down the runway as a huge crack in the pavement loomed before them.

"What about that?" she asked, pointing forward.

"Brace yourself."

She clutched the handle harder, and they hopped over the crack, going airborne for a moment. Then the wheels screeched home again, and the plane started to slow, rumbling down the decrepit landing field.

Gordon grinned. "Smooth as ice."

Her knuckles had turned white on the door handle. "Real smooth."

He taxied down the broken runway to a set of methane tanks at the end. They passed old hangars, most of them collapsed, but a few remained upright. Their walls yawned with huge, rusted holes. Each time they passed one of the erect buildings, Gordon glimpsed nervously into their darkened openings.

"What is it?"

"Just that . . ." He peered into another building, then stopped the plane in front of the methane tanks. His eyes narrowed. "I don't see anyone."

She gave a second look too. "Me either."

"Let's go." He climbed out of the plane and hurried to the tanks. She got out as well, helping him with the bulky refueling hose. As he fitted the connector into the plane's tank, she turned on the pump. It coughed and thrummed, then started up.

"Color me amazed!" he shouted.

"What?"

"They actually left some fuel in here for a change. Usually I have to access the underground backup tanks at this airfield."

As they refueled, they scanned the area nervously. Then H124 realized why there was still methane in the tanks. The sudden roar of dozens of engines fired up from the top of the hill above them. Vehicles streamed down, throwing up clouds of dirt behind them. It was a trap.

"Death Riders!" Gordon cursed. "How much we got to go?"

H124 looked at the gauge. "We're about a third full!"

"Keep going! Just get ready to run back to the plane as soon as you shut off the pump!"

She nodded, as a chilling war cry rang from the Death Riders and their vehicles.

"They'll leave us for dead and take the plane!" Gordon shouted above the din. "How full are we?"

She looked at the gauge. "Almost half!"

"Just a little more, and we're good!"

The vehicles roared onto the airfield, maneuvering between the old hangars. She could see spikes mounted on the backs of their cars, bolstering a series of strange spheres. The Death Riders screamed out as they stood up in massive trucks.

She looked at the gauge. A little more than half full.

The Death Riders thundered closer, now just a few hundred meters away. She could see the mounted spheres better now. Some were red and glistening, others brown-and-black. Some had slick flowing streamers attached. Then she realized that they weren't spheres.

They were human heads.

Chapter 26

H124 watched in horror as the Death Riders drew closer, the mounted skulls on their cars dripping with gore and decay. Some heads had been skinned, revealing gleaming muscle and the white flash of bone.

"Where we at?" Gordon yelled.

"About three-fourths full!"

"Good enough! Kill the pump!"

She shut it off and made for the plane while he dumped the hose and ran to the pilot door, wrenching it open.

She buckled in as he started up the propeller, and they taxied down the runway. "Damn it!" he grumbled.

"What is it?"

"We don't have enough room. We're going to have to spin around."

As he slowed the plane and pivoted it, H124 stared down the runway at the wall of approaching cars. The Death Riders howled and cheered, guns and spears thrust into the air. One of the cars was mounted with a huge gun like she'd seen in Black Canyon Camp. "Will they fire at us?"

"Probably not. They wouldn't want to damage the plane." He leaned forward, building up speed. But they weren't moving fast enough. "Holy hell," Gordon breathed. "We'll have to hop them."

"Hop them?" Her voice cracked.

"Hold on."

He revved the plane and surged down the runway, streaming headlong toward the oncoming marauders. She gripped the seat, watching the distance close between them. They were going to crash. Smash right into them. And their heads would end up mounted on those spikes.

A hundred meters. Then fifty. When they were almost on top of the Death Riders, Gordon pulled back on the stick. Lacking the speed to take off, they darted up into the air, hopping right over the line of cars. He touched down on the other side, racing down the runway, past the old hangar buildings, bouncing over the gigantic crack again. At the edge of the strip, Gordon pulled back on the controls, lifting the plane into the air. She felt her stomach dip toward her feet, then a surge of relief as they careened into the sky.

"Woooohoooo!" Gordon shouted, pumping a fist skyward.

She turned in her seat to look back to the runway. The Death Riders had stopped, a huge cloud of dust settling behind them. One shook his fist at them. She grinned.

"Nice flying!" She clapped him on the back.

"Thank you, ma'am."

She leaned back in her seat. "Do we have enough fuel to make it to the next airfield?"

He looked at the gauge. "We should make it."

She closed her eyes and relaxed her body, listening to the drone of the engine. They flew for an hour in silence, basking in the warmth of the cabin. Then she opened her eyes, staring out into the blue. On the western horizon, gray clouds had started to form, building up into giant anvils.

"Do you remember when the weather wasn't crazy all the time?" she asked.

He scratched his chin. "Not really, though my grandparents told me stories. They said that when they were little, their grandparents grew corn on a little plot of land."

"What's corn?"

"It was an edible plant. Said you could make all kinds of food from it. My grandfather was particularly fond of something called *popcorn.*"

They looked down upon the parched brown land beneath them. There lay miles of dried riverbeds, braiding across the dusty plains.

"They could even make fuel from the corn. Must have been right around here somewhere. They said the whole land was once green, that lots of people grew food out here."

She surveyed the barren wasteland. "Hard to imagine."

"It wasn't the Badlands back then. That name came later."

"What changed? Do you know?"

"My grandparents used to talk about something called carbon capture farms, how they were supposed to change everything, calm the weather and all that."

"And what happened?"

"Well, I guess it didn't work quite the way they thought it would."

"How was it supposed to work?" she asked.

He shrugged. "Beats me. But from what they said, it was supposed to absorb the bad air. Only it wasn't enough. My grandmother used to say it was like trying to patch a leaky boat with a sponge."

She thought of the old PRD with the videos that described geoengineering. "Did they ever talk about some kind of particles that were released into the air?"

He nodded. "Hell, yes. My grandfather used to bitch about that all the time. Said it messed up everything for his grandparents. The Apollo Project."

"Yes! That's it!"

"It was supposed to keep heat trapped way up high, but instead it built up, and came crashing down one day. My grandfather said it was like a scorching tidal wave pressing down on the world. The storms got really bad after that."

"I heard it descended because the people who'd been releasing the particles decided to spend the money on video surveillance instead. So someone else just sent up different particles."

"Figures. My dad used to say that ignorance was one of the paving stones on the road to disaster."

She looked over at him. "Really? What else paved the road?"

He looked far out his window. "Greed, arrogance . . . violence, hubris . . ."

She'd never heard the last word before. "What's hubris?"

"Thinking you're a god," he said.

She squinted in the sunlight, toward the towering gray clouds building in the far west. The tiny plane flew in that direction.

"Should we be worried about those?"

He smiled. "Not until we have to fly into them."

She sighed, readjusting her weight in the seat. The drone of the propeller filled the cabin, and the swaying of the plane made her a little sleepy. She fought the urge to close her eyes, so she studied the ground below. Great expanses of dust billowed upward, sweeping over the hills and valleys. As far as she could see, no twinkle of water caught the sunlight. The storm-swollen rivers of the east didn't extend this far inland; instead the thirsty country choked on dirt and dust.

Still her eyes longed to close, and at last she let them, leaning her head against the seat.

She awoke suddenly as the plane jolted upward. "What's going on?" she said, sitting up straight.

"Will you take a look at that?" Gordon said, pointing down. "Well, I'll be."

She followed his gaze down, spotting a vast stretch of verdant trees.
"What do you make of that?" he asked.

"I don't know."

"I think we need to take a look. You game?"

"Sure."

He brought the plane down near the edge of the trees, wheels touching down on a flat stretch of brown earth. Up ahead the world was green. "What about Death Riders?" she asked.

He opened the pilot door. "Death Riders don't have nothing to do with this." He gave a low whistle, then jogged toward the trees. "Come and look at this, will ya?"

She caught up to him. A sudden gust of wind brought with it a wonderfully sweet smell. It was the best air she'd ever breathed. She felt invigorated. She walked to the edge of the forest and placed her hands on either side of a tree. Its jade leaves rustled in the wind. She pressed her face against it.

"Where did all these trees come from?" Gordon asked, moving among them. "This beats all!"

She followed him, breathing deeply, listening to the sighs of the leaves. After the isolation of her life in New Atlantic, the violence of the Badlanders, the barren landscapes, she felt like she'd stepped into something truly magical. A beautiful sound rang out between the trees. It was as if someone were singing, or perhaps whistling. "What's that?" she asked.

"I don't know."

She followed the sound, walking deeper into the forest. She heard it again and again, originating from somewhere high up. She jumped suddenly. Something flew from one tree to another in the overhead branches. It landed on a limb and began to sing again. She recognized it from one of her field guides. It was a bird. "There!" she said, pointing.

Gordon watched it with her. Then another one joined it, and they sat together on the branch. "Well, will you look at that!" Gordon exclaimed.

Between the trees grew shorter plants. She recognized some of them from the books: ferns, shrubs, and the like. Something rustled in them, and a furry head lifted out. A large brown animal walked past, munching on leaves. From its head grew two pointy bones, with other protrusions branching off. It watched them with big, watery brown eyes, chewing all the while. Then it moved off into the trees.

She looked over at Gordon, who stood there staring, mouth agape. "This is . . ."

H124 turned in a complete circle, the surrounding forest welcoming her. Then she noticed something gray up in a tree. It was smooth and sleek, with a black window in it. Some kind of technology. "Look at that," she said, pointing.

"It's a monitoring device. I've seen them before."

Fear gripped her. "PPC?"

"Nope. Seen one like it in a weather shelter."

"Rover tech?"

"I think so."

She waved at it. "Hey! Can you hear me?"

"Don't think it works like that. It's not a live feed or anything. It just records data now and again. The one I saw seemed to be recording rainfall and humidity."

"So they're monitoring the place." She thought of Raven's video, the one where he mentioned how the Rovers had been talking about planting forests again. This must be one of them. Trees planted to absorb CO_2 from the atmosphere.

"This is amazing," Gordon said. "But where did these animals come from? They died out long ago."

"Maybe the Rovers managed to save some of them."

He stared up at the two birds. "I guess so."

They wandered through the forest, spotting more birds and other four-legged elegant animals. She made a mental note to look them up in her field guide when they got back to the plane.

For a while they sat down at the base of a tree, listening to the singing in the branches, watching the sunlight filter down to the forest floor. She felt something here, something powerful stirring inside her, like a lost piece of a puzzle clicking into place.

"Well, I guess we better mosey," Gordon said, getting up and brushing dirt off his pants.

She stood reluctantly. "All right."

Together they walked back to the plane, taking their time, breathing it all in. A small metal box at the base of one tree caught her eye. She went to it. The box looked identical to the ones she'd seen in the weather shelters that held Raven's video entries. She bent down and opened it, finding a PRD inside. It was newer than the previous ones.

"What'd you find?" Gordon asked.

"Another PRD. I'm going to copy the contents." She started up the PRD, finding it still partially charged. Indeed, it was full of video entries. She pulled out her PRD and paired the two devices, copying over the contents onto her own. Then she gently placed the Rover PRD back into the box and latched it closed.

"What do you think's on it?" he asked.

"If it's like the other ones, it'll have history lessons explaining how the planet got to be the way it is."

"Cheerful stuff, then."

She laughed. "Very cheerful."

They walked back to the plane. She looked forward to watching more of Raven's videos. As they lifted off and flew away, she craned around in her seat to watch the green patch grow smaller.

"That was something," Gordon said.

"Indeed.

They flew on in pleasant silence, staring out as they did. Her eyes burned, and though she fought against it, she slipped into sleep again, dreaming only of green.

H124 jerked awake as the plane dipped. "What is it?"

Gordon gestured ahead. "Snowstorm."

She rubbed her eyes and peered out through the windscreen. Great clouds of gray clustered all around them. She couldn't see ahead, nor the ground below. She didn't understand how Gordon could possibly know where he was going.

He kept glancing nervously at the altimeter and adjusting his controls, looking at the flight plan he'd created on his PRD. "Supposed to be a mountain pass right here. We're almost out of fuel. If I turn back, we're dead in the air." He looked again at the altimeter. "We should be okay."

For a moment she thought he was right. The winds died down a little, and they flew on smoothly. Then a sudden surge of air pushed them down. The plane dipped, then another gust hit them, shoving them down even farther.

"Oh, hell!" Gordon shouted as a third downdraft sent them plummeting out of control. The altimeter said they were low now, too low. He flipped on the landing lights, illuminating the space beneath them.

She saw shapes looming up, strange spires caught in the lights. *Dead trees,* she realized. The plane grazed down among them, their branches scraping and splintering along the bottom of the plane.

Gordon gripped the controls, teeth bared, sweat streaming down his temples. "They just might slow us down enough . . ."

A ripping of metal filled the cabin. She gripped the door handle and seat, feet braced against the floor. The plane screamed toward the ground, the trees below pummeling its underbelly. A tall one loomed up huge in the lights, and she shielded her face as it passed right by the windshield and collided with the right wing of the plane, tearing it off with a deafening squeal. The plane started to spin, thrown violently by the collision, and her head slammed into the passenger window as they hit more trees. Then they bounced, scraping along the ground. Rocks and stumps jarred the plane as it slid, each new strike against a dead tree tossing it about. Her hands flew out, trying to brace herself, one on the door, the other on the instrument panel in front of her. She squeezed her eyes shut, praying for the plane to stop moving. She tried to look over at Gordon, but another collision sent her head snapping back, slamming into the headrest.

They hit with a force so hard that all the air in her lungs rushed out. She flew forward, the seat belt biting into her flesh, her teeth clacking together. Her eyes closed against their will. A rain of glass shattered in on them as something huge splintered through the windshield. It sliced through the side of her face, and after she reached the full restraint of her belt she slammed back violently into the seat. Every bone jarred, every muscle strained.

Sudden silence took over her world. She tasted blood. She sucked in a deep breath, and a sharp pain wracked her chest. The world felt calm, unreal. She opened her eyes, looking around, not comprehending. Where was she? The plane. The storm spiraling them out of control . . .

She snapped her head toward Gordon but couldn't see him. The splintered trunk of a dead tree lay between them. It had speared the windshield and now took up most of the center aisle.

She reached down with trembling hands and unbuckled her belt. "Gordon?" she whispered. She rose up from her seat, trying to see over the trunk. Gordon lay back in his seat, mouth open, blood streaming from his nose, eyes closed. His side of the plane had crumpled inward, smashing his left leg against the twisted metal. His breathing was shallow and rapid.

"Gordon?" she breathed again. He didn't stir. Her face stung, and as she reached up to her cheek, her hand came away red and sticky. Hands trembling, she reached for her door handle and managed to get it open. Her head spun. Her door was undamaged, so she climbed out with relative ease. At once she sank up to her thighs in something cold and white. From the survival manual she'd been reading, she recognized it as snow. She'd never seen it before, and the cold wetness of it instantly sucked the warmth from her body. She shivered as she stepped around the back of the plane, trying to reach Gordon's door. Sinking deeply with each step, she tried to steady herself. Each breath brought a renewed agony to her chest. The cold air stung her face and lungs. Around her hung dense clouds, so thick she could barely make out the area around the crash site. Beyond ten feet, the swirling mists hid everything. It looked like they'd crashed on some kind of rock ledge, with the plane's nose tilted upward. It had slid to a stop beneath a slight overhang of stone, and a dead tree in front of the ledge had gone right through the cockpit.

Teeth chattering, she reached Gordon's door. It had torn off in the crash and lay nearby, dented and twisted. She reached him, already feeling the cold and wet seeping in through her boots.

"Gordon?" she said quietly. Tentatively, she reached a shaking hand through the open door and touched his shoulder. He didn't stir. Blood seeped from his left leg, soaking his jeans. The tree had struck him in the head and sliced up his right shoulder, smearing the ancient dead wood with red.

She could smell methane seeping into the air, and it made her gag. She moved from one foot to the other, rubbing her arms. Her breath frosted in the air, and her nose had gone numb. Gordon wasn't waking up. The sun would soon set, and temperatures would dip well below freezing. If she didn't do something, they'd die of hypothermia. She had to make a shelter, build a fire. But she couldn't risk an open flame here with the methane hissing out. She had to move him.

Staring down at his leg, she saw that it was pinned between the seat and the crumpled cone of the plane. She reached down, finding the lever that controlled how far forward the seat rested. Pulling it, she slid the seat back, gaining enough room for his leg to ease out.

Now she could see more of his wound. Something white and red glistened through a slice in his jeans. She leaned closer, seeing that it was his leg bone, splintered and exposed. Maybe it was good that he was unconscious right now. Dragging him out of the plane was going to be painful.

She felt him over for other injuries, but didn't find any. Hooking her hands under his arms, she carefully slid him toward the door. Then she lifted his injured leg and placed his left foot delicately in the snow, followed by his right one. When he was halfway out of the plane, his head slumped, but he still didn't wake. She grabbed him under the arms again and dragged him out of the plane, looking for a snow-free place to set him down. To the left of the crash site, the overhang continued for about fifty feet. Directly underneath, the rock was void of snow, so she pulled him toward it. The outcrop would protect them from some of the wind, and she could build a fire there.

Gordon wasn't very heavy, but lugging him that far made every breath pure agony. She'd definitely cracked at least one of her ribs, she thought. The blood on her face had started to freeze, crusting over her cheek and ear.

As she dragged him along, she thought of all the corpses she'd moved over the years. Now she hauled someone living, someone she was trying to save instead of incinerate. She had to make it to the protected area, had to find some way to keep them warm.

The light began to fade, and the low, thick clouds dampened the sound around them. It was the purest silence she'd ever experienced.

She stopped for a moment, aching for a lungful of air, and took a series of shallow breaths, nearly hyperventilating in her desire for oxygen. Then she dragged him the rest of the way and propped him up against a rock wall under the overhang. The wind wasn't as bad here, she discovered with relief. Returning to the plane, she rifled through his bag and came away with a thick coat, mittens, a knitted hat, and an old blanket. She put all of these on him, then draped the blanket over him.

Still he didn't stir. She set off to find something to burn.

Thankfully she didn't have to go far for wood. They'd downed enough dead trees on their way. She walked to the plane, grabbing her tool bag with all the books, and assessed the tree that had pierced the windshield. Branches had broken off around the crumpled nose of the aircraft, so she gathered these first. But as soon as she lifted them, she felt the sogginess of the wood. They'd been sitting out in the snow for a long time, and fear stole over her as she realized she might not be able to start a fire at all. She looked around for anything else that would burn. Their clothes were synthetic, the plane metal. If she couldn't get the wood to catch fire . . . She pushed the thought aside and gathered an armful of branches and small twigs, as well as her tool bag, bringing them all back to the overhang. Gordon was still unconscious.

Thirst pulled at her. She drank the last of what she had left in her water bottle. She'd have to filter more later.

Opening the survival guide, she read the steps to building a fire. She took the smallest twigs and ground them to powder, then sprinkled them on the smaller pieces of wood, forming a little interwoven piece that the book referred to as a bird's-nest shape. Then she arranged the bigger branches into a pyramid, with an opening in the side. She pulled out her pocket torch and lit the bird nest. It caught, and in her excitement, she took too deep a breath and cried out in pain. Using two sticks, she transported the bird's-nest into the hole in the wood pyramid. She blew gently on it.

But it didn't catch. When the tinder burned out, the wood hadn't caught.

She tried it again, but the same thing happened. The small pieces would catch, but not the sodden logs.

Referring back to the book, she followed its suggestion to look for slanted trees that might not be wet on their undersides. She left the overhang, tromping through the deep snow. Her feet felt frozen inside her wet boots, and her hands had grown red and painful in the bitter cold.

She crested a small ridge, below which stood a gathering of trees. Some of them had partially fallen, leaning against their neighbors. The book said to tear off bark from the underside, but these trees had lost theirs long ago. They now stood as white, sun-bleached skeletons, silhouetted against the fading western light.

Taking out her multitool, she shaved off pieces of wood. They would make good tinder, but even on the underside, these trees were wet. Lifting her arms sent a searing pain throughout her ribs. She scraped off more and more wood from a few of the drier-looking trees, then headed back to the overhang.

There she repeated the fire-building steps, creating the bird's nest, transporting it to the new pyramid she'd built of shaved wood. But it just wouldn't catch. Her fingers ached in the cold, so much so that she could barely curl them. Soon they felt useless.

She leaned back against Gordon, tucking her hands under her arms in an effort to thaw them. As soon as some feeling returned, she tried again. But the wood was just too wet to catch. She picked it up and shoved it as far under the overhang as she could. Maybe it would dry out. But she knew that in this cold, with no direct sun, the chance was remote.

This just wasn't going to work. She had to get help. They would die out here if she didn't.

Rowan. She had to reach Rowan.

Pulling out her PRD, she used the code system he had installed. She knew he was so far away, had no idea how he'd be able to help. Maybe he knew people nearby. Another pilot, maybe.

She typed out the message using their encryption method. "Rowan, I need your help. Plane crashed. Desperate situation. Lives in danger. Won't make Rover rendezvous. All might be lost. At the following location." She uploaded her coordinates and pressed send.

To cover all her options, she also sent a message to Willoughby. She didn't include her location in case Willoughby had been compromised, but she asked him to contact her.

She huddled up next to Gordon and pulled up the new videos they'd found at the forested site. She clicked on the first entry. Raven's familiar face smiled out at her, but he was older, probably in his late teens. A title glowed at the bottom of the display: *Video Log—Carbon Sink Project 1.1.*

Raven wore a big grin on his face. "My parents and I are about to start tending to the carbon sinks—the forests of trees planted by Rovers two generations ago. The trees have grown to a pretty good height, I hear. We're off to check on a forest that was planted on the eastern side of the country, southwest of New Atlantic. I've never seen anything like it before, and can't wait to get there. After the forest was established, it was populated with a few species that went extinct in recent history—bears, deer, wolves, rabbits, and some birds like woodpeckers and robins. We've preserved DNA from these animals, so we have the ability to grow more. We call it *de-extinction,* a method of replacing species that are necessary for the survival of an ecosystem. I've never seen any of these animals in real life before. Supposedly they're doing quite well in the forest. It's going to be an amazing experience." He reached out and shut off the recording.

Just beyond the overhang, the snow continued to fall, big white flakes drifting down silently, accumulating quickly. The last of the cloud-filtered sunlight faded away, and darkness closed in around them. She shivered, then huddled in next to Gordon's unconscious form and draped the blanket over both of them. Her ribs and cheek ached, and she couldn't get comfortable. Just as well, she thought. If she fell asleep tonight, there was a good chance she'd never wake up. She had to be vigilant.

She clicked on Raven's next entry. His happy face beamed as the camera turned on. Text scrolled along the bottom of the display: *Video Log—Carbon Sink Project 1.2.*

"We're here! I can't believe it," he said, staring around. Behind him she could see a vast landscape of green. "I never imagined how beautiful a forest could be." He held up the camera and revolved it, revealing a densely treed forest. It reminded her of the one she'd seen with Gordon, but these trees were much taller. She could hear the wind sighing in the pines and the caroling of a bird. "This is the forest outside of New Atlantic. I had no idea how amazing it would feel to be here. It's like part of me was missing my whole life, a dull ache inside of me that I couldn't explain. And as soon as I stepped into these trees, everything healed. It's like I belong here, like I've *always* belonged here, but didn't even know a place like this could exist." His white teeth were brilliant against his darker skin.

"My parents and I have been monitoring the animal population and checking on the health of the trees. My mom invented these remote monitoring stations that we can place high up. They record temperature, humidity, and take photos of any animals that walk by. They also record sound, so we can get an idea of what the bioacoustics of the forest are like, how the animals interact with each other, and the sounds they make. It's a living, breathing, honest-to-goodness ecosystem here, something I never dreamed I'd see."

Once again he panned the camera around. H124 felt a little warmer as she watched images of a sun-warmed forest floor, golden beams filtering down through the branches. She could almost smell it. Raven reached out and ended the recording.

Thirst stirred her to action. She'd read in the survival manual that eating snow would only dehydrate her more, so instead she packed her water bottle with snow and then tucked it under her jacket to melt.

It worried her that Gordon hadn't woken up yet. She had to do something about his leg, knew she had to set the bone, then pack his leg in snow. Now would be a good time while he was still out.

She looked over at him, this brave man who had taken her, a complete stranger, on an outrageous quest of mammoth proportion. Without a med pod handy, she knew it was up to her to keep him alive. Using the survival guide, she assessed his wounded leg. The protruding bone told her it was an open fracture. The book said that in most cases, you should leave the bone sticking out, so the patient can later get help to correct it. But if no help was coming, and you didn't have clean bandages or antibiotics to keep infection away, it was better to put the bone back in. That way the body acted as the bandage, and Gordon's immune system would work as the antibiotics. She studied a diagram in the book, then moved into position to adjust his leg.

Taking a series of shallow breaths, she placed her hands on the wound and strained, pressing the bone back inside his leg and aligning it as best she could. Luckily he remained unconscious. Then she gathered the sticks she'd found and tore up one of his spare shirts to tie the broken leg to his good one, as the book instructed. She wiped his blood off in the snow and wrapped the rest of his spare shirt around the wound. Then she checked for a pulse above and below the leg, making sure the splint or the shirt hadn't cut off his circulation. She felt a beat in both places. Now she packed snow around the wound, hoping to bring down some of the swelling.

She settled in next to him and replaced the blanket around them, pressing close so they could share body heat. The fire attempt had been hopeless, and the cold sank steadily into her body. She got up, jumped around, and slapped her arms, but was reluctant to leave Gordon for too long without her body heat to help keep him warm. She sat back down, leaning against him, rubbing his arms and chest. He murmured, stirring gently, but remained asleep. The bitter cold invaded her, but she didn't shiver this time. She read in the survival guide that once you stopped shivering, hypothermia was setting in. She jumped again, jogged around the plane as much as her cracked rib would allow, and sat back down with Gordon.

She couldn't believe how cold it was. Her fingers, face, legs, feet—everything was either going numb or burned like fire. She tucked her hands under her arms again, which helped a little, then clomped her feet on the rock, trying to keep the circulation going. She rubbed Gordon's arms and chest yet again, doing so periodically throughout the night. She felt frozen to her core. But she was still breathing, as was Gordon, and for that she was grateful. She forced herself to concentrate on something else, and took herself out of her body, out of this cold rock enclosure.

She opened her tool bag, rifling through the research she'd saved from the university under New Atlantic: the shiny discs, the small metal devices that had a plug of some sort on one end. She thought of how far she'd come, all the way from her city; there was no way it was going to end like this. She thought of the night she'd spent lying next to Byron, thought of his warmth and how strange it felt to lie so close to someone like that. She thought of the incredible experience with Rowan in the old mine, of how his kisses had sent fire through her core. She started to feel a little warmer. She thought of his eyes, the way he looked at her, the way he smelled. Her heart rate sent a little more warmth spreading through her.

She forced her shoulders to relax and stop cramping up with the cold, but it didn't last long. Soon she was shivering again. Tomorrow she had to be strong and go farther afield in search of firewood. And then she'd figure out her next course of action.

Trying to stay awake, she decided to listen to another of Raven's entries about the forests. If she could imagine herself in that warm place, with the sun on her back, maybe her body would stop shaking so violently. She clicked on the next entry. Text scrolled across the bottom of the display: *Video Log—Carbon Sink Project 1.3.*

But instead of Raven's usual beaming face, he was filthy and exhausted, covered with dirt and what looked like soot. Tears ran tracks down his ash-covered face. He swallowed, his hands shaking so much that the recording wavered. Behind him stretched a desolate, black, charred landscape.

"They've come. We're not sure how or why, but the PPC found out about this place. We didn't think they'd care about it. We were naïve. They came in ships with these giant harvesters in the bottom. They took . . ." He swallowed again. "They took all the trees. Killed any animals they encountered. When they'd harvested everything, they torched the place. My parents . . ." His chin trembled. "My parents tried to stop them. They remotely jammed the ships' controls, but somehow the PPC took over again and kept burning everything. My parents pleaded with them over the comm link. And then, before the PPC left . . ." Fresh tears streamed down his dirty face. "They burned my parents. They launched a stream of fire straight down onto them. I rushed forward, tried to help them . . ."

He put down his PRD, and for several minutes she watched as the display shuddered, his legs kneeling on the burned earth, catching sounds of inconsolable wailing drifting away in the wind. At last he pulled up the PRD again, and she could see his swollen eyes. "I couldn't put the fire out. My parents were screaming, and I couldn't put the fire out. Then they just . . . fell over, crumpled and black, burning out . . ."

He put down the PRD again. She waited. When he lifted it up, he said, "The fire spread. The rest of the plants caught—the shrubs and grasses, incinerated. Everything was destroyed. My mother's data recorders, all the trees . . . I wandered around, looking for animal survivors, but found only charred corpses. Some creatures the PPC had even chased far outside the forest, as if it were a sport. They burned them too . . ."

He slumped his shoulders, hung his head, and let his tears fall. "I don't know what I'm going to do."

And then the recording ended.

H124 straightened up, blinking at her display. Immediately she clicked on the next entry. The title scrolled at the bottom: *Video Log—Carbon Sink Project 1.4.*

Raven appeared on her floating display, looking like hell. One of his eyes was almost swollen shut, and the other had deep black-and-purple bruises all around it. A fresh cut on his cheek spilled blood, and his lip was split open. His face was still covered with dirt and soot. His haunted eyes were rimmed in red. It looked like he was in one of the weather shelters. It wasn't one she recognized, but the shelves of books behind him were a familiar sight. He sighed, trembling. "I thought it was over. The PPC had destroyed everything. The trees, the animals . . . *my parents.*" He looked away briefly. "But they came back. Foot soldiers. They swept the whole area, and I couldn't escape in time. They captured me, beat me. They were going to kill me, so I . . . I got one of their guns and shot a man. I've never hurt anyone in my life. I can still see him, eyes wide with surprise, the sonic weapon throwing him back, blood streaming from his face. I don't know if I killed him. When I threatened to shoot the other two men, they backed off.

"So I ran. I managed to make it to one of our shelters." He paused. "Why did the PPC do this? Of what possible interest could the forest be to them? Why would they take the trees? Why would they even care? It's so far outside their center of control in their cities. I just can't fathom it."

He blinked, the fatigue plain on his face. "I'm going to rest for a bit. I've contacted a group of other Rovers, who I'll rendezvous with. I'm worried about the other forests. I have to check on them."

She pulled the blanket around herself and Gordon a little more, and clicked on Raven's next entry: *Video Log—Carbon Sink Project 1.5.*

This time, when Raven appeared on her floating display, he looked more rested. Enough time had passed from his previous entry that she saw no sign of the beating he'd taken. He looked a little older too, maybe in his early twenties now. His eyes were different, wounded and dark. He didn't smile anymore. A grim determination had set into his features. "I've reached one of our forests here in the west, and all looks okay. I've built more of my mom's sensors and placed them in the trees."

H124 could see other people milling around in the background among a forest of trees, mounting sensors and taking readings. Raven went on. "The PPC hasn't touched the other carbon sinks that were planted, just the one outside New Atlantic. But I did learn why they took all those trees." He clenched his teeth, his jaw set in anger. "Wood came back in style. A fad swept through the PPC execs to decorate their offices in Victorian style. They wanted wooden chairs, wooden desks, and real wood-burning fireplaces. But with most of the trees gone, they were out of luck. Until they happened to spot our forest during a routine New Atlantic perimeter check."

His voice trembled with rage. "An airship had been sent out to make sure the atmospheric dome was in good repair, and the pilot decided he wanted to see exactly what lay outside the city. So he flew a hundred miles out and found our forest. He knew the PPC had been wanting wood, so he went back and reported it. The next day, they sent orders to harvest the wood and wipe out any competition for it."

His eyes went black. "My parents died for *that*. All those animals died, for *that*. For a *fucking fad*." He brought his face closer to the camera. "How are we supposed to save this place, this planet, with *that* in charge?" He looked away and took a deep breath. "We don't believe in violence, though I admit there are times when I'm so angry I'm willing to stoop to it. Instead, we've come up with a way to keep the PPC troops and airships at bay. We've improved our hacking abilities and can take over any airship. During attacks, they haven't been able to regain control. I'm leaving this PRD here. I've made copies for the other forests. I'm not sure who will watch this, but I wanted to keep a record of what's happened here."

One of the people working behind him suddenly ran up. Raven lowered his PRD slightly, but she could still see them.

"What is it?"

"We just got word. A PPC airship was spotted nearby. It's headed this way. We're not sure if it's spotted the forest yet."

Raven called out. "Everybody get your gear. River! Are you ready?"

A woman in the distance nodded, holding up a metallic device.

"Okay, let's move out! We've got to save this place." He looked back into the camera. "If this is my last fight, please, someone try to save this place. Try to save the other forests."

The recording ended.

She looked for the next entry, but there wasn't one. What had happened? They'd obviously been successful in saving the forest, at least for now, because it looked untouched when she and Gordon had landed there. But what had happened to Raven? To the other Rovers? Were they still alive?

She turned off her PRD, returning to the dire reality of her situation. All night she struggled to stay awake, rubbing her arms and legs, as well as Gordon's. When the first gleaming of dawn appeared on the horizon, dread had filled her. She knew they wouldn't survive another night. If she couldn't find firewood, she'd have to think of something else.

Forcing her aching, cold body to move, she rose from her cramped position next to him and began exploring. Her ribs were bruised. Taking tiny breaths, she moved through the powdery snow, feeling the cold wet seeping in through her pants and boots. Every bit of wood she found was soaked. She found some plants that were still alive, leaves covered in snow, but even their wood was thoroughly wet.

She checked her PRD, but found no waiting message from Rowan or Willoughby. She leaned back against the hard granite, feeling colder than she ever thought possible. Pulling her knees up under her chin, she pressed close to Gordon. She went over her options. If she didn't hear back from Rowan or Willoughby, she'd make a stretcher and drag Gordon behind her until they found dry wood. She'd head down the mountain with him, where the snow would be less deep, and eventually reach bare dirt.

She shivered, pulling Gordon's blanket over their bodies. He mumbled something, and she turned to look at him. His mouth moved, and his eyes fluttered.

"Gordon?"

He tilted his head away from the wall. It sagged down to his chest. Then he brought up a hand to his forehead. "What . . ."

He shifted under the blanket, and screamed out in pain.

"Don't move. It's your leg."

"Where are we?"

She looked out at the encroaching mist and saw only a world blanketed by snow. "On a mountain."

"We crashed?"

She nodded.

"Gods, I'm freezing. I can barely move my arms."

"I tried to start a fire, but everything's soaked. I pulled some wood in under this overhang, but it's not drying out."

He readjusted his position and sucked his teeth in pain. "How long have I been out?"

"About twenty-four hours."

He leaned over and dry-heaved. "I feel sick to my stomach."

"You took a bad hit to the head." She reached inside her jacket and pulled out the water bottle of melted snow. "Here. Drink this."

He did so, then handed it back to her, wiping his chapped lips on his sleeve. For a minute he sat in silence, eyes adjusting to the light. She saw sadness in his face, and fear. "So what's the plan?"

"I have two."

That made him laugh and wince at the same time. "Only two? Let's hear them."

"I already called for help, but I haven't heard back. If I don't, I'm going to make a stretcher, and we're going to hike down to a lower elevation."

"You can't drag me all that way!"

She set her jaw. "Oh, I can, and I will. It used to be my job dragging bodies around. It's not up for debate."

He stared at her. "You could die out there."

"*You* could die here."

"You have a much better shot without me."

"I need company."

He appraised her with a shrewd look. "Liar."

"Again, it's non-negotiable."

He pulled the blanket closer. "So what about option one? Who did you call?"

"You might not like it."

"I think I'll probably like it more than our current situation."

"I'm not so sure."

He creased his brow. "Now you've got me curious."

"I called Rowan and a friend I have with the PPC."

His mouth fell open somewhat.

"They're both good people."

"I didn't know they made Badlanders and PPC types in that flavor."

"These guys have saved me before."

She pulled out her PRD from under the blanket. No response yet.

Gordon's head sagged. He shifted his position and said, "Don't let me sleep through the rescue."

She rubbed her arms, then heard Gordon fall into the even breathing of sleep. Her breath plumed in the air.

Darkness enveloped them once more. The second night felt endless. Cold seeped into every pore of her skin, every drop of her blood. It sank into her bones, her brain, her spirit. She'd stopped shivering long ago, and pressed against Gordon for warmth. He dozed, in and out of consciousness, murmuring fitfully, waking up every now and then with a cry of agony.

A few hours into the night, he woke up with a start. "My feet!"

She carefully removed his boots to find his toes frostbitten. Hers weren't much better, but at least she'd been able to stand up, do jumping jacks, and stamp her feet to keep her circulation going. With Gordon's leg as bad as it was, he couldn't do the same. She did her best to rub his toes to get the blood flowing again.

Snowflakes tinkled down almost musically, the snow growing deeper and deeper. The dead forest lay around them, eerily still. All she could hear was the blood thrumming in her ears and Gordon's staggered breathing. A few times it grew so quiet that she could swear she heard the earth turning.

Her body longed to sleep, but she couldn't let it. She had to stay awake, to watch over Gordon, to wake him up now and then. If she slept, she'd freeze, and they'd both be lost, along with any hope of saving the planet.

She gazed up at the clouds, imagining the clear, starlit skies above them, and farther out in space, hurtling steadily onward, that portent of doom racing toward the earth.

She pulled her knees up to her chin, while stamping her feet and rocking back and forth. Cold seeped into her mind and soul. The blizzard gusted beyond their shelter, the thought of it weighing down her shoulders and eyelids. It would be so easy to sleep. Maybe the Rovers already knew about the asteroid. Willoughby said they hadn't given up learning. And the Rover bunker under Delta City certainly revealed that they knew a lot about science. Maybe they already knew, and had already figured out a way to stop it. She didn't need to keep fighting. She could just close her eyes and sleep. Just for a little while. Everything would be fine. She could just lie down on that rock next to Gordon and sleep for an hour. Maybe two.

H124 jerked awake, unaware she'd fallen asleep. Fear coursed through her in a sudden wave. She stood up, peering out into a predawn sky. The storm still raged, the cloud level so low she couldn't see much beyond fifty feet. Gordon moaned, coming to when she stood up. They'd made it through another night. But she doubted they could do it again.

She pulled out her PRD. No message from Rowan or Willoughby. Forty-four hours had passed since she'd sent the SOS. They had a few rations of MREs left, but they wouldn't last long. If she waited here, they might never come, and she and Gordon would grow weaker as their food ran out. If Rowan hadn't gotten the message, or if he couldn't reach her, they could wait there until they died. He must not have gotten the message, because wouldn't he have at least replied by now, even if he couldn't make it? And what of Willoughby? Had the PPC figured out that he'd helped her?

"What's happening?" Gordon mumbled, his speech slurred.

"What's happening is that we're leaving."

"Rescue is arriving?"

"Yeah, and it's us."

"What?"

She looked around at the snow and rock, at the swath of splintered dead trees they'd knocked down in the crash. "I'm going to make a sled so I can pull you. All we have to do is get lower, down below the snow. If we stay up here another night, we're not going to make it."

"You can't drag me down the mountain." Gordon leaned forward, rubbing his arms. He cried out when his broken leg shifted.

She looked him in the eye. "*I can, and I will.*" Snowflakes cascaded down, catching in her eyelashes. "We should go now, while we still have some energy and MREs."

Leaving the overhang, she returned to the plane. From the tail, she collected as much wiring as she could, cutting it with her pocket torch. Then she walked along the line of the crash, selecting the straightest branches that had splintered off, and had soon collected the makings of a workable stretcher. Returning to the dry overhang, she lashed them together with the electrical wire, using two longer pieces of wood as handles.

She was almost done when Gordon closed his hand around hers. "I appreciate what you're doing. But you can't. Go get help, then come back for me."

She looked into his watery blue eyes, his kind face. "If I do that," she said firmly, "you won't be alive when I come back. Without sharing body heat, there's no way either of us would have made it through the last two nights."

He gripped her hand more tightly. "I'm not going to let you sacrifice yourself for me. There's no sense in both of us dying."

"But there's a lot of sense in both of us living, and that's what's going to happen." She tied off the final knot, then stood up. "Now get on the stretcher," she commanded, pointing at it as if she were a military commander.

Gordon looked up at her, then broke out in an involuntary laugh. "Damn, you're stubborn. You could be my kid." His eyes teared in the cold. "If you ever decide you want a pa, I'd be happy to have you as a daughter."

She knelt down and hugged him, feeling his warmth against her cold cheek. "Thank you." She stayed like that for a minute, then stood up. "Now get on the damn stretcher."

He laughed, then shifted his weight toward it. Carefully, she lifted his leg as he eased onto it. He winced, biting back a cry of pain.

Using the seat belts from the plane, she lashed him to the stretcher, then threw her tool bag over her shoulder. Grabbing the two extending handles, she lifted up one end of the stretcher and began to make her way through the deep snow, heading ever downward.

Chapter 27

Sinking into the snow, H124 trudged down the mountain, each step a massive effort. Every breath was a renewed agony as her cracked ribs protested. The deep snow was good for one thing, at least—it kept Gordon's stretcher relatively level as she dragged it over the ground. Had the ground been bare, he would have bumped over every log and rock.

Her breath frosting in the air, she worked her way down the mountain, switchbacking down steep sections. Thirst gnawed at her constantly, and with all the exertion, she couldn't melt water fast enough to drink it. She kept stopping, stuffing new snow into her water bottle, and then tucking it under her jacket to melt.

Gordon drifted in and out of consciousness, groaning on occasion. She thought hypothermia might be setting in for him. At one point he struggled against the seat belts and cried out, "I told him not to go in there!"

For hours she labored on, stopping more and more often to rest and drink. The cold zapped her muscles of strength. She ate the last of their MREs, breaking it in half and forcing Gordon to eat his share. Weakly he pushed her hand away, but finally she got him to chew the ration and swallow it.

As the day wore on, the snow grew less deep. She was making progress. Her lungs burned in her chest, and her body started to tremble with exhaustion. She forced herself onward, stopping more frequently for want of a decent breath. The thick cloud cover continued to send down flurries of snowflakes.

The snow was now only knee-deep. She dragged Gordon down another steep slope, zigzagging across it. More stands of dead trees loomed up out of the mist, gray sentinels in a monochromatic landscape.

Suddenly, far below, she spied an expanse of bare brown earth, and she would have run toward it if she weren't about to fall over with fatigue.

Instead she forged on slowly, step by step, six inches at a time, closing the distance. Tiny breath. Step. Tiny breath. Step. She paused when she reached the next stand of dead trees. If she could make it to that section of bare earth, she had a chance of finding dry wood and starting a fire.

Gordon stirred on the stretcher, murmuring under his breath.

Above her the cloud layer grew thinner, the wind drawing it to the east. All of a sudden she could see an edge of blue sky. Her heart lifted.

She trudged on. Left foot. Right foot. Her arms trembled with the weight of the stretcher. She stopped, setting Gordon down and taking a long drink from her water bottle. She was about to stop and give him a drink too, when she heard something in the distance.

She remained still. Above the eerie stillness of the mountain, she heard thrumming. She strained to make it out. A vibrating, cyclic noise, coming from the east. A layer of clouds still hung low in that direction. To the west she could see blue skies and the sun hanging above a line of snow-capped mountains.

The noise grew louder, moving above the clouds. She lifted her face, and her heart started to hammer. It didn't sound like a plane. It didn't sound like a PPC airship either. She had no idea what it was, as the clouds obscured it.

The sound loudened until whatever it was hovered directly above her, hidden in the mist. Then a machine descended, dipping below the gray clouds. A large propeller spun on the top of it, with a smaller one mounted on the tail. The body of the machine was an oval of sorts, with a large sliding door on one side. Inside the cabin, she saw a woman gripping the control stick. The door slid open, and a familiar face grinned down at her. His blue eyes twinkled beneath a crop of short blond hair.

"Rowan!" she shouted. Unable to control herself, she jumped up and down. "Rowan!" Her ribs cursed at her for the movement, as did Gordon.

"There you are!" he called above the din of the rotors. "Quite a storm!"

"I'm so glad to see you!" She wanted to fall down on her knees and cry. Instead, she knelt by Gordon. "We're saved!"

His eyes fluttered.

"Can you land?" she called up to Rowan.

He turned to the pilot, then pointed at a flat spot a few hundred feet away. The pilot maneuvered the machine down, and a tremendous wind kicked up snow into a fine mist. The pilot cut the engine as they touched down.

Rowan jumped out and ran to her. She met him halfway, her exhaustion forgotten. He gathered her up in his arms. She pressed her face into his warm neck and breathed in his delicious scent. "I am so glad to see you," she said, squeezing him so tightly she felt a sharp stab in her ribs.

"When I didn't hear back from you, I got worried," he said.

She pulled away from him, confused. "Hear back from *me?*"

"After I responded that I was on my way, that I'd found the helicopter."

"I didn't get that message."

He frowned. "Really?"

She pulled out her PRD, checking it. Nothing. He looked at the display too, his face laden with worry.

"What is it?" she asked.

Before he had the chance to answer, another sound drifted down the mountain, a low thrumming that was all too familiar. Her stomach dropped

"An airship," Rowan breathed. "They must have intercepted our signal."

The thrumming grew louder as clouds scudded away in the wind. Descending from that gray layer came a thundering metal airship, identical to the one that had wreaked havoc on the Badlander encampment.

"Maybe it's Willoughby," she told him. But she knew she hadn't given him her location, and dread sank into her gut. Maybe they had tracked Rowan.

Rowan grabbed her arm. "Get to the helicopter, quick! We can try to outrun them."

Already the pilot had restarted the helicopter, spinning the rotors to life.

"But Gordon!"

"I'll get him. Just get to the helicopter."

She didn't like this, but she also knew Rowan wasn't as exhausted or injured and would have an easier time getting Gordon to safety.

She took off for the helicopter, wincing with pain every time she tried to breathe. Rowan dashed over to Gordon. Even as the airship wheeled in the sky, spotting them, she hoped it was friendly. But if it wasn't, there was no more time. They'd be an easy target on the ground, too easily destroyed by the airship's tremendous firepower. Rowan wouldn't have time to drag Gordon to safety single-handedly. Beyond where the stretcher lay stood a massive grouping of boulders. It might provide cover.

She ran back toward Rowan, stooping to grab one side of the stretcher. "We have to get to those rocks!" she shouted. He grabbed the other side of the stretcher, and together they ran for safety.

The helicopter took to the sky, banking away from the airship just as the immense ship fired its first devastating blast. A huge patch of snow and soil blazed up into the air, leaving a gaping hole where the helicopter had landed.

The pilot steered straight for the bank of gray clouds, vanishing into the mist.

H124 leaped over boulders and logs, and they reached the safety of the rocks before the airship was able to fire again. She wasn't sure if they'd seen them. She pointed to a large crevice in the rocks. "Help me hide him in there." Together they steered the stretcher feet first into the dark aperture, then shoved him in until he was out of view.

"We have to draw their fire, distract them," Rowan told her.

She nodded.

"If Marlowe comes back with the helicopter, she can pick us up, and we can find a place to hide out until the airship's gone. Then we can come back and get Gordon."

She frowned. "I don't like this."

His eyes met hers. "I don't either, but it's the best hope we've got."

Gordon stirred in the darkness. "Go!" he said. "This time you have to listen to me. I'll be okay."

She hated this. But if they all stayed there, the airship would find them, and they'd all be dead. "I'm coming back," she told him.

"I know you will," came his voice from the hole.

In the distance, they heard the thumping of helicopter rotors. The pilot hadn't abandoned them.

"Why are they here?"

"They must have intercepted my communications. Learned your location when I sent Marlowe a message for help."

"What will she do?"

"She'll probably circle around to get us. Let's keep moving downhill. Stay close to the outcrop."

She gave another nod.

Rowan peered out. "The airship is higher up, chasing Marlowe. Let's go!"

Gripping her hand, Rowan sped out from the rocks, and together they raced down the mountain, winding among the thickets of dead trees, leaping over logs and rocks. The snow grew more shallow, now only ankle-deep. She tried to keep up with Rowan, but her body trembled with exhaustion, and her ribs throbbed. She couldn't get a good breath.

The airship fired another shot, blasting through the tree trunks. The cacophonous sound of splintering wood filled the air, and H124 looked up to see a mass of trees hurtling down toward them, flames licking up their sides.

"We have to get out of the open!" she shouted. Fiery limbs crashed down around them. One caught her sharply on the shoulder. She staggered forward, landing on her hands and knees. An agonizing pain erupted on her skin, so she rolled in the snow, putting out the flames. Rowan reached a hand down to her and pulled her up. They reached the edge of the trees just as the airship fired again, toppling another section. Flaming logs hit the snow with a hiss and trundled down the mountain slope.

"They've got infrared. It doesn't matter if we're in the open or not. We need something to mask our heat signature."

H124 thought of Gordon, stashed in the rocks. She hoped the cold, snow-covered stone would mask the warmth of his body.

She looked off to the left, where a sheer rock outcrop rose out of the snow. Maybe there'd be another overhang, but if the airship saw them under it, they'd just take out the entire crag. Then she saw a deep crack in the rock, a V-shaped cleft. She could see light streaming through it from the far side. Right now the airship was thundering overhead, changing its direction to match theirs. She dove into some dense brush and crawled forward, Rowan behind her.

"I've got an idea," she said.

Rowan hunkered down, lowering his back below the top of the brush. Snow rained down on them from the leaves. "Let's hear it." He scooped up heaps of snow and piled them on her shoulders, trying to mask her heat.

"We wait here for a few minutes, enough for the airship to move past us. Then we run for that cleft in the rock and jump in. If we can make it to the other side of this outcrop, we might be able to lose them long enough for the pilot to pick us up."

"Even if we do," Rowan said grimly, "what's the long game? They've got us hopelessly outgunned. Even if we elude them for another few minutes, enough for the pilot to grab us, there's no way we can outrun an airship in the open. Not in that beat-up old chopper."

She gripped his arm. "We have to try. We have to draw that airship away from the location and away from Gordon."

The airship stormed past, its low throbbing vibrating in her chest. The snow cover had worked. Through the leaves of the shrub, she watched the gleaming silver ship maneuver farther down the mountain slope. She saw their chance. "Now!"

She burst from the bushes and ran for the cleft. When she got closer, it looked narrower than it had before, a slender V cut into the towering cliff.

It started about five feet above the ground, so she scrambled up the rock, grabbing onto ancient tree roots, and hefted herself into the crevice. Cold and dark enveloped her. She pulled herself up, shinnying along the cleft. Rowan leaped up, and she grabbed his hand, pulling him all the way in. Now her ribs were on fire.

She gazed up. The sky opened up about twenty feet above. The airship would have a very difficult time spotting them in here. The immense size of the cliff meant it would be very cold around them.

She looked to the far end of the V, seeing a patch of daylight not far off. Then a renewed thrumming filled the air. She watched as the daylight across the way was blocked by another massive airship, wheeling slowly in the sky. It rose up, passing overhead, moving back where they'd stashed Gordon.

She met Rowan's eyes in the gloom. "Can you ask your pilot if it's clear out there? I'm sure she's got a better vantage point."

Rowan pulled out his PRD. He started to draft a message to the pilot, then stopped. "No, wait." He switched it off. "We know the PPC didn't track your PRD because it's untraceable. It must have been mine." He stared down at it, looking betrayed. "We always remove the chips, but somehow they're able to hack us."

She pulled out her own PRD. "Here. Use mine."

Rowan took it and sent the message to the pilot.

"I'll look," Marlowe wrote back, "but that second airship ain't far away, and it's tracking me too." Rowan handed back the PRD.

They began to shinny their way deeper and deeper into the crevice, ready to go in either direction.

Then a booming voice swept over the mountain. "We have your friend, the pilot," said the voice. "Surrender now, or we'll kill him."

Chapter 28

She turned to Rowan in the shadows. "They've got Gordon."

His mouth was a gray slash. "They're not going to let him go if you go out there."

"They'll kill him!"

"They'll kill him anyway, if they haven't already."

She bit her lip. "No. I can't just let him die."

Rowan gently took hold of her arms. "You have to think of the big picture. If you go out there, they'll kill both of you. And then who will reach the Rovers?"

She slung her tool bag off her shoulder. "Look. Take this. It's all the research I found on the asteroid. Find the Rovers. I'm going out there. Maybe my surrender will distract them long enough for you to get away in the helicopter."

"Absolutely not." He pulled her close, pressing his face into her hair.

"I won't be able to live with myself if they kill him," she told him.

He pulled back, meeting her eyes. "At least you'll be alive."

She shook her head, placing a hand on his chest. "Rowan . . ."

Drawing her closer, he placed his hand on the back of her neck and pulled her into him, his lips closing on hers. She felt his touch all the way to her toes. She breathed him in, recalling their night in the mine. She wanted to stay with him. Wanted to live. But if Gordon died because she wasn't brave enough to go out there, she'd never be able to forgive herself.

"I have to go," she told him.

He pressed his forehead to her. "No."

"Can you think of anything else?"

He fell silent.

"If we stay here, Gordon dies for certain. If I surrender, there's a chance they'll capture me, and I could escape later."

"From an airship?" he asked incredulously. "Do you know how heavily guarded those things are?"

"I have to take the chance." She gripped her tool bag. "Promise me you'll get this information to the Rovers."

"I don't like this plan."

"Promise me!"

He hesitated. "I promise. But I don't want to lose you."

"Don't give up on me yet. If I can find a way to get both of us off that airship, I will." But her voice faltered a little at the end, and she knew then that Rowan saw how terrified she was. Then she moved past him and jumped down from the crevice into the snow.

"Wait!" he called after her. "We don't even know if they really have him."

"I'll make sure," she said, sprinting up the hill, sticking close to the rock outcrop.

As she drew closer to Gordon's location, she saw one of the gigantic airships had landed in the snow. Three men stood outside, two of them Repurposers dressed in their customary black suits. Keeping Gordon on the stretcher, they dragged him over to a ramp that led up into the belly of the ship. He was screaming in pain as they hefted him up the ramp. The third man, dressed in a gray suit, held a sonic gun on Gordon.

She drew closer, keeping to the rock wall, and stopped with a start. Willoughby. The Repurposers emerged once more from the ship, scanning the snow. "There she is!" shouted one of them. She emerged from the rock, tromping toward them in the snow. Keeping his gun on Gordon, Willoughby gave her a look, but he gave no sign of concern or sympathy.

"You made the right choice," he told her.

With his gun, he motioned her to board the ship.

The Repurposers seized her roughly, forcing her up the ramp. Fear flooded through every vein, leaving a bitter taste in her mouth. She remembered the feel of them as they pinned her down in that alley in New Atlantic, their cold hands on her, shoving her down, the whirring of the glistening tool.

One of their suit jackets flapped open, and she could see the gleaming silver handle of his repurposing device tucked in an inside pocket. She tried to glance back at Willoughby, but the hand was too rough on her neck. Had he really betrayed her?

They shoved her up the ramp into the main section of the ship. While the outside of the machine was all metal and utilitarian, the inside looked like a plush PPC office. Posh chairs, a bar, and media consoles lined the room. Gordon lay on the floor, still lashed to the stretcher. Their eyes met, and she saw tears trickling down his cheeks. His leg wound had opened again, seeping a pool of blood onto the floor.

A pilot sat at the far end of the room, operating a vast console. "Take us up," Willoughby told him.

H124 heard the engines fire up. The floor tilted slightly as the ship lifted off, and the ramp closed, sealing with a clang.

The Repurposers shoved her down into one of the chairs. "Want to do it now?" one asked.

"I don't see why not," said the other. "We have some time to kill."

They looked to Willoughby for confirmation. To her horror, he nodded.

She stood up abruptly, kicking one in the knee, but the other held her fast, shoving her back into the chair. He brought out his tool and fired up the motor. She heard the familiar whirring sound as it came closer to her head. She twisted away her neck, wrenching her hand loose. Then a third Repurposer emerged from a back room. "Looks like you could use a hand," he hissed.

Gordon thrashed in the stretcher on the floor. "Leave her alone! I'll kill you!" He started to struggle up, crying in pain. Then he freed himself from the stretcher and flipped onto his stomach.

The third Repurposer clamped down on her hands, and they forced her onto her stomach as well. Now she heard the whine of the bone saw as the tool moved past her ear.

"I'll kill you!" Gordon shouted from the floor. Her eyes locked on his as he crawled closer, his face a mask of agony.

Then an ear-piercing sound split the air. She felt a racking pain in her eardrums. A Repurposer fell to her side, sprawling on the floor. His eyes bulged out of his head, while blood trickled from his nose and ears. He gasped a final breath, then lay still.

Another blast filled the ship, and another Repurposer crumpled half into the chair, blood flowing from his face. As another whine filled the room, the tool clattered to the floor. The third went down, landing across her body. Willoughby's foot lashed out, kicking the Repurposer off her.

Disoriented from the blast, she looked up. Willoughby stood over her, lowering his sonic weapon. Gordon reached her and clasped her hand.

"What's going on?" she heard the pilot shout from across the room. As she struggled to a sitting position, she saw him rise from his seat, a sonic weapon in his hand. Willoughby spun and fired, knocking the man to the floor.

He knelt down next to her and helped her up. "I'm so sorry," he said. "I didn't want to shoot them while they were so close to you, but in the end I had no choice."

"Thank you," she said, rising on trembling legs, ears ringing. She reached up, feeling blood trickling from her nose.

"They're pretty exact when you aim straight at someone, but there's a little spillover if you're too close."

She nodded dizzily, wiping the blood away.

"Where's the information for the Rovers?" he asked her.

"It's safe." She helped Gordon roll over onto his back, and again he cried out in pain. "Thank you," she whispered to him, kneeling beside him.

Gordon looked up at her with leaking eyes. "Thank you for coming. But you shouldn't have done that. I'm an old man."

"What does that matter?" she asked him.

He smiled.

The ship started to list, so Willoughby rushed over to the flight controls and steadied it. "I hope you don't mean you gave it to that Badlander."

She jumped up. "What?" Hurrying over to Willoughby, she took in the pilot's heads-up display.

Below them, Rowan ran through the snow. Apparently the cliff trick hadn't worked, and he'd been forced to run. She didn't see the helicopter in sight, but she hoped it was still out there to pick him up. A blast erupted from the other airship, blowing a crater in the dirt beside him. He dove to one side, barely escaping. The ship prepared to fire again. He wasn't going to make it.

Willoughby wheeled the ship toward his location.

The second airship fired on Rowan again, striking a dead tree beside him. It erupted in flames, leveling a whole section of the slope. The snow slid downward, sweeping up Rowan with it. She saw him struggling to stay on top of the snow, his arms and legs flailing and kicking.

He neared a steep escarpment on the mountain, a sheer cliff face. The snow carried him hopelessly toward it.

"We have to help him!" H124 cried just as Rowan went over the edge, sailing out into the open air. He vanished from sight, plummeting downward.

Chapter 29

As the airship hovered over the cliff, she ran to the window, pressing her face against it. Relief flooded through her. The helicopter hovered just below the edge of the escarpment. She could see Rowan clinging to one of the landing skids. He swung his body up, into the cabin of the helicopter.

"He made it!" she shouted.

"The asteroid info is on him?" Willoughby asked.

She turned to him and nodded solemnly.

"Then we have to protect that helicopter at all costs." He fired up the weapons panel. The helicopter dashed to one side, and when the second airship tried to maneuver close behind, it proved too unwieldy, banging into the cliff face. It wheeled on the helicopter, preparing to fire.

The helicopter veered sharply away from the cliff, but the airship followed and fired once more. The chopper dodged to the side, and the airship's shot went wide, taking out a chunk of the cliff. Huge rocks rained down beneath them.

Willoughby sent a powerful blast at the second airship. It struck dead on, sending it off course. Flames erupted in the stern. The ship listed farther left. He fired again, blasting a hole in its center. This time it exploded, shuddering down to crash into the jagged rocks of the mountain. Another explosion wracked the air, and debris billowed up, filling the sky with ash and smoke.

Willoughby looked at the infrared display. "What the hell?" A line of bright red shapes was moving in, closing in on their location. "More airships!" Willoughby's mouth fell open. "There must be at least fifteen. Damn it!"

He turned to H124. "I thought if there were only two, I could shoot down the other one. But this?" He looked helplessly at the display.

"Are they after me or Rowan?"

He turned to her. "You. After your pirate broadcast in Delta City, the power didn't go back up. More and more people pulled away from their displays to send each other messages. They weren't seeing to their task windows. The whole northern part of the city went dark, including all power to the PPC Tower. Getting it back up was a monumental task. The media had to debunk your story, going so far as to make up a silly meme about it to discredit you. Eventually power started returning to the city. People lost interest in your story. But the PPC structure was damaged. You undermined them. And they want to be sure it doesn't happen again. I heard they were going after you, and I requested to be on the mission. They almost didn't let me go, being from New Atlantic, as they blamed me for your escape. Said I was incompetent, that I had one shot to make up for it. Thankfully they didn't suspect the real truth. Ideally they'd like to capture you and repurpose you so you can go on one of the chatter shows and say it was all a prank."

The thought made her shiver.

"Can you order the ships back?" Gordon asked from the floor.

"I have no authority here. I'm just along for the ride."

The line of airships closed in.

H124 watched the helicopter speeding away in the opposite direction. Just as she thought maybe they hadn't seen it, the airships picked up speed, fanning out and flanking Rowan's position. They caught up to them in seconds, surrounding the helicopter. She heard their voices come over the comm. "Land now and you will not be harmed." She knew that was complete lie. "Don't land, and we will shoot you down where you are."

"They don't know you're aboard this airship," Willoughby said. "That's good. They think you're on the helicopter."

"That's not good for the helicopter."

Willoughby moved into position near the other airships. There was no way they could take on fifteen of them. Rowan and Marlowe were about to be shot out of the sky, along with all the information that the Rovers would need in order to have any chance of saving the planet.

H124's mind struggled to comprehend what was happening. One second their airship was feet away from Rowan's helicopter, and the next, it veered off wildly, picked up speed and shot away. She went off her feet, then stood up to see that they hovered several miles off, along with the other fifteen ships. She stood on the bridge, blinking quickly.

"What the . . . ?" she heard Willoughby murmur.

A flutter of confused messages came over the comm link, none of them making any sense. "Form up!" came a harsh voice.

The airships approached again en masse, closing in on Rowan. Willoughby followed them. Then once again the engines raced out of control, spinning the ships madly in the air and speeding them away so quickly that H124 had to grip Willoughby's chair to keep from flying backward. When their ship slowed, she looked at the HUD. They were all even farther away, now five miles from the helicopter Willoughby checked and rechecked the controls.

"What's going on?" H124 asked Willoughby.

"I have no idea!" He backed away from the controls. "But I'm no longer controlling the ship."

"What's happening here?" boomed a voice over the comm. "This is Commander Recht aboard Airship 503. Who is doing this?"

"No one, sir," replied another voice. "It's nothing we're doing."

"Close in on the target!" barked Recht.

Moving as one, the airships sped toward Rowan. They caught up with him in no time as he tried to flee south. Willoughby tried to blend in with the other ships, waiting for his chance to do something. "Get ready to fire!" ordered Recht.

"No!" shouted H124 as she saw a blast of fire emerge from the ships. Then their airship dipped, careening toward the ground. Then it veered upward, spinning out of control. She clenched her teeth and squeezed her eyes shut, gripping Willoughby's chair. But she couldn't hold on. She toppled over, sliding violently across the floor and colliding with a wall. All of a sudden the ship stopped moving.

She stood up on shaky legs, and struggled back to the control console. Her airship had been moved so far away, she couldn't see any of the others.

"What the hell?" asked Willoughby.

H124 grabbed her PRD and sent a quick coded message to Rowan. "Are you okay?"

"H?" he replied. "How are you writing me? Are you free?"

"Yes. Did that blast hit you? What's happening?"

"It did . . . we're grounded. I have no idea what's happening with the PPC airships. It looked like they all just went crazy and sped away."

"We're coming to your location." She scanned the sky, then the infrared monitor for signs of the other fifteen ships. The fleet trundled inexorably back to Rowan's location. "Unfortunately, we're not the only ones."

Willoughby turned the ship in Rowan's direction, pushing the airship to such a high speed that she almost lost her footing again. When they got within sight, she saw that the helicopter had been hit. It rested on the ground, with Rowan and the pilot standing beside it. Willoughby set down the airship and opened the ramp. H124 ran down it.

Rowan rushed toward her, taking her in his embrace. "I didn't think I'd ever see you again." He kissed her, his lips warm in the cold air. Then they turned and started running back up the ramp.

Along the way Rowan lifted her tool bag off his shoulder and handed it to her. "I believe this is yours."

The pilot caught up with them, a tall, lanky woman with a crop of short black hair and skin the color of mahogany. "This is Marlowe."

Inside the ship, she shook H124's hand, smiling at her with kind eyes.

"Thank you for risking your life," H124 told her.

"All in a day's work."

From the look in Marlowe's eyes, H124 didn't doubt it.

Willoughby raised the ramp. Inside he pointed up at the infrared monitor. "See that? The airships are about five miles away. And that triangular formation? That's why they brought fifteen of them."

"Hold the formation!" shouted Recht over the comm.

"What is it?" H124 asked.

He fired up the engines and started accelerating. "It's a weapon that requires all fifteen ships to power. It destroys any motorized or computer-aided equipment with a hundred-mile blast. But it doesn't destroy that alone. Anything remotely near its target is utterly decimated. We'd never get far enough away from this ship or the helicopter to leave. We'll get blasted sky-high along with everything else."

He pushed them to maximum velocity. "Hold on!" The force of the acceleration threw H124 off her feet. She slid across the floor, grabbing onto one of the anchored chairs and hefting herself up into it.

"Power the weapon!" shouted Recht over the comm.

"How far are we?" H124 asked.

"Fifty miles out!"

"Prepare to fire!" came Recht's harsh voice.

Willoughby pushed the airship, and she heard the engines screaming below her.

"Ninety miles out!" he shouted.

"Fire!"

A blast hit them violently, tumbling the ship end over end. Everything was chaos. She tried to hang onto the chair. Equipment and carpets and glasses flew past her. Gordon hovered weightless for a moment as the ship plummeted. Rowan grabbed her hand, and she held onto him desperately, her world upside down. She heard an explosion deep in the bowels of the ship, and a blistering wave of heat swept over her.

They hit with such force that she felt every bone in her body shatter. Her head slammed into something hard, and the engines stopped abruptly. A high-pitched whine filled the acrid air, and all went silent. She strained her ears, struggling to hold on to consciousness.

She could hear the blood thrumming in her ears, as well as someone breathing next to her. She opened her eyes, but everything was pitch black. Struggling to lift her head, she almost threw up. Someone groaned in the far part of the airship. She could smell burning circuitry. Something heavy had landed on top of her. She tried to push at it, but her body didn't respond. She couldn't move her arms. The crushing object lay across her legs and torso, pinning her down.

She tried to shift once more, but when she lifted her head, she blacked out.

H124 heard a distant mumbling. She felt warm light on her face. Slowly she opened her eyes. She was out of the airship, lying on the ground. A stand of dead trees rose around her. "I think she's coming around," said a woman's voice.

Then a man, sounding near. "What about the others?"

"Still out," the woman responded.

H124 closed her eyes again, then summoned her strength. She tried to sit up. Couldn't even move.

"Easy now," said the man beside her. She'd heard that voice before. Somewhere. She couldn't quite place it. She lifted her eyelids and stared into the familiar face. It was Raven. But he was older. No longer a teen, but in his twenties. His long black hair hung past his shoulders, framing his tan face.

"It's you," she whispered with a sore throat. She swallowed. "I've been searching for you . . ."

"We were about to leave our camp in this area, but then we intercepted your message to the Badlanders and deciphered it. Said you were looking for us, something about how all might be lost if you didn't find us."

"Yes," she said, fighting to keep her eyes open. Her whole body felt smashed. Every bone and muscle ached. She could barely move. She tried to lift her arm to her tool bag, but it didn't respond. She could still feel the strap across her chest. "Take my tool bag," she told him. "There's information inside . . ."

"About what?"

"An asteroid . . . it's on its way . . . and it'll kill everything . . ."

His warm smile vanished. "What?" He gently unlatched the strap and took her tool bag. She tried to sit up, but a wave of knives went through her entire body.

He placed a soft hand on her shoulder. "Don't try to move. You've got a lot of broken bones, but we'll fix you." He looked into the bag and pulled out the shiny discs, along with the small objects with the sockets.

"Onyx!" he called. In her peripheral vision, H124 saw a woman approach. "Get this back to base immediately. Give it to the encryption team. Looks like very old tech."

"Right!" she heard the woman answer, and her footsteps faded into the distance.

"Rowan? . . . Gordon?" H124 called out.

Raven's kind smile returned as he placed a warm hand on her forehead. "They're both alive. So is the PPC exec. There were others, though, who weren't so lucky. Three men in black, and the ship's pilot. Lucky you were at the edge of that weapon's range, or you'd be gone. Our medics are seeing to the survivors. I know this hurts now, but we'll get you into a med pod as soon as we get you off the mountain."

She glanced to her right, where she saw the great fiery wreck of the airship some distance away, a black plume of smoke snaking up into the sky.

He followed her gaze. "We pulled you out."

"How did you get rid of those airships?" she asked him.

He smiled. "We have a few tricks the PPC doesn't know about."

"Can't believe . . ." she said, taking a deep, painful breath. "Can't believe we found you . . ."

She gazed up at the gray vault of the sky. Storm clouds roiled, bringing down a fresh dusting of snow. It started to collect in her eyelashes. Above those clouds lay the blackness of space. And out there in that void, hurtling ever closer, was the planet killer, intent on wiping out all that she knew.

But now they had a chance.

Acknowledgments

Huge thanks to my editor James Abbate for all of his great work and for believing in this book, and to Martin Biro for making it part of the new Rebel Base imprint.

A lot of research went into this book, and Dr. Patrick Bartlein, climatologist extraordinaire and Professor of Geography at the University of Oregon, was incredibly helpful in this. Many thanks to Joe Jordan, Sr., a great friend and pilot who lent his flight knowledge to the aviation scenes.

My former writing instructors, Joe and Penny, are inspiring teachers who deepened my love of the craft and have remained wonderful friends.

Deep thanks to Jason for being such a stalwart friend, for believing in me and being supportive of my writing, and to the amazing Becky for being such a solid and delightful friend all these years.

Meet the Author

Alice Henderson is a writer of fiction, comics, and video game material. She was selected to attend Launchpad, a NASA-funded writing workshop aimed at bringing accurate science to fiction. Her love of wild places inspired her novel *Voracious,* which pits a lone hiker against a shapeshifting creature in the wilderness of Glacier National Park. Her novel *Fresh Meat* is set in the world of the hit TV series *Supernatural.* She also wrote the Buffy the Vampire Slayer novels *Night Terrors* and *Portal Through Time.* She has written short stories for numerous anthologies including *Body Horror, Werewolves & Shapeshifters,* and *Mystery Date.* While working at LucasArts, she wrote material for several Star Wars video games, including *Star Wars: Galactic Battlegrounds* and *Star Wars: Battle for Naboo.* She holds an interdisciplinary master's degree in folklore and geography, and is a wildlife researcher and rehabilitator. Her novel *Portal Through Time* won the Scribe Award for Best Novel. Visit her online at www.AliceHenderson.com.

Printed in the United States
by Baker & Taylor Publisher Services